SOME ENCHANTED MURDER

AN APPLE MARIANI MYSTERY

SOME ENCHANTED MURDER

LINDA S. REILLY

FIVE STAR
A part of Gale, Cengage Learning

GALE
CENGAGE Learning

Detroit • New York • San Francisco • New Haven, Conn • Waterville, Maine • London

GALE
CENGAGE Learning®

LIBRARY OF CONGRESS CATALOGING-IN-PUBLICATION DATA

Reilly, Linda S.
  Some enchanted murder : an Apple Mariani mystery / Linda S. Reilly. — 1st ed.
    p. cm.
  ISBN 978-1-4328-2681-9 (hardcover) — ISBN 1-4328-2681-6 (hardcover)
  1. Legal assistants—Fiction. 2. Murder—Investigation—Fiction. 3. Missing persons—Fiction. 4. New Hampshire—Fiction. 5. Mystery fiction. I. Title.
PS3618.E564526S66 2013
813'.6—dc23   2012037280

First Edition. First Printing: February 2013
Find us on Facebook– https://www.facebook.com/FiveStarCengage
Visit our website— http://www.gale.cengage.com/fivestar/
Contact Five Star™ Publishing at FiveStar@cengage.com

Printed in Mexico
1 2 3 4 5 6 7 17 16 15 14 13

Some Enchanted Murder

CHAPTER ONE

From the journal of Frederic Dwardene, Thursday, November 9, 1950:

I have never written in a journal before, but today I was compelled to buy one. Where else can I express the giddiness I am feeling right now? In whom could I confide the emotions that some might find improper for a man my age? It began early this afternoon at the bank, when the most beautiful woman I have ever seen walked up to the teller's cage . . .

I'd just plucked a dog-eared paperback off a shelf in the library of the old Dwardene mansion when my cell phone vibrated in the pocket of my wool jacket. I fished it out and saw my aunt Tressa's bubbly visage grinning at me. Her feminized Beatles' do and dazzling smile did not match the voice that bellowed into my eardrums.

"Apple, where are you?" she squawked.

"In the library," I said as quietly as I could. "Is something wrong?"

"Come upstairs," she commanded. "And bring a weapon. Something big. And heavy."

In a flash, I shelved the book. I quick-stepped toward the foyer and hustled up the staircase that curved in a graceful arc to the second story. Although I was long accustomed to my aunt's arachno-encounters, the odd crackle in her tone made the back of my neck tingle.

My foot had barely touched the top landing when my aunt and I collided. She sagged against the papered wall, her neon purple scarf trailing behind her like a psychedelic beacon. One bejeweled hand was clamped over her raspberry-painted lips. Her face was the color of scalded milk.

"Aunt Tressa, are you all right?"

Shaking her head, she grabbed the sleeve of my jacket, nearly wrenching me to the ground. "Oh God, Apple, you will not believe this hideous thing. I swear, it's a foot long. You've got to get it before it—wait a minute, I thought I told you to bring a weapon."

I resisted an eye-roll. "Don't worry, I have a whole pack of tissues in my purse."

"Tissues? You'll need a bed sheet for this one."

"Um, miss? Is everything okay?"

Halfway up the staircase, a skinny, bespectacled man with a brush cut stood staring uneasily at us.

"Everything's fine," I assured him. I didn't dare tell him it was only a spider. To Aunt Tressa, *only a spider* was the equivalent of *only an asteroid colliding with the planet and wiping out the entire human race.*

He hesitated. "Okay, if you're sure . . ."

"I am, but thanks anyway."

With a shrug, the man retreated down the stairs and I turned back to my aunt, who was clutching her prized designer handbag—a gorgeous creation the color of dark cherries and the size of a grocery cart—as if it were a helicopter cable that was going to airlift her out of there. "First of all, it can't be a foot long," I said. "This is an old house. It probably wandered down from the attic."

"Believe me, if this thing wandered in from anywhere, it was someplace a lot hotter than an attic." She aimed her upturned nose at one of the doorways about halfway down the hall on the left. "Go ahead. See for yourself."

The faded oriental runner stretching the length of the hallway softened the clomping of my boots as I headed toward the source of my aunt's distress. When I peeked through the doorway of the room she'd indicated, I couldn't stop myself—I let out a miniature squeal.

The thing was huge indeed, and hideous was probably a benevolent term for the creature strolling languidly across the bedspread of the room's sole bed. About a ninety-four on a creep scale of one to ten, its eight hairy, black-and-orange legs easily spanned the width of my hand. A double shiver raced through me, just as a harsh male voice burst out from the depths of a corner closet.

"Will you people stop making such a racket? You're gonna scare him."

I knew that voice, but at the moment I couldn't place it. A fast glance around the room told me its occupant was preparing to move out. Stacks of sealed cardboard boxes lined one wall. The floor was littered with newspapers that were apparently being used for packing material.

The man belonging to the voice suddenly emerged from the closet, glaring at me from beneath dark bangs that needed cutting a month ago. "Josh Baker," I said dryly. "What are you doing here?" I'd known Josh since he was a tiny terror and I was his reluctant babysitter.

"I live here. At least until Friday I do," he groused. Clearly he wasn't happy about moving out. Or was something else making him so grumpy?

And why was he living here in the first place?

On the bedspread, the monster was on the move, and way too fast for my liking. With an involuntary shudder, I took a step backward. "Uhh . . . is that a tarantula?"

"A Mexican Red Knee," Josh confirmed. "His name is Zorba,

and he's very gentle. I was just letting him out of his tank for a while. I didn't know someone was going to come by and scare the crap out of him."

Aunt Tressa appeared at the edge of the door frame, hanging far enough to the side to keep the tarantula out of her line of vision. "I scared *him?* What about the fright he inflicted on my aging heart? I'm not exactly a spring chicken, you know!"

At sixty-one, Aunt Tressa had one of the healthiest hearts I know, as well as one of the most generous. But she wasn't opposed to a bit of exaggeration when she wanted to slam home a point.

My aunt narrowed her carefully plucked eyebrows at Josh. "Hey, I remember you. You're the little kid Apple used to sit for. The one who ripped off an entire row of tulips from my flower bed right when they'd started to bloom."

A flush colored Josh's cheeks, but my gaze was drawn to the view outside his bedroom window. Bloated white flakes were floating from the sky at a frightening rate. The first snow of the season was already sticking, promising to make driving treacherous. The plows would be along eventually, but in the meantime the New Hampshire roads would have all the traction of a hockey rink.

In spite of the bad weather, people were still milling about downstairs, eyeing the deceased Edgar Dwardene's former possessions. Edgar's nephew and sole heir, and my long-time friend, Blake Dwardene, had opened the once stately home to the residents of Hazleton for the entire afternoon. Everything was for sale, with the exception of Edgar's treasured dagger collection—the deadly knives had been promised to an antique weapons dealer.

"Everything all right in there?"

I turned to see Celeste Frame, Blake's fiancée, standing outside the doorway next to my aunt. Looking trim and fit in a navy cashmere sweater and form-hugging beige slacks, her short blond hair fashionably coiffed, she wore an air of concern on her pretty face.

Aunt Tressa jumped right in. "Celeste, did you know that . . . that *thing* was living here?"

Celeste gave a wan smile. "Yes, Josh got him a few weeks ago. Strange choice for a pet, but to each his own, I suppose."

Josh shot her a dark look.

"So that's why I never saw it when I showed the house," Aunt Tressa said. "Thank God."

As the listing broker, my aunt had dragged at least a dozen potential buyers through the neglected mansion before two doctors from New Jersey, envisioning the possibilities, fell instantly and irrevocably in love with it. With the closing scheduled for this coming Friday, she was already imagining those lovely commission dollars plumping up her bank account. The law firm I worked for, Quinto and Ingle, was handling both the probate and the closing.

"If you ladies don't mind, I'd like to finish packing," Josh cut in.

Celeste tilted her head toward the hallway. "Come on, we can chat out there."

"Bye, Josh," I called to him.

"Yeah, back at ya." He closed the door in our faces.

"I didn't even know he lived here," Aunt Tressa said. "I knew there was a tenant, but he was always out when I brought people through." She shook her head. "Who'd have thunk it?"

"Blake's uncle rented the room to Josh about three years ago," Celeste explained. "I think he was grateful to have company in this dreary old place. I understand Edgar had grown pretty fond of Josh before he . . . well, you know."

Before the poor old man took a fatal tumble, is what she meant to say. Seventy-nine-year-old Edgar Dwardene had died from a fall down the stairs. A younger man might have sustained such a fall with only a broken bone or two, but Edgar landed in an unfortunate position. His neck snapped on impact.

Aunt Tressa's face was beginning to return to its normal color. "Well, I'm out of here," she said. "I came up here to look for Lou, which is what I was doing before I ran into that hairy beast. Any idea where I can find him?"

Lou Marshall was the appraiser for Edgar Dwardene's estate. As of about six weeks ago, he was also Aunt Tressa's new squeeze.

"Lou's in Edgar's study," Celeste told her, pointing in the opposite direction from which we'd come. "Far end of the hall. You can't miss it. *Ooh,* quick caveat, though. Lou and Blake had a bit of a spat earlier, so he might not be in the best of moods."

"Thanks for the warning," I said. "Where is Blake, by the way?"

"In the cellar, cleaning out the last of the old junk, poor baby. He's been complaining all day about all the dirt and dust down there."

My aunt shuddered. "I can only imagine what else is down there."

"Anyway," Celeste said, "if you decide to buy anything, stop in afterward and pay Lou. He's the official cashier."

Aunt Tressa thanked her and hoisted her handbag onto her shoulder. "How about if I meet you downstairs in twenty, Apple? Snow's getting bad outside, so we don't want to hang around too long."

"Sounds like a plan."

Celeste winked at me as my aunt stalked away. "You're coming to our holiday open house tomorrow afternoon, aren't you, Apple?"

Open house. I knew there was something on my agenda for

Sunday. Celeste loved to entertain. Since she and Blake were moving to New York as soon as they closed on the mansion, I knew she was looking forward to hosting this one last party.

"Of course," I told her. "Aunt Tressa and I are both coming. Is there anything I can bring?"

"Absolutely not. All we want from our guests is to show up and enjoy. I have some extra special treats planned. Many of the hors d'oeuvres will be made from my healthy, homemade grain breads."

I bit off a chuckle. The mere mention of the word "healthy" in relation to any foodstuff automatically drew a scowl from my junk food–loving aunt.

"Sounds enticing," I said.

"And the next time you're in the Food Mart, be sure to check out the bread aisle." Celeste beamed with pride. "I have my own display there now. Celeste-y-al Whole Grain Breads." She emphasized the word *Celeste* in the name.

"Hey, that's a great name! I'll definitely check it out."

Downstairs, it felt as if the thermostat had been set on ninety. Dry heat poured out of the ancient radiators in sickening waves. I resisted the temptation to peel off my jacket, which I felt sure was lined with iron.

The entrance door to the library had been propped open with a blue and white pottery spittoon. Filled to the brim with floral-scented potpourri, it made for quite an attractive piece, although I couldn't help picturing a room full of gin-drinking, tobacco-chewing poker players having used it as a depository for stuff I didn't want to think about. A few lone browsers were scanning the shelves, no doubt hoping to snag a valuable first edition, or maybe one of the war novels I'd spotted earlier.

I homed in on the shelf where I'd found the books I was interested in—John Jakes's series based on the American

Revolution. A sign resting on a table announced that paperback books were two dollars each. Since I loved American history—I'd been a history major in college—it was a bargain I couldn't refuse. I gathered up the books, eight in all, and stuffed them inside the tote I'd brought with me.

I was perusing the other books on the shelf when I spied a diminutive figure in a lilac-colored coat standing beside me. "Lillian?"

The elderly woman swung her head toward me. A knitted periwinkle hat sat atop her silvery waves of hair, complementing her coat perfectly. "Why, Apple dear, how are you? How nice to see you here!"

Lillian Bilodeau was a sweet, elderly woman who'd had a cat problem this past spring. As in nineteen cats plus Lillian, all scrunched into a tiny mobile home. Right now she had only one cat—Elliot—a lovable gold tiger.

"I'm great, Lillian." I peered at the white porcelain cat she was grasping in her small hands. About four inches high, it was exquisitely painted and glazed to a shine, its eyes an appealing shade of moss green. In a mansion filled with such masculine accoutrements as daggers and spittoons, the delicate white cat seemed out of place. "Are you buying that? It's lovely."

Lillian nodded. "It's quite a piece, isn't it? It's English bone china, over sixty years old. It's marked twenty-five dollars, but I'm going to ask Mr. Marshall if he might shave off a bit for an old lady. I understand he sets all the prices."

"He does, and I hope he gives you a big discount."

"I'll keep my fingers crossed," Lillian said. "Do you know where I might find him?"

"Someone said he's upstairs, in Mr. Dwardene's former study."

"Thank you. I'll toddle up there and plead my case." She smiled, but this time her eyes held a twinge of anxiety.

"Is everything all right, Lillian?"

"Oh, I'm fine, dear, just a little worried about the snowstorm since I have to take the bus home. Do you think they'll still be running in this terrible weather?"

The bus line that served Hazleton and adjacent towns was normally pretty reliable, but with the roads growing worse by the minute, who knew when or if the next bus might come along? And since it was early December, it would be dark by four-thirty. "My aunt and I will be glad to give you a ride home. You don't need to stress over catching a bus."

Her thin shoulders slumped in relief. "Really? You wouldn't mind?"

"Not at all. How about if we look for you in the foyer in ten or fifteen minutes?"

"That will be perfect. I appreciate it, Apple."

Leaving her to seek out Lou Marshall, I turned my attention back to the bookshelves. My chance to scour Edgar Dwardene's collection was dwindling with every second. I was anxious to see if there were any biographies I might be interested in. I thought I'd spotted one about Benjamin Franklin earlier, and was itching to lay my hands on it.

As I was trying to find the Franklin book, my gaze drifted to a display case that hung on the adjacent wall. Moving a few steps closer, I realized it was one of the myriad antique dagger displays that were distributed throughout the house. This one appeared to be made of solid mahogany, and hand-carved at that. It was impressive, despite the scary-looking knives that hung from its built-in slots.

"I bet you wouldn't want to trip over one of those babies in the dark, would you?"

The voice came from directly behind me. I swiveled to see a blue jean–clad man with thick white hair and a matching beard, round cheeks, and bright blue eyes peering at the row of daggers. Had he been there a few seconds ago? I didn't think so. He seemed to have materialized out of the dust particles on the shelves.

"No, I don't suppose I would," I said inanely, stepping slightly to one side.

Laughter shook the man's pink cheeks. He stroked his jaw. "Yessirree, you could slice right through a hog's neck with one of those little cookie-cutters," he went on affably. "Take it clean off with one swipe." He dipped the tip of his rounded nose toward the long steel blade that hung on the slot farthest to the right. "See that one there on the end? That is a bayonet—German to be exact. World War II vintage. Worth a shiny penny or two, my good lady."

My good lady. Who was this Santa Claus in denim? He talked like a character out of an old movie.

I sneaked a peek at his flannel-trimmed blue shirt. Stitched on one pocket, in flowing red script, were the words *Darby Repairs and Renovations.*

Darby.

The name was vaguely familiar. Unfortunately, I couldn't curl my brain around it long enough to remember where I'd heard it.

"Apple!" I felt a hard finger tap on my shoulder. "It's snowing poodles and purses out there. Maybe we'd better get going." Aunt Tressa looked stressed, and not very happy.

"Everything okay?"

"I guess so. I stopped by to talk to Lou, but he seemed distracted. Something was bugging him, but he wouldn't tell me what it was."

"Strange."

"Yeah. He gave me something, too. Something he wanted me to give to you." She unzipped the battleship that was her handbag, thrust in a hand, and began mining its depths. After

16

at least a full minute she said, "Must've fallen to the bottom. I'll find it later." She pulled out her ruby-red cell phone and did a quick check for messages, her scowl proclaiming she had none.

"What was it?"

"What was what?"

"The thing Lou gave you. The thing you were supposed to give to me."

"Oh." She shrugged. "I don't know. It looked like some sort of greeting card. Remind me to look for it when we get home. By the way, Paul Fenton's hanging around here somewhere. I ducked out of sight when I saw him. I know he's going to give me grief about my inspection."

Aunt Tressa was seriously into the ten-day grace period for her car inspection, which technically should have been done by November thirtieth. Today was December seventh. Paul Fenton, the chief of police, had been dogging her about it since Thursday.

It didn't help, of course, that Aunt Tressa had rejected his invitation to the policemen's ball this past summer. "He's not my type," she'd quipped. "I don't like a man who swaggers, and Paul Fenton has more swagger than a frat boy after a panty raid."

I couldn't argue with that.

Out of the corner of my eye, I caught Darby staring at Aunt Tressa. Truly, seriously gawking, as if his eyelids were propped up with telephone poles.

"Can I help you with something, Mr."—my aunt glared at his shirt pocket—"Darby?"

Darby swallowed. "Yes, ma'am, I mean, no ma'am." His smallish ears flushed pink, and he gave a slight bow. "Jack Darby, at your service." He slid two thick fingers into the back pocket of his jeans, pulled out a business card, and handed it to Aunt Tressa. "You ever need any work done, you call me, any time. My cell number's there, too, in case you ever have an emergency. No repair is too small for Jack Darby. I can do plumbing, electrical, you name it."

A *jack*-of-all-trades, I was tempted to blurt. His whole spiel sounded a little too pat.

Aunt Tressa accepted his card, but the suspicion in her eyes didn't waver. "Thanks. I'll keep you in mind." She turned to me. "Come on, we'd better head home." She gripped my arm and began shuttling me out of the library, toward the foyer. The crowd had thinned. Only about a dozen people still milled about on the first floor.

"Nice meeting you ladies," Darby called after us.

I turned to nod a cordial good-bye, but he'd already disappeared.

"Who was he?" my aunt hissed.

"I have no idea, but his name definitely rings a bell. By the way, Lillian Bilodeau is here. I offered her a ride home."

"I saw Lillian. She was coming out of Lou's office when I was walking in."

"Wait a minute," I said. "I thought you were headed in to see Lou fifteen minutes ago? Lillian only went upstairs a short while ago."

"I stopped to use the bathroom first. After which I decided to spruce up my makeup. After which I decided to fluff up my hair. When I got to the study, Lillian was just leaving."

Her name had no sooner been spoken when I spotted her. Her eyes distant and dreamlike, Lillian walked slowly toward us from the foot of the staircase. The china cat dangled precariously from her fingers. I gently removed it from her grasp. "Here, let me hold that for you."

"Are we leaving now?" she murmured, looking off at a distant spot on the wall behind me.

"Yes, but are you all right? You're very pale."

18

When she finally looked me in the eye, I saw that her lips were trembling. "I'm . . . fine. Getting very tired, I'm afraid."

"We're leaving right now, Lillian," Aunt Tressa soothed, slipping her arm through the older woman's. My aunt had always had a warm spot in her heart for this kind soul who could never turn away a stray cat. "Besides, this place feels like a pizza oven on Venus. I keep getting hot flashes."

I took Lillian's other arm. We had almost reached the front door when a scream ripped through the mansion.

Aunt Tressa gave me a smug look. "I knew that tarantula would cause trouble. Who in their right mind would let a—"

"He's dead!" a voice shouted from the top of the stairs.

Everyone turned to see Josh Baker galumphing down the staircase. "He's dead," Josh repeated, his shoulders heaving, his eyes shiny with fear.

"Hah!" Aunt Tressa stage-whispered to me. "Someone finally nailed the sucker. Probably squirted it with a can of bug spray."

"Josh, are you talking about Zorba?" I asked.

He threw me a dazed look. "Zorba? No, not Zorba. Lou Marshall! Someone stabbed him in the neck with one of those antique knives!"

My aunt's jaw fell open. "Lou? Dead?" She tottered sideways. "Then I"—she swallowed—"was probably the last person to see him alive."

I grabbed her arm to keep her upright, at the precise moment I spotted Chief Fenton striding toward us. "Is that so?" he said, his granite gaze locked firmly on Aunt Tressa's horrified face.

"What I meant was," she squeaked, "I . . . was probably the *next* to last person to see him alive."

But Fenton was already charging up the stairs, his large feet thumping them back two at a time.

CHAPTER TWO

I had just come out of the boardroom and was striding across the bank lobby when I saw her. She couldn't have been more than twenty, twenty-one at most. Her hair was the color of summer sunshine, pulled away from her face and held fast on either side by a pair of pale pink bows. She had full lips and bright blue eyes that I could see even from several feet away. She caught my gaze and quickly looked away, a flush painting her lovely cheeks the same shade as her hair bows . . .

By the time Chief Fenton finished questioning Lillian, Aunt Tressa, and me and allowed us to leave, it was dark outside. Tiny flakes clung to my chestnut-colored hair and continued drifting down at a steady pace. The air felt crisp and invigorating with the scent of the season's first snowfall.

Or it would have, if I hadn't just come from a murder scene.

Parked on the street in front of the mansion, my silver Honda Fit was covered with a thick blanket of snow. Still boiling at Chief Fenton's insinuation that she'd had something to do with Lou's murder, Aunt Tressa shoved herself into the back seat. I took Lillian's tiny arm, guided her onto the front seat, and then placed the china cat in her hands. With an absent look, she slipped it into her coat pocket.

I started the car and flipped the heat on high, then grabbed my windshield brush out of my trunk and cleaned off the car as quickly as I could. My jacket and gloves felt cold and wet when

I finally slid onto the driver's seat. Dry heat blasted out of the vents, warming my bones a little.

I was worried about both of my passengers. Aunt Tressa had been thoroughly shaken by Lou's murder. After the initial shock had worn off, she'd snatched a wad of tissues out of her purse and sobbed for a good five minutes. Then Fenton had pulled her aside and escorted her into the library, closing the door. I don't know what he said to her, but when she stalked out of the room twenty minutes later, I'd swear I saw steam billowing from her ears.

As for Lillian, she'd been far too quiet during the ordeal. Fenton had questioned her, too, but only briefly. According to Lillian, she'd gone upstairs and into Lou's temporary office to pay for the china cat. After he agreed she could have it for ten dollars, she'd given him a ten-dollar bill, thanked him, and left.

But there was something she wasn't telling us. Of that I felt certain.

Fenton had interrogated me too, but his questions were mostly about Aunt Tressa. Had she fought with Lou recently? Were they having problems? Was Aunt Tressa the jealous type?

I answered no to all, but I didn't want him to think I was being defensive, either. I responded to each question as calmly as I could, my heart thumping like a frightened rabbit's the entire time.

Aunt Tressa leaned forward and poked my shoulder. "Look." She aimed a red-gloved finger at a car parked on the street about thirty feet in front of mine. "Isn't that your boss?"

I squinted into the darkness, through the falling snow. Sure enough, Sam Ingle, the attorney I worked for at Quinto and Ingle, was brushing snow off his Buick with a long-handled scraper.

"That's odd," I said. "I don't remember seeing him at the estate sale." He'd told me, in fact, that he didn't plan to attend, since his wife thoroughly disliked "moldy antiques."

Traffic was light as I pulled out onto the icy road. I waved at Sam as we inched past him, but he didn't notice. At least he didn't appear to.

"I'm so sorry to make you drive out to the trailer park in this weather, Apple," Lillian fretted. She twisted her gloved hands nervously in her lap.

"Don't give it a thought, Lillian. I'm glad to do it."

I kept my eyes focused on the slick road, my speed rarely exceeding twenty-five. We passed through Hazleton's small town center, where the one-armed statue of Ezekiel Hazleton, the town's founder, was coated with snow.

Within minutes I was turning onto the narrow drive that led into the Whistle Stop Mobile Home Park. A plow had made a cursory sweep through the park, leaving a narrow ribbon of packed snow that was barely the width of my car. I was grateful that Lillian's small white dwelling was only a short distance ahead on the right.

My Honda skidded slightly as I braked to a stop in front of Lillian's mobile home. I shoved the gearshift into Park and hopped out of the car. I didn't want Lillian navigating the slippery walkway and stairs on her own.

I heard another door open and close. Aunt Tressa's. Wordlessly, she took hold of one of Lillian's arms while I gripped the other. We were helping Lillian climb the two stairs into her trailer when I spotted something stuck in the ground in front of the mobile home. It was a square white sign, its top edge draped in snow. Squinting, I could just make out the words—*Darby Repairs and Renovations*—followed by a phone number.

Darby again.

We followed Lillian inside. She flicked on the wall switch, and a small lamp resting on an end table snapped to life. A gorgeous mound of striped orange fluff immediately jumped onto the table and purred a vigorous welcome.

"Elliot, how are you, baby?" I crooned, lifting the cat gently into my arms. "I've missed you!"

Removing her coat, Lillian gave me a weary smile as Elliot nuzzled my damp hair. "He's glad to see you, too. It's been a while since you've visited us."

I'd actually been there about a month ago. Every so often I drop off a bag of cat kibble for Lillian. I always use the excuse of having picked it up at a BOGO—a buy one get one sale—at one of the out-of-town supermarkets. Aunt Tressa calls it my little pink lie.

Glancing around the small home at the worn but tidy furnishings, I was reminded of the day I first walked in here.

The Hazleton Humane Society had received an anonymous call about a "cat problem" in Lillian's trailer. I'd learned about it from Bernice Jessup, a resident in the convalescent home where I read to a group of seniors every Monday evening. Bernice and Lillian had been close friends since childhood. Bernice had been so concerned about her friend that I offered to help.

Five volunteers showed up at Lillian's trailer that warm Saturday morning. Convinced that we had only the darkest of motives, she first refused to let us in. After much coaxing, we finally managed to reassure Lillian that we were there to help, not to harm, the cats.

The stench of urine had hit us first, so powerful it made our eyes water. The kitties—nineteen in all—were crowded into every nook, crack and cranny. All but one were in decent condition, if stressed from living in such cramped conditions. Lillian, who hadn't realized that the Hazleton Humane Society was a "no-kill" shelter, had collected every homeless cat that wandered into her mobile home park. She couldn't bear the thought of sending any of her babies to the "pound," where she was sure they would all be put to death.

Wearing gloves and masks, we removed all but one cat that day. Later, we returned and scrubbed the trailer from end to end. Elliot, the cat Lillian had adopted as a kitten four years earlier, remained with her. The other cats found loving homes, with the exception of a severely underweight kitty named Smoky, who'd been suffering from feline leukemia. It broke my heart to see him euthanized.

Lillian hung her coat in the small closet near the door. "Would you ladies like some tea?" she offered weakly.

"Thanks, Lillian, but we should be going." It was the first time Aunt Tressa had spoken since we'd walked in. Sadness weighted her usually chipper voice. She reached her arm over my shoulder and stroked Elliot's furry head.

Lillian, looking drained and distracted, was absently fingering an odd-looking pendant that hung from a silver strand around her neck. She toyed with it nervously as she stared off into space.

"I've never seen that before, Lillian," I said, peering more closely at the pendant. It was about an inch in diameter, glowing bright pink, and shaped like a ball of yarn.

"This? Oh dear, sometimes I forget I'm wearing it. I've even worn it to bed a few times without intending to. It was awarded to me for winning last year's Knitting Extravaganza."

"Is that the event your knitting club hosts?" I set Elliot down on the floor.

"Yes." Lillian fingered the plastic pendant. "It has an eensy weensy battery, you see, that makes it light up. Since I don't have any other talents, I'm rather proud of it. Silly, isn't it?"

"It's not silly at all. And I'm sure you have many talents." I didn't know that for sure, but I wanted to cheer her up.

If only she would tell us what was troubling her . . .

Aunt Tressa moved closer to admire the pendant, but I could

tell her mind was elsewhere. When she rubbed her arms and shivered, I suddenly realized how cold it was in the trailer. For her own sake, I hoped Lillian would crank up the heat a notch or two after we left.

"Maybe we should let Lillian get some rest," my aunt said. "We ought to be going, anyway."

Lillian looked relieved, which only increased my concern. Any time I'd ever visited her, she couldn't wait to ply me with tea and cookies. She always hated to see me leave.

Maybe she was simply exhausted, I reasoned. Being questioned by Chief Fenton in the wake of a nasty murder wasn't anyone's idea of spending a relaxing afternoon.

"You'll call me if you need anything, right Lillian?" I said. Her face was drawn. She seemed alarmingly frail, as if a breath of air could blow her across the room.

"Oh, well, I would never want to bother you, Apple. Elliot and I will be just fine, won't we?" She smiled down at her beloved feline.

"It wouldn't be a bother, Lillian. Do you still have my number?"

"You bet I do, right here." She tapped an index finger to her temple. "Yours is easy to remember, because it's the Hazleton exchange, plus eight-six-eight-six. Nineteen eighty-six is the year the ladies and I founded the Hazleton Knitting Club, so I couldn't possibly forget it."

Aunt Tressa waved good-bye and started for the door, but I still had one more question.

"Lillian, I noticed you have a *Darby Renovations* sign in front of your home. Are you having some work done?"

"Oh, yes!" she said, her voice lifting. "Darby is this lovely man I met when I was browsing in the new pet supply store last week. I was eyeing the most wonderful thing for Elliot—a tall carpeted contraption, like a tree, with a little circular house at the top that he can curl up in. It was expensive, though, almost sixty dollars. I was debating whether or not I should splurge for Elliot when this nice man with a white beard standing beside me offered to build me one for only ten dollars. He told me his name was Jack Darby."

Interesting. Ten dollars seemed to be her lucky number today. Or was it so lucky?

And what was this Darby fellow's game? Was he trying to take advantage of a trusting senior?

"Lillian, Jack Darby was at the estate sale today. Did you see him there?"

"He was?" Lillian looked perplexed. "Why, no, I didn't see him at all."

Not surprising, I thought. The man had the knack of disappearing in the blink of a wayward eye.

"I'm sure he'd have said hello to me if he'd seen me," Lillian added. "He's a very polite man. It's peculiar, though, isn't it? I mean, that Mr. Darby would be in the pet store and at the estate sale at the same time I was. What an odd coincidence."

Odd indeed. And more than a little suspect.

"Lillian, if Darby's only building a carpeted tree for Elliot, why did he put a sign out front? I mean, I can't imagine it would take him more than a few hours to build." I chided myself for badgering her, but the whole thing sounded off kilter.

"Oh, that's the beauty part." Her pale blue eyes beamed. "It's not going to be just a tree. Mr. Darby is going to custom build an entire piece of furniture, with a carpeted walkway that goes high over the sofa and a ramp that leads right to Elliot's food dish. It's going to be quite the ticket!"

Hmmm. "He's doing all that for ten dollars?"

Lillian frowned. "Well, yes, I think that's what he said. I hope I didn't misunderstand him."

I hoped so too. Maybe I'd find an excuse to show up at Lillian's the day Darby was building Elliot's carpeted kingdom.

After extracting another promise from Lillian to call me if she needed anything, Aunt Tressa and I headed outside into the cold. I'd lost track of time, but the digital clock in my car flashed 6:16.

"Let's stop at the Food Mart," Aunt Tressa said, referring to Hazleton's only market. "If I'm going to have to fight a murder rap, I'm going to need some sustenance." She snapped her seat belt into place with a loud click.

Starting in the bakery aisle, no doubt. But I couldn't resist a tiny smile.

Aunt Tressa was back.

CHAPTER THREE

I knew I must have appeared to be staring, yet couldn't tear my eyes from her. With a shy smile at the teller, she pulled from her small purse a bank book, along with a five-dollar bill, and set them both on the counter. As the teller made the transaction, I felt myself wishing I could be him, that I could touch the bank book, which moments before she'd held in her slender hand. I knew what I was feeling was madcap. But in that single moment, I wanted nothing more than to marry this woman . . .

The Hazleton Food Mart was hopping.

A plow had swept through the parking lot earlier, leaving the pavement coated with a treacherous layer of slippery, freezing slush. Nonetheless, dozens of cars, trucks and SUVs had slithered over the icy mess, somehow managing to slide into parking spaces. I was forced to park my Honda at the end of a long row. I prayed another driver wouldn't wheel around the corner too fast and skid into me.

"I'll make supper for you tonight," I told Aunt Tressa as we picked our way cautiously across the slick parking lot. "What would you like?"

She heaved a sigh. "Oh, I don't know. After all my talk about needing sustenance, I'm not sure I'll even be hungry. Maybe I'll get a pizza. And I'll pick up a bit of dessert while we're in here."

The deli at the Mart has a deep dish sausage and pepperoni pizza that makes my taste buds dance the tarantella. Since it also contains my monthly allotment of fat calories, I indulge only on rare occasions. Besides, I knew Aunt Tressa could eat the whole thing herself.

"Then I'll get some haddock for myself and a pizza for you," I said. The automatic doors slid open, and a blast of heated air escorted us inside.

I grabbed a hand basket and Aunt Tressa did the same. The market was already mobbed, the lingering after-effect of the blizzard of 'seventy-eight, when almost every store had been forced to close for nearly a week.

We wove our way through the produce section, where I snagged a bunch of bananas and a sweet onion, and Aunt Tressa—who sneered at veggies—snagged nothing at all. She trailed behind me as we approached the fresh seafood counter, her upturned nose already wrinkling at the aroma. She narrowed her eyes at the display case, where fish selections were grouped by species on mounds of crushed ice.

"As far as I'm concerned," she quipped, "this whole display should be labeled the cat food department. I mean, look at that thing!" She pointed at an orange-skinned, polka-dotted creature that was labeled Snapper. "Who'd want to eat that?"

It was an old refrain, but after everything she'd been through today, I was relieved to hear her spouting it for the umpteenth time. "Lots of people. It's supposed to be delicious." As for me, a piece of fresh haddock coated with olive oil and spiced crumbs and baked to perfection was one of my favorite meals.

"After you get your fish, why don't you meet me in the bakery aisle," she said. "I'll pick up some snacks for us. We can get the pizza on the way out."

Ten minutes later, I found Aunt Tressa squinting at the ingredients label on a loaf of bread wrapped in blinding turquoise cellophane. "Look at this, App. It has organic barley malt syrup, organic whole spelt flour, organic cracked wheat . . .

and that's only for starters."

"It's healthy," I pointed out. "Oh gosh, this is one of Celeste's homemade breads. See? *Celeste-y-al Whole Grain Breads*," I read from the attractive, scallop-edged label. *"A healthy, heavenly treat!"*

Aunt Tressa hoisted the loaf in the air. "Healthy, heavenly and hopelessly heavy," she remarked, setting it back on the display rack. "No offense to Celeste, but give me a plain loaf of fluffy white bread any day."

She tossed a package of frosted brownies and a box of almond cookies into her basket. After picking up the pizza from the deli section, we headed toward the checkout. Then I remembered something. "Wait here," I told my aunt. "I have to run back to the seafood section. I forgot the cracker coating for my fish."

"I'll go, Apple. I saw a basket of lemons near the fish display. I'm thinking of baking a lemon pound cake some night this week."

Yumster.

She scooted off while I waited my turn in the "Twelve items or fewer" line. A tap on my shoulder make me swing around.

"Hello, Ms. Mariani," Chief Fenton said gruffly. In one huge hand he juggled a frozen meatloaf entrée, a green pepper and a can of baked beans. "Fancy meeting you here."

Fancy indeed.

"I'm surprised to see you," I said. "I thought you'd still be at the crime scene."

"The techs from the State lab are processing it now. Everything's in competent hands. Where's your aunt?"

Ah, the real reason he got in line behind me.

"She's in the, um"—I crossed my fingers in front of me— "cat food department."

In case he decided to go looking for her.

"Well maybe you can remind her," he said crisply, "that her

Caddy should have been inspected eight days ago."

"She has an appointment on Monday. And aren't you forgetting the grace period?" *And why didn't you tell her that yourself when you interrogated her?* I felt like snapping.

"I'm not forgetting anything." He glanced around to see who might be within earshot, then lowered his voice and leaned close to my ear. "You also might want to tell her to stick close to home, if you get my drift."

Now that perked my dander up. "As in, don't leave town?" I said sharply. The woman standing in line in front of me turned and shot me a glare. I gave her a bland smile, keeping at least a yard behind her as she unloaded the contents of her basket onto the checkout counter.

Fenton flushed slightly. "I'm only telling you what I told her back at the Dwardene place. I don't think she was listening the whole time I questioned her. She kept staring off into space."

"Chief Fenton, a man she cared about was viciously murdered. Don't you think she was probably in shock?"

"Or she was scrambling to construct an alibi."

I threw up a hand. "She doesn't need an alibi! She didn't do anything wrong."

"We'll see," he said ominously. "In the meantime, you be sure to relay my message to her."

With that, he turned and stalked off to a different checkout line, one that was much longer than the one he'd been in.

I paid for my groceries, then waited for Aunt Tressa near the customer service desk. By the time she got through the checkout, she looked thoroughly drained.

As we exited the store, I skimmed my gaze all around. I half expected to see the mysterious Darby pop into my line of vision.

But he didn't, and for that I was grateful.

CHAPTER FOUR

On the pretext of wanting a word with the teller, I strode up and stood slightly to her left, my heart fluttering like a butterfly in my chest. I gave her a polite nod, apologized for the interruption, then proceeded to babble out some imagined task I wished to have the teller assist me with when he was free. Oh, if only she knew that the single task I longed to carry out was to have her for my beloved wife . . .

Cinnie, my orange marmalade cat, was on me like static cling the second I unlocked the door and stepped inside my apartment.

"I know, I know, you're starving." Balancing her on one shoulder and carrying the groceries in the other arm, I trekked into the kitchen. I deposited her gently on the floor, then poured her favorite kibble into her bowl and freshened her water. A wave of mental fatigue—a kind of after-shock—was beginning to slither through my bones.

My aunt had gone into her side of the house to feed Pazzo and Ringo, the two kitties she adopted from the shelter during the adoption fair this past August. Five years ago, Aunt Tressa and I bought the side-by-side duplex we lived in. That was two years after Marty Krichner, my aunt's adoring husband, died from a sudden aneurysm.

Aunt Tressa is more like a mother than an aunt to me, since she reared me from the time I was seven. I was six, just entering the first grade, when my mother left my father and me. She disappeared as effectively as if she'd joined the Witness Protection Program. Not long after that, my father, Vincent Mariani, decided single fatherhood wasn't for him. A year after my mother vanished, he left me in Tressa's care and flew out to Vegas. He's still there, working as a blackjack dealer in a casino on the strip.

I was sliding Aunt Tressa's pizza onto a cookie sheet and popping it into the oven when I heard her kicking off her Beatle boots in my front entryway. Along with the brownies and cookies she'd picked up at the Food Mart, she brought along her fuzzy orange slippers—the ones I call her duck feet.

I'd also poured two hefty-sized glasses of chardonnay. I handed one to Aunt Tressa after she dumped the cookies and brownies she'd bought onto my kitchen table. After a long swig of wine, she dropped into a chair. Her eyelids were puffy, and her nose was red. She'd apparently had another crying jag while she was alone in her apartment.

I squeezed her shoulder lightly. "Aunt Tressa, I'm so sorry about Lou." She looked up at me, her eyes watering. I leaned over and gave her a fierce hug.

I wanted to say more, to expand upon Lou's many attributes. But frankly, I hadn't known the man all that well, at least not in a personal sense. He'd been an estate appraiser for years. My boss, an attorney who specialized in estate planning, had had a fairly long affiliation with him.

In the six or so weeks that my aunt had been dating Lou, they seemed to have developed a special fondness for one another. Lou had even professed to love the Beatles music that Aunt Tressa was forever pumping out of her CD player. My aunt was probably the most fanatic Beatles lover in modern history.

"Thanks, Apple." With a loud snuffle, she tore open one of

the bakery boxes and ripped a brownie in half. "I need an hors d'oeuvre," she explained, as if scarfing down a brownie right before dinner was an aberration for her.

While the pizza heated, I unwrapped the butcher paper that contained my haddock. I grabbed a lemon from the fridge, cut out a wedge with a sharp knife, then squeezed some of the juice over the fish. A light coating of olive oil went on next. Then I dredged the fish through the spicy cracker crumb mixture that Aunt Tressa had picked up for me in the "cat food" section.

I glanced at the knife resting next to the lime. A memory came at me like a comet.

Quick caveat, though. Lou and Blake had a bit of a spat earlier, so he might not be in the best of moods . . .

"Aunt Tress, did Lou ever mention anything about not getting along with Blake?"

She swallowed a huge glob of brownie. "With Blake? No, I don't think so. Although he did mention once that Blake could squeeze a dime until FDR surrendered. But I never heard him say they actually fought about anything."

I extracted a baking dish from my cabinet. "Celeste mentioned that Lou and he had a tiff earlier, remember?"

"Yeah," she said slowly, "you're right. But a tiff does not a murder make."

No, but right now I was looking for motive. "Can you recall who was hanging around Lou's office when you went in to see him?"

She thought about it for a moment. "No one other than Lillian. She was coming out just as I was heading in. She looked odd, too, as if—"

"As if she'd seen a ghost, right?"

"Kind of. She had a spacey look in her eyes."

More like frightened, I thought. I slid the haddock into the oven next to the pizza. "Was anyone else hanging around?"

"A man I didn't recognize came out of the bathroom as I was leaving Lou's office. Short, balding, sort of nondescript."

Which pretty much described at least a dozen of the people I'd seen milling around at the estate sale.

I grabbed some veggies from the fridge and began putting together a salad. "I wonder if Celeste and Blake will still have their open house tomorrow," I said, carving a tomato into five slices. "And before I forget, there's some mail for you next to the toaster. The mailman put it in the wrong box. Again."

She got up and snatched the two envelopes addressed to her off the counter. "Look at this one. Tressa *Kirchner*. They want me to send them a donation but they can't even get my name right." She flipped the envelopes back onto the counter.

I squelched a smile. Either way, I knew she would send them a check. The solicitation was from one of my aunt's favorite children's charities.

Our respective meals came out of the oven at about the same time. After we finished eating, I lifted a curtain and peeked outside the window. The snow had finally stopped. I had to admit it made a lovely winter scene, as if an unseen hand had spread a layer of marshmallow frosting over the town. I was also pleased to see that the plows had done a thorough job of clearing the roads.

And while there was no doubt that the worst thing that had happened today was Lou Marshall getting murdered, I couldn't stop thinking about Lillian—alone in that cold trailer with her cat. She was frightened of something, I was sure of it.

That night, the last thing I saw as I drifted into a fitful sleep was Lillian's fearful expression.

CHAPTER FIVE

In those few moments at the teller's cage, I gained much. First, I saw that her left hand was bare; it bore not a single token of another man's affections. I was also able to see the name on her bank book, as well as her address. She lived in an old section of Hazleton, on a quiet street of predominantly two-family homes. Her name was Dora . . .

On Sunday morning, I was popping bread into the toaster when I heard my aunt's front door open and close. I trotted into my living room and flicked open the mini-blinds on my front window. Outside, snow glistened on the bare branches of the maple trees that lined our quiet street. I spotted Aunt Tressa trudging down our unshoveled front walk in search of the Sunday paper. She found it, halfway between the sidewalk and our front porch.

And then she flew upward, butt over Beatle boots, landing hard in the snow.

I whipped open my door. "Are you all right?"

She waved a hand at me, a signal that she'd survived the fall. Then I saw her face contort as she read the headline through the plastic bag that shrouded the paper. She hoisted herself up out of the snow and clomped back up the walk.

"Look at this!" She closed my front door with a crash and shoved the paper under my nose.

I glanced at the headline as I brushed chunks of clinging

snow off the back of her coat. "Come inside and have some coffee."

In the kitchen, I unsheathed the paper and set it on the table. Aunt Tressa dropped into a chair, and I read the paper over her shoulder.

APPRAISER MURDERED AT ESTATE SALE
Local Realtor claims she was last to see victim alive

Oh, Lord.

The article went on to describe the murder in gruesome, ghoul-like detail.

The eager reporter whose byline appeared under the headline had attended the estate sale with the idea of writing a local feature article.

He got a bigger story than he ever dreamed of.

Apparently, as the police were questioning everyone, a witness to my aunt's "last one to see him alive" declaration revealed this delectable bit of hearsay to the reporter.

"What kind of reporting is that?" Aunt Tressa bellowed. "Totally irresponsible, I say!"

Possibly, but unfortunately, the reporter was simply quoting a witness.

"I wouldn't give it another thought, Aunt Tressa. Everyone in Hazleton knows you would never commit murder." I poured her a cup of coffee and set the sugar and milk on the table.

"Everyone except Paul Fenton."

Oops. Forgot about him. "Maybe. But he can't go around accusing you of murder based on circumstances alone. *Yes,* you and Lou had been dating. *Yes,* you'd seen him only ten minutes before he—"

She looked at me, open-mouthed.

"Never mind. How about a cinnamon roll? I can defrost one in thirty seconds."

"Defrost three." She chucked two spoonfuls of sugar into her mug.

I still can't figure out how Aunt Tressa ended up with the turbo-charged metabolism gene, while I inherited the one with the dead batteries. Her size eight frame consumes enough sugar in a year to keep a chocolate bunny factory up and running. She also lucked out with lush brunette hair that made her wavy, Beatles-style coiffure fluff to perfection around her heart-shaped face—as opposed to my chestnut brown hair, which couldn't hold a curl with a snow shovel.

Which reminded me of the task that awaited me—the first shoveling out of the season.

While the rolls defrosted in the microwave, I smeared raspberry jam on my toast.

"I thought about this all night," Aunt Tressa said. She reached down to pat Cinnie, who'd strolled under the table and was rubbing against her legs. "I wracked my brain trying to remember who else was milling around on the second floor after I left Lou."

"And?"

She shook her head. "Josh was in his room with that"—she shuddered—"creepy monster of his. Celeste came out of one of the bedrooms as I was heading down the stairs. I think I mentioned the bald guy I didn't recognize. And there was Lillian, of course."

Lillian.

"I'm going to call Lillian this morning," I said, removing the buns from the microwave. "I want to be sure she's okay."

"Good idea. I didn't have my head on straight when we left the mansion yesterday, but Lillian did look scared, didn't she?"

"Yes. The question is why."

"Do you think she saw the killer?"

The microwave beeped. I extracted the warm cinnamon buns

and set them on a trivet in front of my aunt. "She saw something, Aunt Tress. I feel sure of it. I just wish I knew what it was." I snapped my fingers. "What about Darby?"

"The guy who gave me his card? What about him?"

"I don't know. He seemed to pop in and out of sight like he was performing a disappearing act. You didn't notice him hanging around the study where Lou was, did you?"

"Definitely not. I'd have remembered that shock of white hair."

I still wasn't ready to cross him off my list of potential suspects. He'd been far too intrigued by those antique daggers for my liking.

My aunt was reaching for a bun when the phone rang. I picked up the receiver and chatted with Celeste for a few minutes, then hung up.

"Celeste and Blake are still going to have their open house this afternoon. She spent all week preparing the food and doesn't want it to go to waste."

"I guess I can't blame her. I'm not much in the mood for it, though."

"I'm sure Celeste would understand if you didn't go. I don't mind stopping by there for a little while by myself."

Aunt Tressa licked sticky cinnamon goop off her thumb. "Nah, I'll go with you. Maybe between the two of us we can do a little spying. Do you think some of the people who were at the estate sale might be at the open house?"

"Maybe, if they're friends of Blake and Celeste."

She smacked her lips. "Let's do it."

CHAPTER SIX

After she left the bank, I hurried back to my office. I pondered what to do next. My schedule has been extremely busy. With the war over, the town is experiencing a building boom. As president in charge of mortgage lending, I attend board meetings almost daily. Every day, new loan applications pour onto my desk. Small tract houses are becoming the rage. Tiny Hazleton is growing . . .

Lillian's cell phone rang six times before it finally went to voice mail. She had one of those services that catered to seniors and charged blessedly low rates. I left another message, begging her to call to let me know she was all right.

I'd been calling her since ten in the morning. It was now ten past two.

"I'm getting a little worried," I confided to Aunt Tressa.

Aunt Tressa shrugged on her coat. "Maybe she went somewhere with her knitting club friends."

"It's possible."

But why wouldn't she have her cell phone with her? Isn't that the point of having one?

"Can you drive again, Apple? I don't want you-know-who to have another reason to hound me."

"Sure. But I'll be glad when you get that sticker."

Celeste and Blake lived in Hazleton's one and only condo development. Known as Cardinal Pond, it consisted of three rows of brick townhouses that formed a U-shape around a man-made pond. The parking lot had been thoroughly plowed and sanded. I located the area marked Visitor Parking and pulled into one of the spaces.

The twin aromas of pine and peppermint swirled around us as we stepped into Blake and Celeste's townhouse. Celeste looked grim and subdued as she took our coats. "Apple, Tressa, I'm so glad you could make it." Today she wore a simple black cashmere dress, adorned with only a jeweled poinsettia pin. Her demeanor seemed a bit more restrained than it had been a day ago. Even her stylish blond hair looked paler and less vibrant than usual.

From somewhere behind me, the opening notes of *The God-father* theme, hummed in an off-key twang, drifted into my ears. I whirled around just in time for Blake Dwardene to plant a noisy kiss on my cheek.

"Apollonia Nicole Mariani, in the adorable flesh." Blake smiled as he encased me in a squishy hug.

Okay, it was true. My dad—whose all-time favorite movie was *The Godfather*—named me after the smoldering Sicilian beauty who married Al Pacino in the film.

"Stop teasing her," Celeste said, swatting Blake lightly on the arm. "Besides, Apollonia is a beautiful name."

At thirty-six, two years my senior, Blake still had the flaxen, surfer-dude locks and long-lashed green eyes that had made him a high school heartthrob. Together, he and Celeste made a stunning—and truly golden—couple.

Today, though, his face appeared drawn, his eyes weary. He looked as if he either hadn't slept at all, or had slept for hours without getting an ounce of rest. "I'm glad you both came," he said. "Tressa, I'm very sorry about Lou. I never had the chance to tell you yesterday."

"Thanks. He was . . . a good friend."

"Have you heard anything from the police?" I asked Blake. "Do they have any idea who did it?"

Celeste nestled closer to Blake. "No," she said. "Chief Fenton and the crime scene people are going back there today. We're hoping they'll finish up so we can move the rest of the stuff out of there tomorrow morning. We'd already scheduled the movers."

"That soon?" I said, surprised.

"I've got to be in New York on Wednesday," Blake said. "I don't want to dump all the last-minute details on Celeste."

"How about some of my homemade eggnog?" Celeste offered, injecting a cheery note into her voice. "It has only a touch of rum, so you won't have any problem driving. Unless you drink a gallon, of course." She winked at Aunt Tressa, then escorted us into the large living room, where jazzy holiday music played softly in the background. On the mantel, above the fake fireplace, a row of white candles winked and glimmered. Several people stood around, clutching cups and plastic plates and chatting in low tones. Their faces were listless, not at all festive. We followed Celeste over to a long sideboard, where platters of hors d'oeuvres rested on both sides of a crystal punch bowl filled with eggnog.

"The eggnog's good," I told Celeste after taking a sip.

"Ditto that," Aunt Tressa said.

Celeste beamed. "Help yourselves to hors d'oeuvres. I made all of the breads and crackers myself with organic flour and grains. And by the way," she whispered conspiratorially, "if you want something with a little more bite, there's a bar in the dining room." With that, she floated away to greet another guest.

Aunt Tressa's eagle-eyed gaze soared over the food-laden trays and landed on a thick cracker topped with a swirly brown mixture. She snatched one. "What do you think this is?"

I took one and tasted it. The flavor was unusual, but I

couldn't place it. "I don't know, but it's good. Try it."

My aunt bit off a half and chomped it into oblivion. "Strange-tasting. Not bad, though."

At that moment, Blake was scurrying past us on his way to the kitchen. I nabbed him and asked him what was on the cracker.

"That's game pâté, imported straight from England."

My aunt's face crumpled like a Ferris wheel whose bolts had given way all at once. She quickly gulped back three mouthfuls of eggnog.

"Really?" I said.

"Yeah, Celeste loves the stuff, but it's pricey as all get-out."

"It's very tasty," I added, grateful that Blake was already scooting away.

Aunt Tressa's face was the color of organic flour. She wiped her lips with a red paper napkin. "Did I," she said shakily, "just eat *game* pâté? Little-animals-that-walk-in-the-woods pâté?"

I winced. "Kind of. You don't have to eat the rest of it."

She looked around surreptitiously. "What am I going to do with it? I don't suppose they have a dog."

"Afraid not."

"How about a tarantula?"

"Here, put it on my plate."

She obliged, and I covered it discreetly with my napkin. Sometimes I wondered who got custody of whom all those years ago. "All right, now let's mingle," I said. "Keep your ears open for any scuttlebutt about . . . you know what."

"That's right, we came to spy." She glanced around. "You'd think we'd know some of these people, wouldn't you? I don't recognize a soul."

"Maybe they're colleagues of Blake's."

Blake is a manufacturer's rep for several high-end vitamin companies. Although he and Celeste both attended Hazleton

High School in the early nineties, they'd never spoken a word to each other until about two years ago, when Blake went into The Grain Factor to keep an appointment with the regional marketing manager, who turned out to be Celeste. They clicked instantly and began seeing one another. As my aunt is fond of saying, *chalk another one up for Cupid.*

"Even Celeste's mother isn't here," Aunt Tressa said. "Doesn't she live in Hazleton?"

I'd wondered about that myself. "As far as I know she does. She's either remarried or living with a boyfriend. I'm not sure which."

Aunt Tressa and I split up and I puttered around the room, smiling politely at everyone and wondering who the guests were. As far as I could recall, none of the people who'd attended the estate sale were here. Sam was noticeably absent. I had this weird sensation that the guests were all ringers, replacements for the ones who'd originally been invited.

Starting to grow bored, I meandered back to the punch bowl for more eggnog. En route, I passed a cluster of framed photos that sat on a low chrome-and-glass table. I bent down to take a gander at them. In the center of the table, a silver, heart-shaped frame bore a faded color snapshot of a sixty-something woman sitting on a flowered sofa, her arm wrapped possessively around a gawky, preteen girl—Celeste. In contrast to Celeste's sad smile, the woman wore a vivacious grin, belying the world-weary glaze in her careworn blue eyes.

Another photo caught my eye—this one of Blake and an older man standing in front of a log cabin. I couldn't help smiling at the image of a much younger Blake, his blond hair curling around his neckline, a mischievous gleam in his eye.

"Ghastly photo, isn't it?"

I turned to find Blake hovering behind me with a glass of something crimson in his hand.

I laughed. "Are you kidding? You look exactly like you did in high school. Macho man with an attitude. *Machotude.*"

"Come on. Was I that bad?"

"Worse, actually. Always kissing the girls and making them cry." I pointed at the photo. "That's your dad, isn't it?"

"Yep." Blake grinned. "That's us at his fishing cabin in Weare."

I remembered Albert Dwardene from Blake's high school graduation party. Always quite the character, he'd whisked off the dress shirt he'd been wearing that day and donned one of his wife's bikini tops. He paraded around like that for a good half hour before Blake's mom dragged him inside by the ear and ordered him to change.

My own dad didn't quite make it to my high school graduation. A big convention in Vegas that weekend prevented him from flying east for the event.

It was a convenient excuse, anyway.

"Do you still have the cabin?"

"Unfortunately, yes." Celeste squeezed in between us and slid her arm through Blake's. "I've been begging him to sell that old place, but Blake says it's his haven."

He tapped her lightly on the nose. "It *is* my haven. Some day, when you're tired of the rat race in Manhattan, you'll appreciate having a love nest on the lake we can escape to."

"Love nest! It doesn't even have a kitchen, just one of those horrid wood stoves." Celeste shuddered. "Not to mention that I saw a spider there last summer the size of a tractor."

"Yikes, don't tell my aunt," I said.

"Tell your aunt what?" Aunt Tressa ambled into the mix holding a plate covered with cheese chunks, rolled ham slices, and black olives.

"Oh, I was just telling Apple—"

The doorbell rang three times in quick succession.

"Sounds like an anxious latecomer." Blake excused himself and went to answer the door. Seconds later, a loud voice erupted.

"But your uncle *gave* me that car," the voice boomed. "Not only does it belong to me, but I've already sunk about eight hundred bucks into it! Why should I pay anything for it?"

I recognized the voice right away—Josh Baker's.

"First of all, calm down." Blake's tone was one of controlled fury.

After that, he must have dragged Josh into another room, because somewhere a door closed. Hard.

The guests had all turned and were gawking in our direction. Celeste's face flushed pink. "It's all right everyone," she called to the group. "He's just a disgruntled tenant of Blake's." She excused herself and fled toward the kitchen.

Aunt Tressa offered me an hors d'oeuvre from her plate. "Well, flippity doodah, that was embarrassing."

"I feel bad for Celeste," I said, taking a small square of cheddar. "She looked mortified."

"What do you suppose Josh was so riled up about?"

"I don't know, but it was obviously something about a car."

Josh had always been somewhat of a sulky kid, and I'd heard his temper explode on more than one occasion when things didn't go his way. And, if I remembered correctly, he'd always been a car aficionado.

But none of that explained his bursting into a private residence and verbally attacking Blake.

The background music grew suddenly louder, the bass a tad bolder. Celeste, I was sure, had adjusted the volume on the CD player to mask any unpleasant voices that might drift into the areas where the guests were still mingling.

"Maybe we should think about leaving," Aunt Tressa said.

"I'm all for that. When Blake is free, I'll ask him to fetch our coats."

Celeste returned to the living room bearing a large tray. Wearing her best hostess face, she ambled among the guests, offering up tiny round carrot cakes and chocolate truffles. Aunt Tressa eyed the tray hungrily, but my appetite was gone.

"Oh, Apple, at least try something," Celeste pleaded. "I made the carrot cake with organic carrots and pure Tahitian vanilla. And Tressa, the filling inside these truffles is my own concoction, made from the most delectable cocoa—grown in Trinidad—that you've ever tasted."

Aunt Tressa wouldn't have cared if the cocoa had been grown in the Bronx. She snagged a truffle and bit off a large half.

I removed a miniature carrot cake from the tray and took a bite. "Mmm, this is scrumptious." And it was. It was one of the best cakes I'd ever tasted.

"So's the truffle," Aunt Tressa said, dabbing at her lips with a holiday napkin.

"Thanks. Once we're settled in New York I'm going to create a line of desserts to go with my—"

"—take it to small claims court! Don't think you're getting away with this." It was Josh again, this time stomping toward the front door, his face flushed with fury. When I fell into his line of vision, he momentarily froze.

"Do whatever you want," Blake said, one fist clenched at his side.

Josh hesitated, but only for a moment. His dark gaze seared through me before he stormed out and slammed the door.

"Excuse me," Celeste said quietly. She set the dessert tray on a side table and hurried over to Blake, but he was already stalking toward the kitchen. Celeste followed him.

"So much for our coats," Aunt Tressa said.

Several of the guests began making noises about leaving. The incident with Josh had clearly made everyone uncomfortable.

"Don't worry," I said. "It looks like other people are getting ready to go, too."

By the time we'd gotten our coats and thanked Blake and Celeste for their hospitality, it was dark outside. A chill wind nipped at our faces as we made a brisk dash for my car. As soon as I cranked the engine, I flipped the heat on high and dug my cell phone out of my purse. I tried Lillian's cell number again. After four rings, I snapped the phone shut.

A bad feeling was beginning to gnaw at me.

"She's still not home," I told my aunt.

"Then let's go over there. For all we know, she could have fallen and broken something and can't get to her phone."

Oh, Lord. That hadn't even occurred to me.

I turned sharply out of the parking lot and headed for Lillian's. It was four fifty-nine when I pulled up in front of her trailer. In each of the small windows, a dim glow filtered through the lowered shades.

"Good, there's a light on," Aunt Tressa said. "She must be home."

But any relief we felt was short-lived.

I leaped up Lillian's front steps and was tapping the metal door with my knuckles when I realized something—the door was already open, about a quarter of an inch.

"Lillian?" I called through the crack.

No answer.

I felt Aunt Tressa's hand on my back, and we both rushed inside.

The light came from the small lamp that rested on an end table next to the sofa. No other lights were on. I felt a chill zip down my spine.

"It feels like Antarctica in here," my aunt said with a shiver.

"Lillian?" I could hear the rising hysteria in my voice.

Aunt Tressa barged across the small living room, and I followed on rubbery legs. We paused for a moment, looking all around.

The door to Lillian's bedroom was open, as was the bathroom door. My heart nearly stopped beating when I peeked into her bedroom.

Lillian's bed was unmade.

And it looked as if she'd left it in a hurry.

A thin blanket and a knitted, yellow-and-white afghan were tangled around the top sheet. Had Lillian been thrashing in her sleep? Or had someone rousted her out of bed in the dead of night?

A painted white bureau in the corner of the room was adorned with a vinyl jewelry box, a framed black-and-white photo of a white cat, and an old-fashioned hand mirror and hairbrush. Nothing appeared to be disturbed there, at least as far as I could see.

A miniature lamp with a frilly shade sat on Lillian's night table. I spied something on the floor between the bed and the night table. Bending closer, I saw that it was a plastic alarm clock, its cord still plugged into the wall socket.

"What do you think happened?" my aunt said, directly behind me.

I jumped. "Lordy, you scared me. I don't know what happened, but I don't like this at all."

"Yeah, I agree." My aunt followed me out of the bedroom.

The bathroom was spare, with only a few toiletries atop the vanity and a box of yellow tissues on the toilet tank. Gingerly, I peeked behind the shower curtain. I was relieved to find the tub empty.

On the other side of the bathroom was another door—a closed one. A spare room of some sort, I suspected. Given the size of the trailer, it had to be tiny. I turned the knob, afraid of what might await me on the other side.

But it was only a storage room. An ironing board leaned against one wall, and a few cardboard boxes sat on the floor. A large shopping bag bulging with skeins of pastel yarn rested on one of the boxes.

I closed the door.

A sudden thought struck me. I dashed back to the kitchen area and yanked open the coat closet. "Aunt Tressa, Lillian's lilac coat is still here." I turned around. "Aunt Tressa?"

My aunt was standing beside the sofa, peering at the crumpled scrap of paper in her hand. "Look at this, Apple. It's a napkin from some restaurant."

"Where did you find it?"

"Right here. On the floor."

She smoothed out the napkin and handed it to me. It was white and somewhat greasy, made of flimsy stock. Printed diagonally across it, in bright red script, were the words *Darla's Dine-o-Rama ~ New Hampshire's best eats!*

"I've heard of this place. Isn't it in Hampstead, or Atkinson?"

"Shush for a minute." Aunt Tressa grabbed my arm so hard she almost pulled me to the floor. "Did you hear that? Something squeaked."

"No, I—"

Oh, God.

That wasn't a squeak. It was a meow.

Shoving the napkin into my coat pocket, I raced back to Lillian's bedroom. I dropped to the floor and peered underneath the bed. My gaze was met by a pair of glowing eyes.

Elliot shot out as if he'd been launched by a catapult. He stopped short when he reached Aunt Tressa, then rubbed vigorously against her boots. She bent and lifted him into her arms. "Oh, sweetie, you must be so cold," she cooed, rubbing Elliot's face against her own.

"He's probably hungry, too." I remembered when we'd passed by the kitchen that his food dish had been empty.

Cuddling Elliot against her faux fur coat, Aunt Tressa carried him into the kitchen. While she fished through the cabinets looking for cat food, I took one last look around.

And found something that sent my insides plummeting.

On the floor next to the sofa, tucked behind the end table, was Lillian's handbag.

Sheer instinct told me to inspect it, but somehow it seemed wrong, intrusive. Nevertheless, I reached down and grabbed it, then flicked open the latch. After a quick glance inside I went into the kitchen.

"Aunt Tressa, I don't think Lillian left voluntarily. I found her purse next to the sofa. With her house key inside."

She dropped the bag of cat food she was holding, sending kibble in forty directions.

I whisked my cell phone out of my purse and punched in 9-1-1.

CHAPTER SEVEN

The next few hours felt endless. I reviewed loan applications half-heartedly, focusing instead on the vision that kept drifting before my mind's eye. I pictured Dora in a checkered blouse and white pedal pushers, her golden hair unpinned and flowing loose about her shoulders. I saw the two of us picnicking on the shore of a sun-dappled lake, munching on sandwiches and sipping lemonade as we made plans for our future . . .

"Much as I hate to break it to you ladies, there's no law against an eighty-something-year-old woman leaving her purse and her cat and going out somewhere."

Aunt Tressa and I were huddled in the cold in front of Lillian's trailer, watching as Chief Fenton flicked the beam of his flashlight all around in the snow. He'd already been inside the trailer. After a few cursory looks around Lillian's tidy, sparsely furnished rooms he'd deemed there'd been no foul play.

The beam from his flashlight, diluted by the glaring headlights from his cruiser, crawled over my right front tire. Fenton stooped down, and with a frown ran a long finger over the tread. He stood slowly, his expression grave.

My insides did a cartwheel. "Did you find something?"

"I don't think this tire will pass inspection."

I gawked at him. Lillian was missing, and he was wasting valuable time examining my tire! "It already passed inspection,

Chief." I didn't even attempt to filter the irritation from my tone.

"When, Ms. Mariani? Ten months ago?"

"It was this past September. My entire car, for that matter, passed with flying colors."

"Nonetheless, safety should always come first and—"

"Paul, have you not heard a word we've said?" Aunt Tressa stomped over to him, her Beatle boots puncturing the hardened snow with every exasperated step. "A woman does not—I repeat, does *not*—leave the house without her purse or her coat. And she left her bed unmade!"

In Aunt Tressa's world, leaving home with an unmade bed was on par with going to work in only your bra and panties.

"So? I got a nephew who's never made his bed in his life. Every time he stays with me—"

"You're forgetting that the door was ajar," I interjected, my patience wearing thinner by the nanosecond. What did it take to convince this man that something had happened to Lillian?

"I'm not forgetting anything," he said coolly. "A female adult, and a very mature one at that, has left her home for who-knows-what reason. I'm sure she had another coat she could wear. Maybe she's staying at a friend's. Maybe she's even staying at a *male* friend's, if you catch my drift. Bottom line, ladies, I've got to wait at least twenty-four hours before I can do anything."

"What about the napkin, the one from Darla's Dine-o-Rama?"

Fenton smirked. "I suppose you think a stray napkin on the floor is supposed to be some kind of clue."

"I don't know what it is, but can't you at least check it out? Can't you even consider the possibility that Lillian might be in trouble?"

"Can't *you*, Ms. Mariani, consider the possibility that your friend might've eaten at the restaurant, taken a napkin home, and then dropped it near her sofa?"

My brain was ready to burst out through the back of my skull. It was time for a tactical change. "What about this . . . Darby person?" I said, pointing at the sign in front of the trailer.

"What about him?"

"I think you should question him about Lillian. He promised to build an elaborate walkway for her cat for ten dollars. Does that sound logical to you?"

"No, but I don't see the connection. You're grasping, Ms. Mariani. And you're coming up with big old handfuls of air. But let me say this." Fenton pointed a finger at me, a gesture I did not appreciate. "If your friend does turn up missing, then I'm going to be looking at her from a whole new angle."

"What are you talking about?" Aunt Tressa said.

"I mean, maybe she had a reason to want Lou Marshall out of the picture. Maybe your sweet little old lady is a cold-blooded killer."

Aunt Tressa threw up her arms. "And maybe you left your common sense home in a bottle by the door. Because you cannot, *cannot* seriously believe that Lillian Bilodeau has the temperament, let alone the strength, to stab someone."

He glared pointedly at her. "I believe everyone has the capacity to kill. Now, if you ladies are through—"

"We're not through," I said, moving toward the trailer. "With Lillian missing, I'm certainly not going to leave Elliot alone."

Fenton moved toward me, but I scurried up the stairs before he could stop me. "Who's Elliot?" he yelled.

"Lillian's cat," Aunt Tressa informed him, clumping right behind me. When she reached the doorway, she turned on her black-booted heel. "Don't worry. We won't swipe the silver."

CHAPTER EIGHT

This evening, at home alone, I have begun to plan how I will approach Dora. Aside from her name and where she lives, I know little about her. With whom does she live? Her parents? Does she have a bevy of overprotective brothers who will cringe at the idea of a man my age courting their sweet sister?

Cinnie eyed Elliot from the arm of my sofa as he poked his nose around the living room, exploring the trappings of his temporary new digs.

Aunt Tressa grinned. "I think they like each other. At least there isn't any hissing going on."

"Yet," I cautioned.

Before coming home, we'd made a brief stop at the market for kitty litter and cat food. Having an extra mouth to feed now, I didn't want to risk running short. With everything we'd had to juggle getting into the house, including one very confused cat, I'd left the ten-pound bag of litter in my car. Tomorrow would be soon enough to retrieve it.

After I put away my coat, I carried Elliot into the kitchen to show him where the cafeteria was located, then into the bathroom to show him the . . . well, bathroom. He offered up a few cursory sniffs in the direction of the litter box, then sauntered back to the living room to see what Cinnie was up to.

"Lord, what a stressful day," my aunt drawled, pouring herself a glass of spring water from my fridge. "No wonder I'm starving. How about I throw together some kooky macaroni for supper? I haven't made that in a long time."

Aunt Tressa didn't enjoy spending a lot of time on food preparation. She has flashbacks of her mother always toiling over the stove, using every pan in the house to cook the elaborate meals she was known for. Since Aunt Tressa had always gotten stuck with dishwasher duty—a chore she despised—she now favored simple meals with little fuss.

But kooky macaroni was an easy, delectable concoction Aunt Tressa invented when I was a kid.

"Right about now, a plate of kooky macaroni would really hit the spot." I set down a second dish of kibble and an extra bowl of water for Elliot.

"Uh-oh, I just remembered. My dishwasher's been leaking for the past few days. Mind if I cook everything here?"

"Be my guest."

"Okay, back in ten," she said, already striding toward the front door. "I've got a new package of ziti, and I want to feed the monkeys first."

The monkeys being Pazzo and Ringo, who'd recently perfected their high-wire act on Aunt Tressa's new valances. The word "pazzo" was Italian for crazy, and it fit the rambunctious little feline to a tee.

I put away the cat food I'd bought, then set a pot of water on to boil. After that I went upstairs to change. My thong had been crawling up my . . . well, you can imagine, so I abandoned it in favor of a pair of cotton undies. Right now, having a no-show panty line was low on my list of priorities.

As I threw on a holiday sweater and a pair of comfy sweatpants, I couldn't stop thinking of Lillian's sparse trailer, her purse tucked behind the sofa. For safekeeping, I'd hidden the purse in one of her dresser drawers before we left.

Where are you, Lillian? Please be all right . . .

Downstairs, I extracted a jar of black olives from the back of the fridge and set it on the counter. From the cabinet beneath my kitchen sink, I pulled out the old coffee can I'd stashed there, tore off the cover, and whipped out the plastic bag that housed my secret stash of gummy snakes. I grabbed a teal-colored reptile—yum, blueberry—and stuck it into my mouth. I'd barely finished chomping it and returning the can to its hideout when Aunt Tressa returned. With all the nagging I did about the junk food she ate, I didn't want her to catch me scarfing down these sugary bad boys. I'd never hear the end . . .

My aunt had changed into a pair of snug black stretch jeans, which she'd topped off with a screaming-red sweater emblazoned with glittery white snowflakes. A huge pair of silver reindeer dangled from her ears, their cloven feet resting on her shoulders.

"I got the ziti"—she plopped her culinary supplies onto my counter—"two packages of shredded cheddar, a jar of marinara sauce, and, best of all, a bottle of port wine."

I was grateful she'd brought along the port. I made a mental note to add wine to my grocery list.

"Just since we've been gone," she griped, "I've gotten seven messages on my answering machine. All from reporters, two of whom were from Boston TV stations. Can you believe the gall?"

I could believe it. That's what reporters did. But since it didn't seem like the ideal moment to voice that particular opinion, I poured us each a glass of port instead.

Aunt Tressa dumped the entire box of ziti into the boiling water. "I need something to nosh on while I cook," she announced, opening the cabinet doors over my sink. Finding nothing of interest, she moved on to the cabinets above the counter, scanning the contents of each one with all the intensity of a DEA agent searching for illegal drugs.

I leaned against the counter, a million thoughts circling my brain like birds with no place to land. "What I want to know," I said, "is why Chief Fenton refuses to admit that something happened to Lillian. I mean, how could it be more obvious?" I took a sip of port, which sent a delicious flare of warmth coursing through me. "What I also want to know is why he made that crack about looking at her from a whole new angle. Did he think that was going to intimidate us?"

A hand on her hip, Aunt Tressa fixed me with one of her looks. "What I want to know is why you don't have any more of those cookies with the cinnamon buds in them. Didn't you buy a bag last week?"

"You ate those, remember? There's a box of those garlic chips you like on the left. See it?"

"Found it." With a wicked wiggle of her eyebrows, she plucked the box from the cabinet and poured a mound of crackers into a bowl. "To answer both your questions: because he's crazy, that's why. He's been chief in this small, nearly crimeless town for so long that he can't see the florist for the peas."

I roared. "I can't believe you remembered that!"

When I was in the fourth grade, I had an art teacher who told me that the pretty horse I'd so painstakingly drawn with my colored pencils looked like a dragon in the final stages of death. Indignant, I'd stomped into the house after school, slapped it onto the fridge with a wad of tape, and announced to Aunt Tressa with all the wounded dignity of a nine-year-old that Mr. Conner couldn't see the florist for the peas.

Thoughts of Lillian intruded, sobering me immediately. She'd always seemed so delicate, so frail. I couldn't imagine anyone wanting to harm her, unless . . .

Unless, I realized grimly, she could identify the murderer.

"Aunt Tress, what if Lillian saw the murderer? And what if the murderer knows she can identify him?"

"Then she could be in trouble," my aunt said. "But we

already knew that, didn't we?" She looked away, then, "I think you should call Daniel."

Daniel.

The name gave my heart a forceful kick, sending it running for safety behind my rib cage.

Daniel Pryce and I met at Lillian's several months ago. It was a few weeks after the other volunteers and I had removed the cats from her trailer.

Concerned about Lillian, who'd been traumatized over the negative publicity from her cat ordeal, the director of the Hazleton animal shelter had contacted the New Hampshire Bureau of Elderly and Adult Services. The Bureau sent a social worker, Daniel Pryce, to investigate her situation. Kind and capable, with eyes the color of a quiet gray sea, Daniel showed up on a drizzly afternoon when I was dropping off a bag of kibble to Lillian. Right from the get-go, it was kismet.

Or *kiss-met*, as Aunt Tressa likes to call it.

We clicked, strong and hard, like a seat belt that jerks you backward too tight.

Daniel hailed from a small but close-knit family, and had always known precisely what he wanted. A woman he could love and cherish, and with whom he could share the joys—and trials—of married life. Add a kid or two to the picture, and his life would pretty much be perfect.

It was a grand plan, with only one huge glitch.

Me.

Don't get me wrong—I'd been crazy about Daniel. But trust was a humongous issue for me. My mother and father had both bailed on me. How could I be sure he wouldn't do the same? What if I possessed some deadly flaw that I wouldn't discover until it was too late?

So I'd kept my foot firmly on the brake, trying to slow the relationship to an easy pace. Daniel, meanwhile, had shifted into high gear, zooming toward a wedding date and happily ever after. I did the only thing I could think of to slow him down.

I broke it off.

I cleared my throat. "I can't call Daniel. I don't even know why I should."

"Because he cares about Lillian, App. I think he'd want to know that she could be in trouble. He might even be able to help."

Part of me, probably the bigger part, knew she was right. But the part that was still that scared, abandoned little girl said, *No, don't go there. It'll hurt too much to see him . . .*

"I'll think about it," I finally said.

She sighed. "Fair enough."

For a while we were quiet, busying ourselves with our own tasks. Aunt Tressa ripped open the packets of cheese, while I dug out my large casserole dish and coated it with a non-stick spray. I pulled out my colander and set it in the sink.

Aunt Tressa chuckled when she spied the colander. "My Nana, your great-grandmother, could never remember what that was called when I was a kid. In that darling accent of hers she'd say 'Teresa, get me that thing. You know, the-pasta-she-stay-the-water-she-go thing.' Cracked me up every time. Too bad she died before you were born. She was such a sweetheart."

I sometimes forget that my aunt was christened Teresa. When she started her realty business in the late eighties, she decided to have her name legally changed. Her personality, she'd claimed, didn't fit her original saintly appellation.

Personally, I think she just liked the name Tressa.

"Remember when the Beatles came on the *Ed Sullivan Show* for the first time?" Aunt Tressa said, her face taking on a dreamy expression.

"I don't, but—"

"It was my Nana who watched it with me. My folks had fled

upstairs, leaving the two of us alone with our old black-and-white TV. I sat on the floor, as close to the TV as I could get, while Nana sat behind me on the sofa. The music was so fantastic that I was jumping all over the place, practically tearing out my teased hair. When I turned around, Nana was smiling and clapping to the beat of 'She Loves You.' Like it was the best song she ever heard, you know?" Her eyes glistened with unshed tears.

"That's a beautiful memory, Aunt Tress."

And while the stories about my great-grandmother made me smile, I felt a dull ache grip me inside. I barely remembered my own mother, let alone Aunt Tressa's mom, who died when I was ten.

I twirled the remaining port in my glass. "Aunt Tress, did . . . Sharon ever cook for me?"

Aunt Tressa stiffened. Then she turned and looked at me thoughtfully, a wistful smile on her lips. "Your mother? Sure she did, all the time. She was actually a fairly decent cook, when she put her mind to it. And in those days, you weren't easy to please. Back then, you were as fussy as they come."

"*Moi?*"

"Yes, you."

"But I like everything!"

She shut off the burner and dumped the ziti into the colander, sending waves of warm steam spiraling toward the ceiling. "Not then, you didn't. You were a royal pain in the petunia, as your grandfather would say."

"So what did she cook?"

"Oh, the usual stuff kids like. Hot dogs in a blanket. Mac and cheese—homemade, not from a box. And since you weren't so hot on fruits and veggies in those days, she used to find ways to sneak them into your food."

I grinned. "Really? How?"

"Well for one thing, she'd slip paper-thin slices of banana into those peanut butter and marshmallow sandwiches you loved so much."

"Did I notice?"

"If you did, you didn't complain. Oh, and the mac and cheese? She'd chop broccoli into miniscule pieces and mix it in. When you asked her what the green spots were, she'd tell you, with a completely straight face, that they were the flavor buds that made the macaroni taste so delicious."

What are those green dots, Mommy?

Those are just flavor buds, sweetie. They make the macaroni taste extra special!

A sudden lump clogged my throat. In a memory as clear as glass, I could see Sharon standing at the kitchen counter wearing pink shorts and a skimpy halter top, her caramel-colored hair pulled into a loose braid, a wooden spoon waving from her hand as her sandaled feet boogied to a tune on the radio.

I'd forgotten how pretty she was. The photos I had of her had been unceremoniously ripped from their frames and shoved into a box that was now stored in the attic—a punishment for her long-ago abandonment.

"You haven't talked about her in a long time," Aunt Tressa said, layering the cheese and marinara sauce into the ziti.

"Once in a while I think about her, wonder where she is. For all we know she could be living a block away." I opened the fridge and stuck in my head. "I mean, after all this time would you even recognize her?"

"That's a tough question, App." My aunt shrugged. "Who's to know how much she's changed in twenty-seven years."

I pulled a tub of whipped butter out of the fridge and closed the door. "Tell me honestly, Aunt Tress, how hard did Dad *really* try to find her?"

Aunt Tressa's hand paused mid-stir. The question clearly

bothered her.

"Here's the thing, App. Your mom, well . . . she left your father a note."

"A note?" I stared at my aunt, whose complexion was now verging on tomato red. "She left a note and no one ever told me?"

"You were six, Apple."

"Am I six now?"

When she didn't answer, I gritted my teeth. "What did the note say?"

"It's ancient hist—"

"What. Did. It. Say."

Aunt Tressa squinted at the tangerine-painted wall above my stove, as if she could see those long-ago words scrawled there like faded graffiti. "I don't recall precisely, but essentially she told him she was leaving for a while to take care of something very important. Something extremely personal that only she could handle. She would be back as soon as she could."

"That's it?" I said.

"Pretty much. I'll admit it was cryptic. It didn't seem like something Sharon would do, but the note was definitely in her handwriting. Even the police didn't find any reason to believe she didn't leave of her own accord."

"How did Dad react?"

She set her wooden spoon on the counter. "At first he was frantic. He couldn't imagine what could be so personal that she couldn't tell him about it. All sorts of terrible things went through his mind."

"I can imagine."

"He tried getting in touch with her family in Maine, but it took him two days just to track down her folks' phone number. It wasn't like it is today, where everything's on the Internet. Anyway, when he finally reached her mother, she said they hadn't seen Sharon since before she got married."

"Why was my . . . why was Sharon estranged from her family?"

"No one ever knew. She refused to talk about it." She opened my oven and slid the casserole dish inside. "Every so often I'd catch this look on her face, like she was remembering something—something terribly sad. But don't ever think she didn't love you, Apple. You were everything to her. She told me that more than once."

My throat felt taut. "But she left me anyway."

"I can't explain that. I only know that whatever dire circumstance made her leave that day, it wasn't something she chose willingly. I think she always intended to come back, but for some reason she couldn't."

I nodded dully. If I dwelled on it long enough I'd start to get maudlin, and right now that was the last thing I needed. "Shall we skip the salad tonight and go straight for the carbs and the fat?"

Aunt Tressa gave me a relieved smile. "I'd say that sounds like a plan."

I defrosted some crusty rolls, warmed them on a cookie sheet, and set them in a basket on the table. Twenty minutes later, we were devouring the oven-baked kooky macaroni as if we hadn't seen food in a week. I was rubbing my stomach, lamenting about having overindulged, when a crash from the living room snapped me out of my fat-induced funk. I jumped up and dashed to the scene of what I was sure was a minor disaster.

A sigh of relief escaped me when I saw what actually happened. Aunt Tressa had apparently left her designer bag balanced on the arm of the sofa. It now lay on the floor in a disemboweled jumble. While Elliot chewed happily on an aquamarine eye pencil, Cinnie munched to her heart's content on a miniature Three Musketeers bar, paper and all.

I couldn't help myself—I burst into giggles.

When I finally got myself under control, I noticed that Aunt Tressa was just standing there, gawking at the mess. Then she slapped the side of her head so hard I was afraid she'd given herself a concussion.

"App, I almost forgot! That letter, or card, or whatever it was Lou gave me, is still in my bag!"

CHAPTER NINE

I sit here now at my writing desk, emptying my soul onto paper. It is very late, past midnight. Could it be but a mere half day ago that I first saw my love? Is it possible that my heart was so irrevocably captured in that tiny space of time?

My aunt stooped and gently tugged her massive handbag away from the cats. After excavating through its remaining contents, she managed to unearth a worn yellowed envelope. It was rectangular, about five-by-seven, and clearly decades old.

Aunt Tressa flipped it over. "There's no stamp or postmark, so it was obviously never mailed." She read the faded ink on the back of the envelope. "*To my love,* it says."

"Okay, now I'm intrigued."

We sat on the sofa. I turned on another lamp.

The envelope had already been opened, its top edge bearing an even slit. One corner was slightly torn. With her thumb and forefinger, Aunt Tressa extracted a faded card. "Hey, look, it's a valentine. See the picture?"

On the front of the card, two sweethearts in old-fashioned garb gazed adoringly into each other's eyes. A crimson heart was superimposed behind them like a bloated red halo. In the upper right corner, a chubby, winged cupid with a mischievous smile aimed its arrow directly at the couple.

Aunt Tressa opened the card.

The printed message on the right-hand side, in elaborate red lettering, was a simple *Happy Valentine's Day.* But the homespun poem on the left, handwritten in a precise script, was far more curious.

> *You've dwelt within my heart, dear love*
> *From that first and shining day*
> *Your eyes of blue and locks of gold*
> *Within my dreams did reign*
> *And so, dear sweet, to you I pledge*
> *My essence and my soul*
> *Now we shall dwell within this home*
> *Which shall be yours to hold*

I gave out a low whistle. "Wow. Someone had it bad for someone."

"I'll say. That's the worst poem I've ever read."

"Is there a date on the card?"

Aunt Tressa flipped it over, then tipped it closer to the light. "It's hard to read, but I think it says one-nine-five-one. Nineteen fifty-one."

"Let's see, Edgar Dwardene was seventy-nine when he died. In nineteen fifty-one he would have been"—I subtracted in my head—"seventeen or eighteen."

"Hard to believe a seventeen-year-old would write this."

"I know," I agreed. "It sounds more like someone wrote it in *eighteen* fifty-one, not nineteen fifty-one."

"I wonder whatever came of their love affair," Aunt Tressa mused dreamily. "If it *was* a love affair. I mean, why did Edgar still have this? Why didn't he ever give this valentine to the object of his affections?"

"Maybe he did and she threw it back at him. Maybe that's why he never married. Or maybe Edgar didn't even write it. But Aunt Tressa, more important: why did Lou give it to you in the first place? Tell me exactly what he said."

She blew out a breath. "Let me think. It was something like, 'Give this to Apple for me, will you?' I'm pretty sure that was it."

"But why me?"

She shook her head. "I'm as clueless as you are. The look on his face was weird, though. Almost like . . . I don't know. It's hard to explain."

"Did he know I collect antique postcards?" Buying old postcards had been a hobby of mine for the past few years. One of these days I planned to mount them all into a giant collage and have it framed.

"I might have told him that. I suppose he thought you could add this to your collection. It is pretty unique."

I picked up the envelope and flipped it over. On the front, near the edge where the envelope had once been sealed, eight numbers had been scribbled with a felt-tip pen. If I was interpreting the hasty penmanship correctly, the numbers were 1199-0540. "I wonder what these numbers mean."

Aunt Tressa peered at them. "That sort of looks like Lou's writing, but I'm not sure." She shrugged. "Eight numbers. So it can't be a phone number."

"No. Even if you left off the last zero, phone numbers never start with a one."

Then something else caught my eye. A faint brown line, slightly darker than the paper, skirted the borders of the envelope.

"Something else was in here," I said. "See? It left a mark." I showed her the darkened lines that suggested another card or paper had been inside the envelope.

"Hmm," was all she replied.

Hmm, indeed.

Whatever had been inside the envelope had been there long enough to make those dark lines. Had Lou Marshall been the one to remove it?

If so, was it important enough to have gotten him killed?

CHAPTER TEN

On the wall above me, the oil painting of Sapphire Lake that I completed this past spring beams down at me. I struggled for months getting the hues just right, but I am pleased with the results. Gazing at it now, I realize what is missing—two lovers strolling along the shore, their arms wrapped leisurely around each other's waists. Dora and me . . .

I jerked awake in the middle of a goofy dream. I'd been slicing a tomato for a salad when my small kitchen knife suddenly morphed into an enormous black dagger. Over a foot long, it seemed to weigh as much as my car. I kept trying to slice the tomato with it, but it was like lifting an anchor. Then something crawled down my back . . . a tarantula—and fortunately I woke up.

Sheesh, what a nutty dream. I turned over and screwed my fuzzy gaze in the direction of the only window that faced the street. It was too early for any daylight to be seeping through the mini-blind, but since it was Monday, staying in bed was not an option.

Elliot jumped onto my shoulder, while Cinnie sidled contentedly onto my pillow and began chewing a strand of my hair.

"Is that a hint?" I said groggily.

I shot a glance at my clock—it was six eighteen. Shivering, I tossed aside the covers, cast a baleful glance at my treadmill, then threw on my robe and slippers and trekked downstairs.

Cinnie and Elliot pranced along in front of me, beating a path directly to their food bowls. First order of the day: turn up the thermostat.

In the kitchen, I replenished the cats' food and gave them fresh water, then made a fast breakfast for myself. My reliable coffeemaker, which operates on a timer, was dutifully giving off aromatic waves of a scrumptious French roast blend.

By the time I'd showered and changed, Aunt Tressa was already in the driveway, warming up her car and scraping the frost from her windshield. The moment I opened my front door she waggled her scraper at me, then pointed at her watch.

"Coming, Saint Punctual," I muttered to myself.

The plan this morning was for me to follow her to the dealership where she was having her Caddy serviced and inspected, then give her a lift back to her realty office on Aubrey Road in Hazleton—just three streets away from the law firm where I worked.

Aunt Tressa is overly attached to her Caddy, since it belonged to the man she'd loved more than a never-ending live Beatles concert—Marty Krichner. When he died of an aneurysm seven years ago, she spiraled into a gripping depression. During those months, I worried about her constantly. She could barely haul herself to the office every day, let alone muster any enthusiasm for selling homes. Nothing seemed to snap her out of it.

Then, one afternoon on her way home from work, a car whipped out in front of her, forcing her to slam on her brakes. She started to curse at the driver when the license plate suddenly snagged her attention. It had exactly three letters—Marty's initials. To her it was a sign that he was watching over her, a loving, caring angel.

He was also giving her a mild kick in the tailpipe, she'd decided. By the next morning she was her old self again. Within a week she'd landed two new listings.

The sun was beaming from a gorgeous blue sky, glinting off the stretches of snow that lined Route 121 as I drove toward the dealership where my aunt got her car serviced. By the time I pulled up in front of the service entrance, Aunt Tressa—hard to miss in her faux mink coat and an orange scarf that could easily substitute as a runway beacon—was waiting for me.

"We have to pick it up no later than five-thirty," she said, hopping into my front seat.

"Won't it feel good to finally have that sticker?" I said.

"Yeah." She snickered. "But I'll miss tormenting Paul Fenton by reminding him I'm still in the grace period. The man is obsessed with inspections."

Right now he's more concerned about murder, I thought, choosing not to voice that particular sentiment.

"You know, last night I got thinking," Aunt Tressa said, sticking the end of her seat belt into the slot, "about that Darby guy."

Uh-oh. The sly glimmer in her eye made me nervous. I hoped she wasn't hatching some devious plan.

"And I came up with a plan."

Here we go.

"He made it pretty clear on Saturday that he was smitten with me."

"Smitten?"

"Yes, smitten," she said defensively. "So what I have to do is use that to our advantage."

"And you do that how?"

"By luring him to my apartment on a pretext, so I can do a little interrogating of my own. Paul Fenton isn't the only one in this town who can ask questions. I can do it, too—with a little more flare and a lot more subtlety."

"Subtlety? Like the time you told Jodie Breenlow her *crass* was showing?"

My aunt sniffed. "That was different. She'd put that obnoxious anti-gay bumper sticker on her car only days before her sister was marrying her life partner. Her crass *was* showing. I was simply pointing it out."

"You're missing the point," I said. "What if Darby is actually dangerous? What if he's the one who—" I stopped myself from hurtling over the edge of that one. "Okay, let me ask you this. What are you planning to use as a so-called pretext?"

"Hah! That's easy—my dishwasher. I told you it was leaking. And he told us he does plumbing repairs, remember? No job too small!" she mimed in a perky tone.

I heaved a useless sigh. It was obvious she already had her mind made up. "So what are you planning to do, get him to fix your dishwasher, then cozy up to him and then make him spill his guts?"

"Whatever it takes. Look, App, I know it's too late to help Lou, but what if that man did something to Lillian? Right now, Paul Fenton won't even entertain the idea that something's happened to her. Who's going to help her if we don't?"

I hated to admit it, but she was right.

"I'll go along with it," I said, "as long as you let me know when he's coming over. I want to be sure I'm home when he's there."

She didn't answer.

"Aunt Tress?"

"I know, I heard you. I was just thinking that Lou's birthday was coming up next week. I'd originally planned to bake him a coconut cake, but then . . ." She shook her head.

I reached over and squeezed her arm, and for a while we drove in silence. Since we were running early—it was only eight thirty-five—I decided to swing by the Dwardene place to see if anything was happening.

Minutes later, I pulled alongside the curb in front of the

mansion, just as a large white truck was swinging out of the driveway. The truck merged into the morning traffic and headed toward the center of town. What I didn't see was any logo or banner on its side panel. Was it a state police crime scene van, traveling incognito?

I slid my gearshift into Park and sat for a moment, staring at the house. As mansions go, the Dwardene residence was actually fairly small. Built over a century ago in the Second Empire style, it had a central portico with two paired columns supporting a shallow balcony. On either side of the entrance was a tall shuttered window with a horizontal hood. The mansard roof, gracefully sloped and topped by a lantern-like structure, lent the dwelling the look of a fancy wedding cake, albeit one long abandoned by a loveless bride and groom. The facade, once showy and dramatic, now drooped like a tired old woman propped up by a pair of canes. A huge mound of snow had blown onto the front steps, giving the house a neglected look.

Behind the mansion was a two-car garage that was only partially visible from the road. Squat and plain, it bore no resemblance to the dwelling. Clearly it had been built for functionality and not for style. Another truck—this one a rugged-looking flatbed—was backed up to one of the bays.

"That looks like a tow truck," Aunt Tressa said, stepping out of the car. "Let's check it out."

A feeling of gloom crept over me as I trudged up the paved drive behind my aunt. Thankfully the driveway had been plowed, but it was slippery in spots. I warned Aunt Tressa to watch out for icy patches.

On the hood of the flatbed, two large foam cups sat alongside a white paper bag. As we drew closer, I caught a glimpse of a vehicle inside the garage, but couldn't discern any particular make or model.

A tousled head of bright orange hair popped up like a jack-in-the-box from behind the truck, giving my heart a jump-start. Dressed in work blues and sporting grime-covered canvas gloves, the man speared us with a suspicious glare, then came around to the side of the truck where we were standing. "Help you ladies with something?" he barked.

"Um, no, we were just—" What were we doing, other than being outrageously nosy?

"Never mind, Chet, I know these two," came an exasperated voice from around the other side. Josh Baker, who'd apparently been stooped behind the tow truck, stood and glowered at us— his usual cordial greeting of late.

"Hey, Josh," I said brightly. "We were driving by on the way to work and wondered what was happening. We noticed a white truck pulling out of the driveway."

Pulling off his leather gloves, Josh strode toward us. "Yeah, that was a moving truck. They loaded up as much of Edgar's furniture and stuff as they could fit. They'll have to make at least two more trips to get the rest of it out of here. Good ol' Blake used his influence with the chief to get the crime scene released in a hurry, didn't he?" he added with a sneer.

I wondered if Josh was imagining that, or if Blake was really that tight with Chief Fenton.

Squinting against the bright sun, I peered into the garage. A single overhead bulb shone over a huge, cream-colored vehicle that looked straight out of a forties' gangster film. "Wow," I said. "Was that Edgar's car?"

Josh turned his back on me and walked into the garage, where Aunt Tressa was already peeking through the windows of the mammoth vehicle.

"Technically, yes, but originally it belonged to Frederic Dwardene, Edgar's uncle."

Frederic Dwardene. I knew the name from the title search I'd done on Edgar's property. If I remembered correctly,

Frederic died in the early fifties. Since he'd been a widower with no living children, his entire estate went to his brother Mason—Blake's grandfather.

"What is it, a Nash?" Aunt Tressa's designer sunglasses were pressed to the passenger-side window.

Josh stroked his hand lovingly over the car's curved front bumper. "Of course not. This stunning creation is a nineteen forty-seven Hudson Commodore Six sedan. Isn't she the most spectacular thing you've ever seen?"

Maybe not the most spectacular, but I couldn't help admiring the gargantuan hunk of Detroit metal, only a foot or two shorter than a cruise ship. "It's a beautiful car, but does it run?"

"Not yet," Josh said, "but I've been working on the restoration. I've already sunk several hundred bucks into it, and that's only on minor parts."

I peered at the horizontal slats of chrome that formed the impressive grille work. "The grille has a bit of rust, but the body's in decent shape. It doesn't look as if it's had much exposure to the elements."

"It hasn't. It was only four years old when Frederic died. No one really drove it much after that, which is part of the problem. Cars need to run. Their engines need regular lubrication. Anyway, Edgar told me he'd never liked this car. Fortunately for me, he never bothered to get rid of it." His voice broke. "He told me that it was mine, no strings attached."

Aunt Tressa opened the Hudson's passenger-side door, and I saw one leg swing up behind her. For a moment I thought Josh would have a bird, but instead he said sharply, "What are you doing?"

Bending over the passenger seat, Aunt Tressa called out, "Wait a minute." Seconds later she emerged clutching a scrap of yellow cloth. "When I was peeking through the window I noticed something stuck under the seat. I wanted to see what it was."

Josh and I both leaned in for a closer look. It appeared to be a woman's hair bow.

"How did you even spot that?" Josh said, irritation threading his tone.

My aunt grinned. "I have eagle eyes." She held it up for a better look. Attached to a rusted metal clip, the threadbare bow appeared to be made of satin—very old and faded satin. Aunt Tressa got a wicked gleam in her eye. "Looks like Frederic might have been entertaining a lady friend back in the day."

"Just toss it," Josh said. "There's a waste can in the back of the garage."

Aunt Tressa slipped it into her coat pocket. "I'll throw it away when I get to my office. So where're you working these days, Josh?"

Josh observed her silently for a moment, then said, "I'm in the IT department at Diamond Crown Insurance. Actually, I am the IT department." He turned his gaze on me. "Can I talk to you for a second, Apple?" He shot a glance at my aunt. "Privately."

I shrugged. "Why not?"

In truth, I was grateful for the opportunity to chat with him alone. I had a few questions of my own for him.

We moved away from the garage, toward the front of the flat-bed truck. Chet, the tow truck operator, was leaning against the driver's-side door, slurping coffee from one of the foam cups. He appeared content to have a few minutes of downtime.

Josh flipped off the top of the other cup and took a sip. Then he opened the white bag and pulled out the oddest-looking pastry I'd ever seen. Long like a cruller, it had one thick end that bulged with thousands of chocolate sprinkles. Josh shoved the chocolate end into his mouth and tore off a huge wedge, reminding me of how he'd loved chocolate *anything* as a kid.

"Sorry," he mumbled, then swallowed. "I didn't have

breakfast and I'm starving." He stuck the pastry back in the bag and set the coffee down on the hood. "Let's go over here," he said, ambling away from the truck.

I followed until he stopped short in the driveway. Josh lowered his voice. "Is it true your law firm's handling the closing of Edgar's house?"

"It is. Sam Ingle's been Edgar's lawyer for years."

"Yeah, that's what I thought. Look Apple, I wanna know something. Did Edgar really die without a will?"

I nodded. "Yes, he did. Sam had been prodding him for years about doing a will, but Edgar kept putting him off."

Josh kicked at a chunk of ice with the toe of his boot. "That's what I heard, but I didn't believe it."

"It's not that unusual," I said. "Lots of people put off making a will. They think there's plenty of time. Then when the unthinkable happens . . . well, unfortunately it's too late."

"I never figured he'd take a fall down the stairs the way he did. For an old guy, Edgar was in pretty decent shape." Josh shook his head, and his eyes turned shiny. "I was the one who found him, you know, when I got home from work that day. God, it was awful. His eyes were open . . ." He looked away, and my heart ached for him.

"He wasn't just a landlord. He was a friend, wasn't he?" I said quietly.

Josh heaved out a breath. "Yeah, he was. Truth be told, Edgar was more like a father to me than my real father was. We talked about a lot of stuff, you know? I know Blake thought I was just taking advantage of the old guy, but it wasn't like that. I helped out a lot around here. Picked up Edgar's groceries for him, kept the lawn mowed in the summer. Even planted those girly pink impatiens he was so nutty over."

"At least they weren't tulips."

Josh gave me a crooked smirk. "No, they weren't tulips."

Josh had been an exuberant seven-year-old the day he sneaked into Aunt Tressa's flower bed and snapped eight red tulips off their stems. Larceny accomplished, he skipped happily home, waving his purloined bouquet like a Fourth of July sparkler. My aunt, who never missed much, spotted him running down the sidewalk. Josh's mom later apologized, confessing that her darling boy had picked them for her birthday. Aunt Tressa grudgingly forgave the rascal, but she never forgot it. Those tulips were the only things she'd ever been able to grow.

"Why did you ask about the will, Josh?"

"Because no one believes Edgar gave me the Hudson. It's my car, and now I'm stuck paying for it. It isn't fair!"

"Edgar never put anything in writing?"

"No. And the car was too old to have a certificate of title." Josh chewed at his lower lip. "I keep thinking about something. What if Edgar had written his own homemade will? Would it be legal?"

"Depends," I said, wondering where he was headed with this line of questioning. "If the will was witnessed, the witnesses would have to come forward and confirm that Edgar was in his right mind and not under any duress when he signed it. After that, it would be up to the probate court judge to either allow it or disallow it. Why, Josh? Where are you going with this?"

"I'm not sure," he said. "It just seems weird that a guy who was so successful in business wouldn't have been savvy enough to leave a will. I keep wondering . . . look, I know this is going to sound paranoid. But what if Blake—or his lackey, Lou Marshall—found a homemade will when they were going through Edgar's papers? And what if Blake didn't like what the will said and destroyed it?"

"I'm sure Blake wouldn't do that," I said. "And Lou Marshall was a reputable appraiser. I've never heard anyone say a word against him."

Josh scowled. "I should've known you'd defend Blake. You two are old high school buddies, aren't you?"

"That has nothing to do with it." I was getting testy myself.

"Never mind, then. Sorry I even asked."

He started to stalk away, but I wasn't through with him. I caught the sleeve of his jacket and pulled him backward. "Wait a minute, Josh. I have a question for you, too. Why did you crash Celeste and Blake's party yesterday? That was a very embarrassing scene you created."

Josh flushed. "Yeah, well, I intended it to be. I wanted to shame Blake into admitting that the Hudson was mine. I thought if I did it in front of a crowd, he'd tell me to just keep the flipping car and get out of his life. And I'd have a room full of witnesses to hear him say it. Instead, he pulled me into another room, where he proceeded to chew me up one side and down the other. Greedy little weasel."

I shook my head. Josh had always been rash, with emotions that ran hot and cold. But he was brainy, as well—far too smart to think that such a childish act would result in any real satisfaction.

"Even if you had a beef with Blake," I said, "you should've taken Celeste's feelings into consideration."

Josh remained silent.

After a few moments I said, "I gather you agreed to pay for the car."

He glared at me. "I had no choice."

"Where are you going to live now?"

"I found an apartment in Hooksett. After spending the past two nights at my mother's, it'll seem like a resort. She freaked when she saw Zorba. But at least she's letting me garage the Hudson at her place." He stared over my shoulder. "Hey, your aunt is giving you the evil eye."

I looked at my watch—it was eight fifty-two. "Yikes. I have to get to work. One more question. What do you know about Darby?"

"Jack Darby? He built all the custom display cases for Edgar's dagger collection. He finished them right before Edgar died." Josh shook his head soberly. "Poor old guy didn't get to enjoy them for very long. Why are you asking about Darby?"

"Um, he promised to build something for a friend of mine. I wanted to be sure he was reliable."

"I don't know the guy personally," Josh said, "but he's a fantastic carpenter. Not the speediest, but definitely the best I've ever seen. The man works magic with wood."

Aunt Tressa was tromping toward us now. As her own boss, she could pretty much set her hours, but she knew I had to answer to Sam Ingle.

"You're going to be late if we don't get our butts in the car," she said, gliding past Josh and me like an oversized flying squirrel. "Nice seeing you again, Josh. Don't be a stranger."

When she was out of earshot, Josh looked at me. "Your aunt's a trip."

My aunt is actually a journey—of fun, frivolity, and most important, of love. She was always there when I needed her, and as a kid I was needy a lot.

But the hint of derision in Josh's tone irked me.

"The same *trip*," I said, "who washed and dried your corduroy pants the day you fell in that scummy pond behind our house? The one your mom was always warning you to stay away from?"

Josh flushed pink, then gave out a strangled laugh. "Geez, I'd forgotten about that. What was I—eight, nine? I was trying to catch tadpoles in a jar that day. I panicked when my foot slipped and I stumbled backward and fell. Your aunt came to the rescue with her trusty washer and dryer. She definitely saved me from a major scene with my mom."

Mission accomplished. I waggled my fingers. "I have to go, Josh. Thanks for chatting with me."

"Yeah, likewise."

I heard his boots crunch over the frozen driveway as he retreated toward the garage.

In the back of my head a nagging voice whispered.

Could the hyperactive little kid I once babysat be a murderer?

CHAPTER ELEVEN

From the journal of Frederic Dwardene, Friday, November 10,
1950:

Today I looked up the record on Dora's savings account. She
has an accrued balance of exactly $229.48. Once we are mar-
ried, she can spend her money buying trinkets and other luxuries
for herself. For I will see that she has all the necessities of life.
She shall want for nothing . . .

The law firm where I worked, Quinto and Ingle Professional
Association, was located in an old but well-maintained brick
building on Center Street—Hazleton's main drag. Dating back
to the early nineteen hundreds, it boasted a pair of mini-
gargoyles above the red-painted wooden door and a brass door-
knocker that evoked eerie images of a tortured Jacob Marley.

Sam's one-time partner, Felix Quinto, retired two years ago—
exactly one week after we'd celebrated his eightieth birthday. A
kindly man, he'd always enjoyed doling out big Christmas
bonuses whenever the firm had had a good year. For the past
year or so, Sam had been half-heartedly looking for an associate
to help him with the estate-planning portion of the practice. So
far, none of the resumés that crossed his desk had managed to
excite him, so for now he continued to fly solo, shouldering the
workload himself. With the economy in a rut, it was do-able.

I climbed the worn marble steps at exactly one minute before
nine and swooped through the front door. Heidi Smith, the

receptionist, was already waving a yellow slip of paper at me. "Mrs. Shepard wants you to call her the second you get in," she droned. "She's, like, going nuts about her closing."

I took the slip from her as I unbuttoned my coat. "I'll call her," I said. "Have a good weekend?"

"Not really." She adjusted the almost life-sized plastic reindeer that was attached to her black sweater above her collarbone. "My mom got this, like, awful flu, and I had to practically wait on her hand and foot. Not to mention clean throw-up off the bathroom floor. I mean, it was like, puke city all weekend. I thought I'd gag my guts out." She rolled her eyes, the lashes of which had enough mascara to form two new Zorbas.

"That's too bad," I sympathized, feeling my breakfast starting to meander in a northerly direction. "I hope she's better."

"Not much," Heidi said. She coughed violently into her only free hand, the other being wrapped around a huge powdered doughnut. "I think I'm getting it now, too."

Great. Thank you for coming in today to share it with us. "Sam in yet?" I asked, backing away as politely as I could.

"Yeah, and he doesn't look happy." She bit off a wad of the doughnut and slugged it down with a mouthful of coffee. "Not that he ever does."

I tamped down a smile. Sam was a dear, but he tended to be moody. I had a feeling this was going to be one of those days.

Directly behind Heidi's curved reception desk, a carpeted hallway with two offices on either side extended toward the back of the building. The first office on the right belonged to Vicki Pomeroy, Sam's administrative assistant. Tall and pencil-thin, Vicki was somewhere in her forties—exactly where, no one had ever been sure. She wore her ginger-colored hair styled in the shape of an upside down fishbowl, and her eyeglasses had tiny wings sprouting from each corner. Since the day Sam decided she should have her own office instead of a cubicle in the reception area, Vicki had elevated herself to the position of associate without ever attending law school.

"Hey, Vick." I poked my head into her office and gave her a little wave. On the wall behind her was a large, framed photograph of a great blue heron soaring low over a sun-speckled pond. She'd taken it herself with her fancy digital camera and was immensely proud of the result.

Vicki glanced up at me, her fingers tapping her keyboard at a steady, efficient pace. I thought she looked a little haggard, not her usual energetic self. "Morning, Apollonia. Running a bit late, are we?"

Technically I'd arrived on time, but Vicki had a way of making me feel I should apologize for just about everything. And for some reason, her manner toward me had cooled over the past several weeks. Why, I had no idea. If I'd done something to offend her, I couldn't imagine what it was.

"I had to drop off my aunt at the car dealership this morning," I murmured, bumbling out a half-hearted excuse. "You know how the traffic is on—"

"Did you hear all that hacking that girl is doing out there?" she interrupted. "I've told her at least a thousand times to take zinc, but does she listen? No. I take two zinc tablets a day and I'm never out sick. Never."

Two zincs a day? That sounded like an awful lot of heavy metal to me.

I waited for a break in her tirade and then slunk into my office, which was directly opposite hers. I hung my coat on the funky purple coat rack I'd picked up a few years ago at a flea market in Exeter. After logging on to my computer, I headed for the tiny kitchen at the end of the hallway. I was making myself a single-serving cup of vanilla-nut coffee when Sam came in, his mug clutched to his chest like a shield.

"Morning, Sam." I sipped the delicious brew in my cup, my

taste buds reveling in the flavor.

"Morning." His eyes looked saggy as he prepared himself a mug of our coffee supplier's "double-trouble" blend. "Got a minute?" he said.

"For you, two minutes." I was trying to lighten the mood, but his solemn expression didn't change as he turned and trudged out of the kitchen.

Sam's office was at the end of the short corridor that led back from the reception area. His pale green walls bore evidence of his undergrad degree from UConn and his law degree from Franklin Pierce. His bookshelves—lined with legal volumes, including the New Hampshire statutes—held a myriad of framed family photos. Sam had an adorable family, something I occasionally found myself envying. His wife, Mary, was a first-class sweetheart, and their nine-year old twins, Sarah and Sophia, were as cute as they come.

Sam closed the door behind me. A shaft of sunlight streaming through the window played over the debris on his paper-strewn desk.

"Terrible about Lou Marshall," he said quietly.

"Yes, awful. He and my aunt were good friends."

"How's she taking it?"

"Okay. It hit her hard at first, but she's a tough lady. They hadn't been dating all that long, but still . . ."

"She go to work today?"

"Oh, yes. We dropped off her car for inspection this morning at the dealership where she gets it serviced. In fact, do you mind if I leave a few minutes early this afternoon? I need to get her back there by five-thirty, and the rush-hour traffic on Route 121 is brutal."

"Of course." He waved a hand. "You don't even need to ask."

"Thanks, Sam." I waited, knowing there had to be a reason for the summons into his office.

Finally, he said, "Apple, did you talk to Lou at all? On Saturday, I mean."

I shook my head. "No, I never got the chance. Aunt Tressa spoke to him briefly, but she said he seemed distracted. In fact—" I slapped my forehead with my palm. "Great gobs of gobbledygook, I never paid for the John Jakes books I bought! Or didn't buy. Or—oh, you know what I mean."

"I wouldn't worry about a few books," Sam said.

"But technically I pinched them. I'll settle up with Blake or Celeste before they leave for New York."

"Go back to what you said about your aunt. She thought Lou seemed distracted?"

I nodded. "That's what she told me. She only spoke to him for a few minutes. It wasn't long after that we heard a scream and—"

Sam's face paled. He looked away. Something was clearly troubling him. Whatever it was, he was having a devil of a time spilling it. Had he realized that we'd seen him leaving the mansion after the murder? Had he been trying to keep his presence there a secret?

In fact, when *did* Sam arrive at the mansion that afternoon? Prior to when we spotted him scraping snow off his car, I didn't recall seeing him at all. Had he been in the cellar with Blake, sorting through Edgar Dwardene's dusty artifacts? Considering how fussy Sam was about dirt, I couldn't picture it.

Hoping to ease his pain a bit and maybe loosen his tongue, I steered the conversation sideways. "Sam, did Lou always handle his estate sales that way, letting strangers traipse all over the house like that? It seemed, well, a little odd to me."

Sam scrubbed a hand over his left eye. "That's the way Lou liked to handle those open house sales. Blake wasn't happy about it, but Lou told him it would be done his way or no way at all. He could be a stickler when he wanted to be."

Interesting. Could that be the little spat Celeste had referred to on Saturday?

"So Blake objected to the way Lou was doing it," I said.

Sam swallowed a mouthful of coffee and nodded. "Blake figured people would rob him blind. Slip little trinkets into their pockets and such. I think that's why he asked Paul Fenton to be there. He figured folks would be less likely to pilfer with the police chief strolling around." Sam set his mug on his desk, then reached into his jacket pocket for his cell phone. He raised it up, his finger poised over one of the buttons.

For a second, my heart rate spiked. Why was he holding his phone that way? Was he going to take my picture?

Holding my breath, I waited. Sam opened his mouth to say something, but nothing came out. His shoulders slumping, he slipped the phone back into his pocket.

"Sam, what is it? What's wrong?"

"Never mind, it's nothing," he said, his words suddenly clipped, his expression tight.

"Are you sure?"

"Positive. Go back to work."

"Okay, I'd better call Mrs. Shepard anyway. Heidi said she wanted to talk to me the moment I got in. If you think of anything I can help you with, let me know."

Sam nodded at me and smiled, but what I saw in his gaze was unmistakable: fear.

CHAPTER TWELVE

From the journal of Frederic Dwardene, Sunday, November 12, 1950:

A magnificent musical opened last year on Broadway. Though I haven't seen the play, I have heard the music, and it is marvelous. As I write these words, I am playing my favorite song— "Some Enchanted Evening"—on my phonograph. Powerful and beautifully sung by Ezio Pinza, the words resonate. For yesterday I saw a stranger, a beautiful, captivating stranger. And now that I've found her, I will never let her go . . .

Celeste called mid-morning and asked if I could have the seller's closing documents ready for Blake to sign by Tuesday morning. He was planning to leave for Manhattan that same afternoon, as long as another snowstorm didn't threaten to roll in.

For a typical closing, the buyer has approximately four thousand documents to sign, give or take a few affidavits. Mortgage loans come with an enormous amount of paperwork. In the hour or so normally allotted for a closing, it all has to be signed, initialed, and notarized, and then photocopied for the buyer.

The seller, fortunately, has only a few affidavits and tax forms to sign, along with a statement of the settlement figures. And, of course, a deed. Since Blake had been appointed administrator of his uncle's estate, he would be the one signing the deed. And since Sam represented the estate, it was the firm's responsibility to prepare it for Blake's signature.

I promised Celeste I would have the seller docs ready for Blake to sign Tuesday morning. She also asked if she could stop by the office in the afternoon to deliver a tasty surprise. I assured her it would be a welcome distraction.

The Dwardene file sat amid the pile of other file folders stacked on the corner of my desk. I snatched it out of the heap.

The file was divided into two sections—one for the probate, the other for the title search and sale of the mansion. I was flipping through the probate file, refreshing my memory, when a name leaped up at me like a frog off a lily pad.

Darby Repairs & Renovations.

That's where I'd seen it before—in Edgar Dwardene's probate file!

When Darby built the custom display cases for Edgar's dagger collection, he apparently sent an invoice to Edgar to the tune of almost three thousand dollars. Before Edgar had the chance to pay the bill, he fell and broke his neck.

After the estate was opened in the Rockingham County Probate Court, Darby sent his invoice to Sam, who represented Edgar's estate. Blake was appointed administrator, and after the inventory was filed the bill was paid from the assets of the estate.

Strangely, Edgar Dwardene hadn't died with a whole lot of liquid assets. For a man who'd once owned a successful insurance business, his savings account had been puny. He'd also owned a number of speculative stocks, but in the recent economy those had taken a serious dive.

The mansion—the real property—was the estate's primary asset.

A disturbing thought struck me. By now the news of Lou's murder must have reached the buyers. Would they still want to go through with the closing? Or would they try to renege?

If they pulled out of the deal, it would be a crushing blow to

Aunt Tressa, who would lose a sizeable commission. And for Blake and Celeste it would be devastating.

I made a mental note to ask Celeste about it when she stopped by.

With everything I had to do, the morning passed quickly. I tried calling Lillian several times, to no avail. My stomach felt sick as I imagined all the things that could have happened to her.

Around eleven thirty, Aunt Tressa called me. "How about lunch at Rosie's?" she said. Something in her tone suggested she had news to share. "I have two things to tell you. Well, three if you count my new listing."

"A new listing? That's great, Aunt Tress!" Another house sale would be a boon for her, since real estate sales had slowed in recent months to the pace of evolution. "Can't you tell me the other two things now? The suspense is killing me."

"Nah. It'll give us something to talk about over lunch. I'll walk down to your place and meet you around ten to twelve. We can scoot over to Rosie's from there."

"Be careful on the sidewalks. They're not cleared everywhere. Oh, and a word of warning. Your BFF Heidi might be coming down with a flu bug. If I were you, I'd refrain from doing your usual huggie-pie dance with her."

From the day Heidi first met my aunt, she'd bonded to her like a blob of gum that won't come off your shoe. Now, any time Aunt Tressa walks through the door, Heidi leaps off her chair and embraces her as if she'd just returned from a ten-year expedition to the South Pole.

"Thanks for the warning. I'll try to keep my distance. Even though I never get the flu."

Predictably, Miss Punctuality whizzed through the front door at eleven forty-nine. I'd waited in the reception area for her, hoping I could head off Heidi at Contagion Pass, but she wasn't to be deterred.

"Mrs. Krichner!" Heidi bolted from her chair, nearly trampling me in the process, as she galloped around the reception desk to throw her arms around my aunt.

Aunt Tressa was ready for her. Before Heidi could complete her end run, my aunt coughed vociferously into an eggplant-colored cocktail napkin. "Hi, Heidi," she said wanly. "Better not get too close. I think I'm coming down with something."

"Oh, don't worry about it." Heidi encircled Aunt Tressa in a hug that would have put a polar bear to shame. "My mom, like, puked her brains out all weekend, so I've probably already got it!"

On that appetizing note, we bade Heidi good-bye and fled as graciously as we could.

"A purple napkin?" I said dryly as we walked toward Rosie's.

Aunt Tressa crumpled the napkin and tossed it into a nearby trash receptacle. "It was all I could come up with on short notice. Would you have preferred toilet paper?"

I laughed as I opened the glass front door to Rosie's, which was a short walk from my office. The café, a popular lunch place, shared a building with an old-fashioned shop that specialized in penny candy and other sugary delights, including my secret faves—gummy snakes. The tinkle of a tiny cow bell announced our arrival as we stepped inside the café.

Rosie, the café's Ecuadorian owner, was a lover of all things cowboy, or rather, cow*girl*. Greeting us warmly, a braided leather headband holding her dark springy curls at bay, she escorted Aunt Tressa and me to our favorite table near the window. Multiple circles of turquoise-studded silver marched along each arm as she handed us a list of the daily specials. From the kitchen came the luscious aroma of deep-fried empanadas and tangy salsa, tantalizing my taste buds and firing up my appetite.

"Good special today, Tressa." Rosie's snow white teeth

beamed a grin. "No fish. Just nice melted cheddar and ham in a giant flour tortilla, exactly how you like it."

"Sold!" my aunt said. "With extra cheese, a large order of seasoned chips, and a cinnamon coffee."

"I'll have a fish taco, Rosie, and a side of slaw. And spring water will be fine." Rosie's chef—her brother Pedro—was known for his scrumptious fish tacos. Prepared with delicate chunks of cod baked in a light cracker coating, they were one of my favorites as well.

"You got it." Rosie scooped up the specials cards and hurried off, the clump of her azure cowgirl boots reverberating off the black-and-white linoleum.

I shot a glance out the window. The sky was thickening into a mass of dense clouds. Next to the one-armed statue of Ezekiel Hazleton—the town's founder—a lone man sat huddled on a bench reading a newspaper.

About thirty years ago, the story goes, an elderly gent was bickering with his wife as they drove through town. The man lost control of his car, which jumped the curb and slammed into poor old Ezekiel. Ezekiel toppled, amputating one outstretched granite arm as he hit the concrete pad below. Since then, he'd been known as the onesy.

"So tell me," I said, shrugging off my coat. "What's your news?"

Aunt Tressa slung her faux mink over the brass hook above the booth. "First of all," she said, plopping back into her seat, "I have an appointment this evening with one Jack Darby."

"Darby? He's coming to your place? Tonight?"

"Yep. I told him my dishwasher was leaking, and oh, dear me, I simply didn't know what to do or whom to call! And then I remembered his business card! What a lifesaver!" Her voice had morphed into her damsel-in-distress flutter, a tone she used quite effectively when she wanted to.

"I see you've already forgotten," I pointed out, "that tonight is my reading night at the nursing home. I don't want Darby coming over when I'm not there."

Aunt Tressa waved a multi-ringed hand at me. "Don't be ridiculous. I don't need a protector. I can handle myself perfectly fine."

I blew out a frustrated breath. "Didn't we talk about this? Didn't we agree that Darby might be dangerous?"

We paused as Rosie delivered my water and Aunt Tressa's coffee. The scent of cinnamon wafted around us, making me hungrier.

Aunt Tressa took a sip from her steaming mug. She was trying to ignore me, but I didn't intend to let her off the hook.

"What time is he coming?" I said.

"Um, around seven, I think."

"You don't know?"

"Okay, seven."

Why was this turning into a grilling session?

My Monday night reading group at the Hazleton Convalescent Home always starts promptly at six, and I'm usually out of there by seven.

"That might be okay, then. I shouldn't get back much later than seven fifteen or so. We should devise some kind of signal in case you get into trouble."

Rosie came along with our lunch platters. "Here you go, ladies. Enjoy!"

"Thanks," we both chirped.

"What kind of a signal?" Aunt Tressa grabbed her fork and sheared off a chunk of oozing tortilla.

"How about a sharp knock on the wall?"

Aunt Tressa rolled her eyes. "And how do I discreetly achieve that? Pretend to trip over a lamp cord so I can body slam the wall?"

"It doesn't have to be that dramatic. You're very creative when you want to be, so just think of a way to signal if you need me."

"Okay," she agreed, a bit too easily. She popped a seasoned chip into her mouth.

I sampled my fish taco, which was warm and spicy and over-the-rainbow delicious. "What was your other news? You said you had three things."

"Oh. Right. I got bad news about the Deville. The service manager from the dealership called. He said my uptake manifest has leaky caskets. It's going to cost over a thousand to fix."

"Leaky caskets?"

"I'm pretty sure that's what he said."

I'm far from a mechanic, but I was almost sure they'd told her that the intake manifold had leaky gaskets.

"Anyway, it's a pretty big job, so they won't be able to finish it today. Do you mind being my chauffeur for another day?"

"Of course not." Then, cautiously, "Not to beat an old rug again, but are you sure you want to invest that much in the Caddy?" It killed me to see her pour that kind of cash into a car with well over a hundred thou on it.

She flashed me a look. "I'm not giving up Marty's car, so don't even go there."

We finished up our lunches. I passed on dessert while Aunt Tressa slugged back another cinnamon coffee and a slab of coconut cream pie.

"Why don't I give you a ride back?" I said. "It's getting too chilly to walk."

Aunt Tressa buttoned up her coat. "I'll take you up on that."

The public parking lot for people who worked downtown was located across the street behind the Hazleton post office. We scooted across Center Street at the crosswalk.

On the next corner was an antique shop that had opened

several years ago—From Trunk to Treasure. I'd poked around in there on numerous occasions. Once or twice I'd picked up a kitschy trinket for my office. Today, a homemade sign posted in the huge, glass front window caught my gaze.

COME IN AND BROWSE—
NEWLY ACQUIRED ITEMS FROM THE
EDGAR DWARDENE ESTATE

"Isn't that interesting," I said.

"Let's pop in."

Before I could respond, my aunt was barreling through the front door.

I guess we were going in.

On the windowsill, just inside the store, sat a cut glass candy dish filled with wrapped red-and-white mints. I snagged one, unwrapped it, and popped it into my mouth, then slid the cellophane into my coat pocket.

A plump, seventy-something woman with jeweled eyeglasses immediately rushed over to us. It made me wonder if we were the first customers she'd had all day.

"Hello, I'm Moira Tatum," the woman gushed. "Please feel free to look around. I'll be happy to answer any questions. Did you see our sign in the window? Just this morning we got in some fascinating artifacts from the Dwardene mansion!"

"Yes, we noticed," I said. "In fact, we saw a moving truck leaving the Dwardene house early this morning. You certainly managed to get everything set up quickly."

"Oh, well, not much of it is in the shop yet. The larger pieces are still in the back room, and there's much more to come. The moving truck has already been here twice. Thank heaven we have a huge storage area on the other side of this building. But anyway, let me show you some of the smaller items. I've already begun setting up a display." With a sly little grin, she crooked a finger, enticing us to follow.

In the rear of the shop, an entire corner had been devoted to the Dwardene estate.

"Several small boxes of miscellaneous items came in this morning with the larger items," Moira explained. "Oh, I couldn't wait to get my hands on them! I adore rummaging through people's old baubles and such. Imagine my delight when I saw so many personal things! Phonograph records, letters, you name it. If you see anything you like, just give a holler, and we'll work out a fair price."

We both thanked Moira, and she left us to browse on our own. I glanced at my watch. "We can spend about fifteen minutes here, then we've got to make like a Hollywood power couple and split," I told Aunt Tressa.

"Suits me," she said distractedly. She sauntered over to a rack that held old vinyl records and began flipping through the albums.

I homed in on some wooden boxes—each about a foot square and half as deep—that rested on a rectangular table.

The first box contained a myriad of assorted junk. Letter openers. Tattered bookmarks. A slew of vintage buttons. Nothing that really jingled my chimes.

The second box was far more intriguing, the contents more personal. Fishing through, I found about a dozen old date books. Each one was black and had the words *Hazleton Savings Bank* imprinted on the front in elegant gold leaf, with the year imprinted below that.

Curious, I opened the one labeled *1950*. Several entries had been made on each page. In places the ink was badly faded, almost indecipherable. But most of the entries were quite legible, composed in a firm hand. There was nothing out of the ordinary about the lunch dates, medical appointments and the like that filled the date book. It was the handwriting itself that caught my attention.

It was the same flowery script that composed the valentine Lou had given to Aunt Tressa.

Setting the date book aside, I dug deeper in the box. Toward the bottom, I discovered a small stack of dog-eared cards tied with a now threadbare ribbon. I pulled it out carefully. When I saw what they were, I smiled—old report cards from Hazleton Elementary School. Leaving the ribbon intact for fear it might disintegrate, I flipped gently through the stack. At the top of each card, the student's name had been written in block letters—Kenneth Dwardene.

Kenneth.

I didn't recall his name from the title search. I wondered what branch he occupied on the Dwardene family tree.

"Hey, App, get a load of this."

I looked over and saw Aunt Tressa holding up a turquoise box, about seven inches square. It was a set of records—old forty-fives—from the musical *South Pacific*.

"That's quite a rare find, I'm told." Mrs. Tatum had come up behind us holding a large painting, which she propped on the floor against a nearby sideboard. "I'm not an expert on records, but I know this is a very special collection."

"This musical came out around the time I was born," Aunt Tressa said. "I saw a local production of it in Manchester when I was a teenager. It was good, but according to my grandmother, it certainly wasn't Mary Martin and Ezio Pinza."

Moira's eyes rolled dreamily. "I was a young girl when the play first hit Broadway. I never got to New York to see it, but I saw the movie years later." She sighed. "How sad it was, yet how wonderfully romantic. All those beautiful songs! I couldn't stop thinking about it for days afterward."

I was preparing to signal to Aunt Tressa that we needed to leave when I spotted something else in the box—a burgundy-colored leather journal. As Moira waxed nostalgic about the musical, I pulled out the journal and perused the pages. Like the date books, the entries had been composed in the same flowery handwriting as the valentine.

"Excuse me." I gently interrupted Moira. "May I buy this?"

Moira lowered her eyeglasses and squinted at the journal. "Why, certainly. How does twenty dollars sound?"

"Would ten be okay?"

She smiled. "Yes, I guess ten would be fine. I assume you mean cash, of course."

"Of course."

I was opening my handbag, ready to follow Moira to the register, when my gaze landed on the painting she'd propped against the sideboard. For a moment, my breath caught. It was a portrait, done in oils, of an absolutely stunning young woman. The artist had portrayed her seated on a tufted sofa, her legs tucked delicately beneath her. A waterfall of golden hair, pinned back above each ear with a pair of yellow bows, flowed over her slender shoulders. The bright yellow jewel suspended around her neck complemented her sun-colored dress. Her eyes had been painted an almost unnatural blue. In her lap sat a large white cat—a Persian.

"Ah, I see you've spotted the portrait," Moira said, lowering her voice. She shook her head meaningfully, yet I sensed a lilt in her tone. "This was in the room, you know, when that appraiser was murdered the other day. Terrible thing, wasn't it?"

Aunt Tressa stared at the portrait. "Yes, horrible," she said mechanically.

Moira's eyes glittered. "If either of you is interested, I'm sure we could work out a fair price."

Aunt Tressa swallowed but said nothing. She seemed speechless, and I wasn't sure why.

"Do you know who the artist was?" I asked, put off by the

woman's keenness to wring even a modest profit out of the murder.

Moira grinned. "Why yes, it was Frederic Dwardene. I believe he was Edgar Dwardene's uncle. He was quite a fine artist in his day, I understand."

I stooped down to get a closer look at the signature. In the bottom left corner of the painting, the initials FD had been inscribed in black.

"Well, you ladies take your time. I'll be up front when you're ready."

After she left, I said to my aunt, "Are you okay?"

Aunt Tressa nodded slowly. "She's right, you know. I saw this portrait in the study the day Lou was killed. It was propped against the wall with a bunch of other paintings, right next to the mahogany desk." She swallowed hard, then reached into her coat pocket. She removed the tattered bow she'd found in Josh's old clunker and extended it toward the painting.

Though faded and frayed, it was a dead ringer for the hair bows of the woman in the portrait.

Chapter Thirteen

From the journal of Frederic Dwardene, Tuesday, November 14, 1950:

I've decided to paint her, though I'm sure that even my capable brushstrokes can never truly capture her sweet and tender beauty. I worked on the painting very late tonight, until my eyes could no longer stay open. But when the day comes that I ask her to marry me, I must have it ready to present!

Aunt Tressa's realty office was located at the corner of Center and Aubrey, on the second floor of a restored Victorian. Years ago she'd had the opportunity to buy the place, and had even placed a deposit with the seller. Then the inspection report came in. While the house boasted a plethora of charming features, the vintage plumbing and electrical systems weren't among them. With visions of having to sink a queen's ransom into renovations, Aunt Tressa passed on the deal. Not long after that, a local periodontist with cash to spare bought the house, restored it to its full glory, and turned it into two offices. Aunt Tressa—Krichner Realty—rented the second story. With its own private entrance in the back, it made the ideal office for her.

I swung into the driveway and pulled around to the rear parking area, which was reserved for Aunt Tressa's customers.

"Oh, no," Aunt Tressa said.

One glance in the direction of her office and I immediately saw the source of her dismay. A man in a brown ski jacket and corduroy trousers was sitting on her top step, sobbing his eyes out. It was Wilbur Speen, a young man who lived with his mother in a nearby apartment complex.

"Poor Wilby," I said, slamming my gearshift into Park. "We'd better find out what's wrong."

"I can handle it, Apple. You'll be late getting back."

"A few minutes won't hurt. I'll let Heidi know."

I made a fast call to the office, then followed Aunt Tressa across the parking lot toward the entrance to her office.

Wilby looked miserable. His eyelids were puffy and swollen, and his runny nose looked like a maraschino cherry.

My aunt plunked down beside him on the top step and slipped her arm around his shoulders. "Wilby, what's the matter?" she said kindly. "Why all the tears?"

Wilby wiped his eyes with the back of his bare hand, then held up a greasy, orange-stained bag marred by a distinct footprint. "My mom gave me money for lunch before she left for work," he said, his voice laced with sobs. "Seven whole dollars! She said I could buy two pizza slices from the market and I'd still have enough left for a candy bar."

I sat on the step on Wilby's opposite side. "So did you buy the pizza, Wilby?"

He nodded, then burst into a fresh round of tears. "Yeah. And a chocolate bar with peanuts. I got eleven cents change. Wanna see?"

"No, we believe you," Aunt Tressa said. "What happened then? How did your lunch get squished?"

"When I was leaving the market two boys saw me. They were hanging around outside. I think they were high school kids. I tried to walk around them, but they blocked me. Then one of them, the big one, grabbed my pizza bag and threw it to his friend. I told them to give it back, but they just kept laughing at me and throwing it back and forth and calling me *dummy* and '*tardo*.' "

This story was making me more furious by the second. "Didn't anyone try to help you?"

With a loud sniffle, Wilby shook his head. "No, there wasn't nobody else around. I tried not to act scared, but I couldn't help it. I started to cry and cry and cry. It musta made them mad 'cuz then the skinny one grabbed my glove right off my hand. And my house key was in it! Then they stepped on my pizza and ran away with my glove and now I can't get back in our apartment!"

Aunt Tressa looked mad enough to spew poison darts from her eyeballs. "It's all right," she soothed. "You can spend the afternoon with me. I have some frozen pizza in my fridge upstairs. I'll microwave one for you. How would that be?"

Wilby swiped his coat sleeve over his eyes. "Okay. But will you call my mom for me? I'm afraid she might get mad about the key."

"She won't get mad, Wilby," I said, praying I was right. "She'll know it wasn't your fault."

"I'll call your mom and explain everything," my aunt assured him. "Wilby, did she ever think about getting you a cell phone?"

He shook his head. "No. Even if I had one, I prob'ly couldn't figure it out. My mom's has lots of buttons and stuff on it."

"It's easy. I can show you," Aunt Tressa said. "I have one at home I'm not using anymore. Why don't I ask your mom if you can have it? She'll need to sign you up with a service provider, but I can help with that, too."

Wilby's face brightened. "That would be real good, Miss Tressa. Then if I needed to call my mom or the cops or something, I'd have my own phone."

Aunt Tressa smiled and they both stood up. With Wilby's problem temporarily resolved, I left the two of them and headed back to my office.

Or at least I started to.

What stopped me dead was a black-and-white police car blocking my exit, Chief Fenton sitting at the wheel.

Once again, I put my car in Park and hopped out. I stomped over to the cruiser and waited for Fenton to get out. With agonizing slowness, he opened his door and unfolded his long legs, like a spider crawling out of a drain. I practically lunged at him, pouring out Wilby's story of harassment by the teenage bullies.

This time, I had to give the chief credit. He listened carefully, then pulled out a notebook and made some entries. "I'll look into it, Ms. Mariani. It shouldn't be too hard to identify these two punks. In fact, I already have a good idea who they might be."

"Good. What then?"

He smiled, but his eyes were granite. "Then I have myself a little confab with their parents, throw a good scare into them. Believe me, after I get through with them they won't be hassling anyone again for a long, long time."

With a shiver, I wondered if he was planning to resurrect the guillotine and use it on the two scalawags. I could see it now. *Thwump!* Head roll. *Thwump!* Head roll.

I thanked him for his help, but my assault wasn't over. "Now what about Lillian Bilodeau? I called her several times today, and she still doesn't answer."

Fenton regarded me for a calculated moment. "I stopped over there this morning. And you're right, she still isn't home. I interviewed some of her neighbors—the few that were home— but no one saw or heard anything useful. An elderly man a couple of trailers away thought he heard a motor idling when he got up in the night to use the, um, facility, but that was about all."

"Did he look out the window?"

Fenton shook his head. "Afraid not."

I sagged, and felt my knees wobble. I was more convinced than ever that something bad had happened to Lillian. "Have you called all the area hospitals?"

"That's next on my agenda, Ms. Mariani."

Then what are you waiting for? I wanted to scream.

"I assume you'll call me and let me know what you find out? There aren't that many hospitals in this vicinity. I shouldn't think it would take too long for the police to make a few inquiries."

The chief glowered at me for a long moment.

"If you wouldn't mind, that is," I added, trying to soften my approach.

Fenton shot a look toward Aunt Tressa's office. "I'll contact you when we know something," he said tightly.

"Thank you, Chief. I appreciate that. For what it's worth, I think Lillian might have seen who killed Lou Marshall. She acted very subdued when we drove her home on Saturday. She wouldn't admit anything was bothering her, but I think it's because she was scared."

He pursed his lips for a moment. "You may be right, Ms. Mariani. It's entirely possible that your friend witnessed a very brutal crime. The preliminary results from the medical examiner showed that whoever stabbed Mr. Marshall did it with massive, aggressive force. Even with a rush of adrenaline, it's unlikely that a small-boned woman in her eighties could have accomplished that."

I opened my mouth to agree, but he held up a finger. "I said it was unlikely, not impossible. We're still investigating every potential angle. Which brings me to the purpose of my visit. Is

Tress—Mrs. Krichner in her office?"

I hesitated. "Um, yes, she's there with Wilby. Why?"

He glared at me. "Why? Because I have some questions for her, that's why. What are you, her nanny?"

I felt myself blanch. Why would he say such a thing? Of course I wasn't her nanny.

Grappling for an answer, I managed to stutter out, "I . . . I don't want you upsetting her, that's all. She's been through enough these past few days."

"I'll take that into consideration, Ms. Mariani," he said, with an annoying little smirk. "I certainly wouldn't want to be accused of upsetting any of my suspects."

"Aunt Tressa is not a suspect," I flung back, "because she didn't do anything wrong. And you're blocking my car. I'm already late getting back to work."

He gave a sharp nod. "I'll be out of your way in a moment. But know this: until I have the murderer *or murderess* in custody, everyone is a suspect. That includes you, Ms. Mariani."

CHAPTER FOURTEEN

From the journal of Frederic Dwardene, Wednesday, November 15, 1950:

I have made some quiet inquiries. Dora lives with only her mother in a two-family home on Harris Street. Her father died years ago in an accident at the paper plant where he worked. Her mother never remarried, and works for a local beautician. As for my Dora, she works at the sweater factory in Manchester, and rides the bus to and from every day . . .

Seriously late now, I practically flew back to the office.

By the time I sailed through the front door, Heidi was coughing into a tissue so large it could have served quite adequately as a baby blanket. Her mascara had degraded into messy black clumps. She looked like someone in the final stages of bubonic plague. Even her plastic reindeer was looking unwell.

She was obviously too ill to be working, which made me feel all the more terrible for getting back so late.

"Why don't you go home?" I said to her. "You need to get some rest and get rid of that bug. Vicki and I can listen for the phone."

"No, I'm okay," she choked out. "If I go home, I'll probably just have to clean more of my mom's throw-up."

Poor thing. Heidi could be flaky at times, but she could also be sweet and considerate.

"I'm not taking no for answer," I said firmly. "Now go get your—"

"Hey, everyone!"

Celeste Frame stepped into the reception area, a bright green tote draped over one arm. Wearing a red wool cape, a chic white beret, and black velvet gloves, she made me think of a cheery elf.

I greeted her and she gave me a quick hug. Heidi warded her off with a raised hand and a cough.

"Heidi was just packing up to leave," I explained. "She's picked up a nasty bug."

"Poor girl," Celeste said. "I wanted it to be a surprise, but I'm giving all of you some of my nine-grain sweet buns with my special glaze to take home. They freeze very well, so you can save them for when you feel better."

Heidi eyed the green tote suspiciously. "They don't have, like, bran in them or anything, do they? Bran does these really weird things to my colon."

Like make it work?

Celeste looked at me, her smile frozen in place. She turned back to Heidi. "Well, no, they don't have bran, exactly. I make them with unbleached all-purpose flour, milled flax seed, almond flour, and the most delectable Tahitian vanilla you've ever tasted. Trust me, you'll love them!"

Her complexion now slate gray, Heidi rose abruptly. "I gotta go," she blurted as she raced for the bathroom. We heard the door slam shut.

"Wow, she really is sick, isn't she?" Celeste said.

"Yeah, she is. She took care of her sick mom all weekend and now she's got it. She needs to go home."

Celeste reached into the tote and pulled out a plastic container with a red bow and a green foil tag affixed to the top. The tag read *To Heidi with appreciation. Celeste and Blake.* She winked at me, then reached over the reception counter and placed it on Heidi's desk. "She can look forward to these when she's better."

"You're a sweetheart, Celeste. How do you find time to do all this baking? Aren't you moving in a few days? You must have a ton of packing to do!"

Celeste grinned. "First of all, baking healthy, delicious foods is my life's passion. As for the packing, we've rented out the condo furnished, so most of our things are staying put. And the moving company we hired is actually going to do the packing for us, so that's a huge help. The loft in Tribeca won't be ready for at least two months, but we've rented a furnished place for the interim. By the time the loft's ready, Blake will have received the proceeds from the estate so we'll be in good shape. Meanwhile, I'll be busting my buns—pun intended—getting my bakery and catering service off to a start." Excitement beamed in her lovely blue eyes. "The competition will be fierce, but I'm relishing the challenge."

"You and Blake must be so psyched."

"Oh, we are! Blake has worked so hard to get where he is, Apple. And it's always been my dream to live in New York. We're both thrilled about the move."

Celeste had grown up with her mother and grandmother in a tiny apartment over Hazleton's only dry cleaning establishment. I could only guess how the stench of the chemicals must have permeated their living quarters. It was easy to imagine why she was so anxious to move into a spacious loft in tony Tribeca.

"Are you getting married in New York?" I asked.

"Yes. The ceremony will be small but extremely elegant." Her expression clouded. "I only wish my gram had lived long enough to enjoy all this with me. I would have brought her to New York with us, taken her to Broadway plays. We could have seen all the sights together, eaten in some of the great restaurants . . ." She broke off, her eyes growing misty.

"You and your grandmother must have been very close," I said.

"We were. Some days I miss her terribly. She was my rock."

Vicki came out of her office just then, one hand clamping a tissue over her nose and mouth, the other clutching a stack of papers. She tromped over to Heidi's desk and dropped the stack into a wire basket marked FILING.

Celeste smiled and gave her a little wave. "Hi, Vicki. Nice to see you again."

Vicki looked up sharply. When she saw Celeste, her cheeks burned pink. She muttered a quick "Hello" and then hustled back to her office.

Celeste gave me a pained look, then quietly said, "I think I know what that was about. Can we chat privately for a few minutes? In your office?"

"Sure."

Vicki's door was open. She barely gave a nod when I asked if she'd listen for the phone. I escorted Celeste into my office and closed the door.

"I feel so bad," Celeste said in a soft voice, taking a seat opposite my cluttered desk. She set her bag on the floor. "Vicki was at the estate sale on Saturday. I think she left before you got there, but I'm not sure. Anyway, at one point I'd gone upstairs for something and I overheard her talking to Lou Marshall. She was trying to persuade him—no, it was more like *begging* him—to go bird-spotting with her. Poor Lou kept mumbling excuses, but Vicki wouldn't let up. Oh, Apple, she sounded so desperate. My heart nearly broke for her. It was so obvious she'd had a huge crush on Lou. She must be devastated by his death."

Well, this was news.

Over the years, Lou had been in our office a number of times.

Had Vicki been admiring him from afar? Could she have fallen for him without anyone ever noticing?

The more I considered it, the more I could envision the possibility. Vicki had always guarded her private life closely. She lived alone with two parakeets in the home she'd inherited when her mother died. No one from the office, as far as I knew, had ever been invited inside. If Vicki had developed feelings for Lou, she wouldn't have shared it with any of her co-workers. Of that I was certain.

"Do you think she knew you overheard her?" I said.

Celeste sighed. "I do. I was standing right there when she came out of the study. When I saw her stricken expression, I felt so bad. I tried to play dumb by babbling about something innocuous—the weather or something—but she obviously knew I'd heard the whole exchange. And the look on her face . . ." Celeste shook her head. "If ever I saw unrequited love, that was it."

If Celeste's observations were correct, then Vicki had to be suffering terribly right now. If she'd truly loved Lou, or even thought she'd loved him, she must feel shattered by his death.

"I'm sorry, I didn't mean to depress you," Celeste said, a bit more cheerfully. "I brought packages of my holiday sweet rolls for everyone, including Vicki, because you've all helped Blake and me so much these past months." She reached into her bag and drew out a large plastic container festooned with a forest green bow. The foil tag read *To Apple. Thanks for Everything. Celeste and Blake.* With a self-satisfied grin, she set it on my desk. "You get the biggest one, since I know you'll share with Tressa."

"Thanks, Celeste! I can't wait to try them."

"I've got one for Sam, too. And Vicki. You can give Vicki's to her later."

"What's the Hazleton Food Mart going to do without all

your delicious breads?" I teased.

She laughed. "They'll survive, but I promised the owner one more batch of my whole-grain breads before I leave for the big city, so I'll be spending the rest of my day baking."

I wondered how she managed it all. The woman was a whirlwind.

"Celeste, I don't mean to change the subject, but before I forget—have you heard from your buyers lately? Do they know what happened at the mansion on Saturday?"

Celeste leaned back in her chair. "Oh, believe me, they know. I spoke to them at length on the phone this morning."

"And?"

"Apple, these people are doctors. They see death every day. Naturally they were upset that someone was murdered in the mansion, but it certainly didn't kill the deal. Oops, sorry—bad choice of words. Anyway, they assured me that neither of them believes in ghosts or spirits or any of that woo-woo nonsense. They're looking forward to moving in and turning it into their dream home. They have plans to do some major rehabbing with the place."

Well, that was a major relief. For all of us.

Celeste shifted slightly in her chair. "Until Saturday, I never realized you knew Josh Baker so well. Has he always been a friend?"

I shrugged. "Sort of. He's about seven years younger than I am. When he was a kid, I used to sit for him whenever his mom had to go out."

Celeste chewed her lip thoughtfully. "This may sound strange, but . . . well, was he mean or nasty as a kid?"

I frowned at the question. "Josh? No, not at all. He was overactive, that's for sure. My aunt always called him a rascal. But I never saw him hurt anyone or anything." I chuckled. "Except for Aunt Tressa's treasured tulips." I related the story of Josh pilfering the tulips to give to his mom for her birthday. "Why do you ask?"

"It's just—oh, it wasn't anything serious, really. This past spring I was at the mansion one day doing some cleanup. I went outside to dump a pile of newspapers in the trash, and found three dead baby birds in the barrel. Poor things had been sealed up tight in a clear plastic bag, nest and all." She touched her abdomen lightly. "It was . . . nauseating."

I swallowed. Was she implying that Josh had killed the birds? Or worse, suffocated the live babies in a plastic bag? On purpose?

"It was originally my idea," she said, "to let Josh stay in the house until it was sold. Leaving the mansion empty would've made it a ripe target for intruders." She sighed. "In retrospect, I'm not so sure it was a good idea. There's something about that guy that . . . I don't know, I can't put my finger on it. He gives me the willies."

"Does Blake feel the same way?"

"More or less. From the beginning, Blake never trusted Josh. He couldn't understand why a young guy like that would want to live with an old geezer like Edgar."

I shrugged, but the whole conversation was making me distinctly uncomfortable. "Cheap rent?" I offered. I saw no need to disclose what Josh had told me—that he'd viewed Edgar as somewhat of a father figure.

"You could be right." Celeste waved a gloved hand. "Anyway, it's all water over the falls." She rose and glanced around my disorganized office, her gaze landing on all the homey touches I'd added over the years. "You really love this job, don't you, Apple?"

"Actually, I do. Call me boring, but I get a lot of pleasure from helping people with their real estate transactions. And I love doing title searches. Each one is like its own little snippet of history."

"About seven years ago, when I was between jobs," Celeste said, "I did some temping. I ended up working for the real estate partner at a law firm in Concord while his paralegal was out having a baby. He showed me how to do online title searches. I got very good at it, and he wanted me to stay on permanently, but all that attention to detail bored me silly."

I laughed. "Oddly, that's the thing I love most—all those dastardly details. So when did you start working at The Grain Factor?"

"It was April Fools' Day, four years ago. I'd gone in there one day for some organic flour. Oh, if you could have seen how dismal and tacky the displays were! It was so disorganized—the whole place looked like something out of the Wild West. Ideas began sparking in my brain like firecrackers. I knew I could transform the store into something warm and welcoming, a place where everyone would want to shop. I introduced myself to the owner and asked him if I could design a new layout for the store, and show him ways he could expand his product line. A week later I was hired. Within two years we'd opened three more shops in New England."

"That's a wonderful success story. So tell me, how did you and Blake, um, hook up?"

Celeste smiled and her eyes lit up. "After The Factor expanded, we began carrying some high-end vitamins, and Blake came in one day with his product catalogs. I recognized him instantly. He hadn't changed all that much since high school. When I told him who I was, his jaw nearly hit the floor. It was a comical moment."

I could well imagine. This stunning woman sitting before me was the polar opposite of the somber teenager with the frizzy hair and crooked teeth and thrift shop wardrobe she'd been in high school. "Celeste, I'm so happy for both of you. I wish you every success in New York. So who's replacing you at the grain store?"

She laughed. "You make it sound like a place to buy cattle feed."

"Oh, I didn't mean—"

"Don't worry. I know what you meant. Actually, I've been grooming one of my sales clerks to step into my shoes when I leave. She's a sharp cookie, a real go-getter. I have every faith she can handle the position." Celeste looked at her watch. "Hey, look, I've got to scoot to the dry cleaner to pick up some things I left in storage. Would you see that Sam and Vicki get their presents?"

With a promise to deliver her culinary gifts, and also to have documents ready for Blake to sign in the morning, I walked her out to the reception area. I was glad to see that Heidi had gone home to get some much-needed rest.

It was only after Celeste was gone that I realized I'd never told her about Lillian being missing.

Maybe it was just as well. With everything Celeste had to do to get ready for their big move, she didn't need one more thing to worry about.

I decided I should apologize to Sam for coming back late from lunch. Sam was always flexible about things like that, especially since I always made up the time. Still, it wasn't fair for me to take advantage.

Sam's door was partway open, but his light was off. I peeked inside, but he wasn't there. I set Celeste's gift container on his desk and retreated.

Vicki was in her office, keyboarding away at the speed of sound. A steaming mug of fragrant chamomile tea—the only beverage she ever drank—rested near her elbow. On the wall behind her, the great blue heron was still in glorious flight over the shimmering pond. I entered the room quietly and set the gaily wrapped container, this one with a gold bow, on the corner of her desk. The tag read: *Happy Holidays, Vicki—Celeste and Blake.* "For you," I said.

I scurried back to my office.

Back at my desk, I dialed Lillian's cell number again. Again, it went to voice mail.

I spent the rest of the afternoon working on the Dwardene closing documents. Sam came back around three, slipped silently into his office, and closed the door.

With Sam and Vicki both incommunicado, I felt as if I was working in a morgue. At five past five, I packed up and left. I didn't even bother to let Sam know that I wouldn't need to leave early after all.

CHAPTER FIFTEEN

From the journal of Frederic Dwardene, Friday, November 17, 1950:

Through a private source, I have learned that Dora's shift at the factory ends at 5:15. The stop where she waits for the bus to Hazleton is one block from Manchester's bustling Elm Street. Today I parked my car across the street from the old brick factory. I watched the workers stream out a side door at the end of the long work day. They strode in groups or in pairs to catch a bus or trolley, or in some cases to walk home. But Dora, my Dora, walked alone . . .

"Here's our Apple!" Bernice Jessup beamed at me as I walked into the main dining room of the Hazleton Convalescent Home. "Six o'clock on the button."

I loved coming here every Monday evening to read to my group of seniors. The weekly reading club was made up of six women and one man. Not one was a minute under eighty. They were always so tickled to see me—it made me feel like a rock star or a famous writer.

Minus the talent, of course.

I'd been looking forward to this evening more than usual, mostly because I needed a mental break from the drama of the past two days. Aunt Tressa had been unusually tight-lipped when I drove her home after work. She'd fluffed off Paul Fenton's visit to her that afternoon as "another silly goose chase" and refused to discuss it further. The more I prodded, the more she'd clammed up.

My seniors were all seated at the far end of the room, adjacent to the Home's industrial-sized kitchen. Their respective chairs— mostly wheelchairs—formed a semi-circle around the padded, straight-back chair reserved for me. After peeling off my coat and gloves and greeting each of them warmly, I sat down. In Bernice's lap was a jumble of multicolored yarn, representing her latest knitting project.

A young nurse's aide came by and offered everyone fruit cups and wafer cookies. "No thanks, I'm fine," I told her.

"What chapter did we end on last week?" Irma Blakeley bleated after everyone had helped themselves to snacks. "Wasn't it when that young guy with the fancy car choked on some- thing?" She popped a grape into her mouth and crunched it between her dentures.

For the past three Mondays, I'd been reading Agatha Chris- tie's *And Then There Were None* to the group. So far it was a hit. Everyone was having fun tossing out guesses as to who the murderer was. Only Roger Landry, the group's sole male member, had wanted me to read a romance this time around. But the women had clamored for a mystery and outvoted him six to one.

"Let's see." I flipped open to the bookmarked page. "Looks like we ended with chapter four, so we'll begin chapter five."

When I reached the end of chapter seven, I closed the book and looked up. Everyone clapped except Irma, whose head lolled to one side as she dozed. For the next ten minutes or so the group chatted about the chapters I'd read. At ten to seven, two aides came in to wheel everyone back to their rooms. I bade the members of the group good night, all except for Bernice. I always stayed a few minutes longer to visit with her. Bernice had helped me form the reading group, and we'd developed something of a bond.

Tonight I had a dual reason for wanting to chat with her. I knew that Bernice and Lillian were long-time friends.

"That was wonderful, Apple," Bernice said when I pulled my chair up alongside her. She had soft gray curls that framed her careworn face. "You have such a good speaking voice."

"Thanks, Bernice."

She patted my arm. "And as much as I know you enjoy reading to us, I'm sure you have better things you could be doing with your free evenings."

"Not true. I love coming here and visiting with all of you." I looked at the clump of yarn she was working on. "Is that the baby afghan you're making for your new great-grandson? It's coming along nicely."

Bernice sighed. "It would move along a lot faster if I didn't have to struggle with these gosh-darn arthritic fingers. At the rate I'm going, he'll have it in time for college. I'd give a kidney to have Lillian's fast fingers. Why that woman can knit faster than anyone I've ever seen!"

Lillian and Bernice had been friends since they were girls. They'd worked together at Princess Sweaters in Manchester—the factory that once produced a popular line of clothing. I remembered my aunt telling me how she always loved shopping in the outlet that was part of the old factory building.

"Lillian and I worked in the winding room. Worked darned hard, too, not that you'd know it from our pay envelopes. Summers were a brute in the factory with no AC, but we did what we had to. Ah, well, that was all a long time ago."

I couldn't help smiling. Bernice loved telling stories from her younger days. She somehow managed to make grueling work and skimpy pay sound pleasingly nostalgic.

Snapping back to the present, I felt a dead weight drop inside my stomach. Bernice didn't know Lillian was missing. And there was no way I could tell her. It would only worry her needlessly, and for what?

No, for now I would keep Lillian's disappearance to myself. But maybe I could do a little digging.

"You've known Lillian a long time, haven't you, Bernice?"

"Oh my, yes. We go back to the days when the trolleys still ran in Manchester. Oh, I wish you could have seen Lillian back then, Apple. Such a sweet, lovely girl she was. Prettiest little thing you ever laid eyes on. The men at the factory were always gawking at her, but she never so much as looked them in the eye. She was painfully shy. Truth be told, I was always a bit jealous of her," Bernice said with a chuckle. "Isn't that awful?"

"Not at all. It's a normal human emotion. How many years did you work together?"

Bernice stared at her knitting. "Oh, let's see. Must've been thirteen or fourteen years we worked together at the sweater mill. I got married in nineteen fifty-three, but I stayed on another eight years or so. After that I took a job at one of the shoe factories, where the pay was a bit better."

"I'll bet you missed her."

"Sure did. You never saw a worker as reliable as Lillian. I swear, she never even took a sick day. Healthy as a groundhog, she was. Oh, well, there was that one time back in the early fifties—fifty-one, I think—when she took a long leave to help out her sick aunt in Scranton. The aunt had had a stroke, as I recall, and had no one to care for her. Lillian took the train to Pennsylvania. She was gone for the better part of a year, but as soon as she came back she went right back to work. For a long time she seemed real sad. The aunt had died, you see, and Lillian took it hard. Very hard."

"That's too bad," I murmured.

"Well, it was a long time ago," Bernice said. "Lil still visits me once a month, like clockwork. Always sneaks me some of those scrumptious butter cookies I'm not supposed to have, God love her."

I wondered when Lillian's next visit was due. If she didn't show up on her regular day, whatever that was, I was sure Bernice would worry.

"Bernice, didn't you once belong to the Hazleton Knitting Club?"

"Yes I did, back when my Howie was still with me." She crossed herself. "I think he liked it when I had my weekly night out with the ladies. Made him feel less guilty for playing cards with the boys all the time. But I left the group years ago, after my arthritis starting getting bad. I couldn't keep up with the other knitters. Since everything we made was for charity, I wasn't able to contribute much."

I squeezed her hand sympathetically. "Do you miss it?"

"In a way I do. But there was always a backbiter or two in the group. That part I don't miss at all."

"I guess every bunch is bound to have one."

"But I do miss the camaraderie," Bernice said wistfully. "We always held our knitting club meetings at the library. Afterwards we'd pop across the street to the cafe that used to be there. It was always so pleasant, chatting with the other knitters while I pampered my sweet tooth with an ice cream brownie. In a way, that's the part I miss most. You know, the friendships."

"That's understandable. Did you and the ladies ever go to a different place to have your dessert? To a restaurant out of town, maybe?" *Like Darla's Dine-o-Rama?*

"No, not that I can recall. None of us ever wanted to drive too far, especially at night. It was much easier to grab a snack right here in Hazleton."

That made sense. Perfect sense.

Which made the napkin from Darla's all the more troubling. Call it a gut feeling, but I felt sure that Lillian had never been inside the place.

So who left the napkin in her trailer?

CHAPTER SIXTEEN

From the journal of Frederic Dwardene, Saturday, November 18, 1950:

My Hudson is an impressive vehicle. I've kept it in fine shape since purchasing it three years ago. Today, I drove past Dora's house several times, hoping to catch a glimpse. It was nearly dark when I finally saw her step out onto her front porch. I pulled my car over to the side and stopped. I watched as she called out a name several times. Minutes later, a large white cat ambled out from behind a shrub. Laughing, Dora hurried down the front steps and swept the cat into her arms . . .

A light-colored van was parked in front of the duplex when I swung into my driveway. I assumed it belonged to Darby, though in the dark I couldn't make out the lettering on the side panel.

My imagination began spiraling out of control. Wasn't a van the perfect vehicle for snatching a woman from her home and driving her to God-knows-where? Didn't the serial killers on those creepy crime shows always drive vans?

I pulled up beside the duplex and killed my engine. Without my aunt's Caddy moored there, the driveway looked vast and empty. I slid out of my Honda and slammed the door hard, just in case Darby was paying attention. It wouldn't hurt to let him know someone else was around. And close by.

Something about the guy bugged me. Bugged me like a tiny

sliver wedged under my skin that I couldn't grasp hold of and remove.

Sure, he'd seemed polite enough. Too polite, in fact. And Aunt Tressa was right when she said he was smitten with her, though at the time I hadn't wanted to encourage her by agreeing.

For sure, there was one thing that didn't make one iota of sense—his ten-dollar deal with Lillian. What would he gain by charging next to nothing to build an elaborate play area for her cat? Certainly there wasn't any profit in it. Was he using it as a ploy to get into her trailer?

If that was the case, then Lillian had something he wanted. And since Lillian subsisted on her Social Security and savings, I couldn't imagine what it was.

I trudged into my house, kicked off my boots, and shed my outerwear. Cinnie and Elliot were curled up together on my overstuffed chair as if they'd been best buds for years. I grinned at the pair, but seeing Elliot reminded me all over again that Lillian was missing. As for Elliot, he had to be wondering where she was, and why he'd been relocated to this strange new environment. I comforted myself with the thought that he seemed cozy and content, all curled up in a furry orange ball with his new squeeze.

In the kitchen, I threw some low-fat cookies on a plate and made myself a mug of tea. I hauled it all into the living room, where I plunked down on the sofa.

The Monday night TV lineup was abysmal. I clicked the remote distractedly, training my ears for any signs of distress seeping from Aunt Tressa's side of the house.

Nothing.

And that's when I remembered the old journal I'd bought at the antiques shop earlier in the day. This was as good a time as any to see if it contained anything interesting. But where had I put it?

Aachh. It was on the back seat of my car. I'd tossed it there when I was driving Aunt Tressa back to her office.

I pulled on my winter boots and scooted out into the cold to fetch it. The winter sky was crisp and clear. A white nugget of moon hung low over the trees.

A minute later I was sitting yoga-style on my sofa. After a soothing sip of tea and a bite of a vanilla-flavored cookie, I opened to a random page.

Saturday, November 18, 1950.
The painting is coming along nicely. The white cat gave me an idea. I will paint Dora seated on my tufted blue sofa, the white cat nestled in her arms. How impressed she will be when she realizes how much I know about her . . .

The painting.

From the description, it had to be the one Aunt Tressa and I had seen in the antique shop. Whoever Dora was, Frederic Dwardene had obviously been in love with her. I skipped to the next day's entry.

Sunday, November 19, 1950
Today my heart was shattered. I drove past Dora's house several times, but the weather was cold and rainy, and she never appeared. Around 3:20, after I had driven past the house for the fifth or so time, I spotted in my rearview mirror a rusted old Chevrolet. It stopped in front of Dora's and a young man hopped out. I drove once around the block. The old Chevrolet was still there. I parked several yards behind it, then sat and waited. It was dark when he finally emerged, and this time I saw that he wore an army uniform. He was a soldier! Even with only the moon for illumination, I could tell that he was

dark-haired and handsome . . .

Ah, so Frederic had had a competitor for his beloved Dora's affections. This was getting juicy. I flipped to the following day's entry.

Monday, November 20, 1950
Thanksgiving is only three days away. I'll be forced to endure another excruciating dinner with my brother Mason, the boor. At least his wife Eleanor is a dear, if a bit simpering. Their younger one, Albert, is a mischief-maker. The elder boy, Edgar, seems stodgy for 18, but then some children are born old. Seeing them always reminds me of my darling boy Kenneth. If he'd lived, he would already be 21 . . .

Kenneth.

The same name on the old report cards I'd perused at the antique shop. Frederic Dwardene's somber words "if he'd lived" suggested that the child hadn't made it to adulthood.

My tired brain strained to visualize the limbs of the Dwardene family's scrawny tree. A prolific bunch they were not. Mason would have been Blake's grandfather, so Frederic had been Blake's great-uncle.

I kept reading.

Wednesday, November 22, 1950
My Dora came into the bank again today. With Thanksgiving tomorrow, she no doubt received her pay envelope a day early. She obviously uses her lunch break every week to ride the bus to Hazleton to make her deposits. How sweet that she patronizes her local bank over one in Manchester, which would be far more accessible during the day! My numerous strolls through the lobby paid a dividend, for I spotted her just as she entered. She wore a yellow knitted hat that perched prettily on her hair, and

gloves that matched. This time I greeted her personally, pretend-
ing to have ambled into her path as she walked up to the teller.
She smiled kindly, but I could see she'd been crying. When I
inquired if she was all right, she poured out her heart to me.
And then I learned the most wonderful thing—he's gone! The
soldier is off to war! Four days from now he will be in Korea,
far, far away from my Dora. I pretended, of course, to be
thoroughly sympathetic when she told me about her departing
soldier. In truth my heart was singing . . .

Friday, November 24, 1950
I am fully into the painting now, steaming along magnificently.
I don't think I've ever painted so swiftly, or so well. But then, I
have a date with destiny. I have decided that on February 14,
1951, I will ask Dora to marry me . . .

Curiosity blooming, I flipped ahead a few pages. Frederic's
writing style seemed more reminiscent of the *eighteen* fifties than
the nineteen fifties, which made the diary all that more intriguing. I was really getting into Frederic's love life when a deep-
throated laugh—thoroughly masculine—filtered through the
wall.

Muting the television, I set down my tea and tiptoed over to
the wall that separated my apartment from my aunt's. I pressed
my ear against it, feeling like some nosy character in a sitcom
spying on a neighbor.

Clop.

Clop.

It sounded like a knife cutting something. Hard.

My mouth went as dry as the Gobi. I squashed my ear harder
against the wall.

"Let it be—" Darby's voice.

Let *what* be? A sudden knot of fear clogged my throat.

Then Aunt Tressa's voice, ". . . that one, too . . . we can work it out . . ."

Dear God, work *what* out? Was she trying to convince him not to hurt her?

At that moment, the music started getting louder. And louder. My already mashed ear vibrated like a tuning fork as John Lennon's voice exploded through the wall, bellowing out a plea for help.

Help.

Help!

Suddenly, I got it. Aunt Tressa was signaling to me, exactly the way I'd asked her to. She'd turned up her CD player loud enough that I couldn't possibly miss the Beatles belting out "Help!" through the partition wall.

For a second or two, my head spun. A wave of pure terror rushed through my veins, surging to the tips of my toes and back to the top of my head. I knew I shouldn't have allowed her to meet Darby alone. I felt like kicking myself all the way to Pluto.

Panicky now, I snatched my portable phone off its cradle on the coffee table and punched in 9-1-1.

"What is the nature of your emergency?" a calm female voice inquired.

I burbled out a story about someone threatening my aunt and possibly killing her, and demanded that they send a SWAT team or the equivalent right away.

"Ma'am," said the annoyingly composed voice. "I'm dispatching a patrol car to your location as we speak. In the meantime, I need you to take a few deep breaths, calm down, and describe what happened."

What was she, a cop or a kindergarten teacher?

"I don't have time to breathe or to calm down," I sputtered. "My aunt is in deadly danger. I'm hanging up now and going over there."

"Ma'am," she pleaded. "Do not hang—"

I slammed the phone back in its cradle and raced into the kitchen. Frantically, I looked around for something I could use as a weapon. The ballpoint pen sitting on my counter didn't look especially menacing, nor did the rubber spatula. I had a drawer full of sharp knives, but after what had happened to Lou Marshall, I couldn't bring myself to even consider using one as a weapon.

No, I needed something heavy.

My gaze landed on the wooden rolling pin that hung from the utility rack next to my stove. I'd made exactly one pie in my life—an apple-rhubarb culinary disaster that even now sent shudders through me—which is the only reason I owned the utensil in the first place. I snatched it off the hook, then opened my junk drawer and fished around until I found Aunt Tressa's house key.

Armed now with solid wood and a means of access, I rushed out my front door in my red-stocking feet and onto the front porch. "Aunt Tressa, open up," I said, pounding on her door.

I thought I heard someone call out my name, but with the music so loud I wasn't sure.

With a shaky breath, I slipped the key in the lock and turned it. I quietly rotated the knob. Holding the rolling pin high in the air, I stepped inside the apartment just as Aunt Tressa whipped open the door.

With all the grace of a wounded pterodactyl I dove into the room, landing *kerplunk* on both knees on my aunt's lemon yellow carpet. The rolling pin twirled away, coming to an abrupt stop on the leg of her kidney-shaped coffee table.

"Apple!"

Aunt Tressa's cry pierced my eardrums at the same time I felt two strong arms hoisting me off the floor. Darby held me aloft as if I were made of toothpicks, performed a graceful half turn, and then set me down in the old wing chair that once belonged to my great-grandmother.

I sat there, humiliated, as he leaned over and stared into my eyes, searching, no doubt, for some telltale sign of insanity. Or maybe he was looking for signs of sanity—at this point I couldn't be sure. "Are you all right, young lady?" he inquired in the singsong tone generally reserved for the happily demented.

"I'm fine," I mumbled, rubbing my throbbing knees. "I thought . . . when I heard the song 'Help!' blasting through the wall—"

"You don't like that song?" Darby asked soberly, a hint of amusement waltzing in his deep blue eyes.

I wanted to melt through the floor. Disappear down a well hole. Fall into a freshly dug grave.

Aunt Tressa, all decked out in a clingy red sweater and a pair of off-white stretch pants, turned down the music, then came and perched on the edge of the wing chair. "Are you sure you're okay?"

"Yes, I'm fine," I groused. "It's only a couple of bruised knees. I'll survive."

Feeling utterly mortified, I did a quick survey of the room. Resting on the coffee table was Aunt Tressa's ancient cutting board—circa nineteen seventy-five—with a massive block of cheddar roosting on its center tile. Next to that was a sharp kitchen knife, along with three or four wedges of cheese that had been lopped off the mother lode, explaining the *clop clop* sounds I'd heard earlier. Two mugs of cocoa crowned with globs of melted marshmallow sat on either side of the board. Aunt Tressa and Darby had obviously been having a grand old time before I came charging through the door.

I wondered where Pazzo and Ringo had disappeared to, and was about to inquire when Aunt Tressa's front window shade began pulsing with blue light.

Shoot! Shoot on an oyster cracker.

"Is that a police car?" Aunt Tressa bleated, stomping toward the door.

"Um, Aunt Tress, there's something I have to tell you . . ."

Too late. The doorbell rang and she flung open the door. Two grim-faced police officers stood on the porch. One was positioned slightly behind the other, his hand poised over his nightstick. Both looked ready to do battle.

My aunt's jaw dropped. Darby gave out a chuckle, but he had to do some fast talking to persuade the police not to haul him in for questioning. It took the three of us nearly twenty minutes to convince the zealous officers that my 9-1-1 call had been a false alarm. Aunt Tressa allowed them to do a walk-through of her apartment. I was pretty much forced to do the same, since the call had originated from my home telephone.

It was almost quarter to nine when the officers finally drove off and I was able to breathe a sigh of relief. I couldn't help thinking what a fine giggle Chief Fenton was going to have when news of this little escapade reached his ears.

"Aunt Tress, I'm so sorry." I slid a slice of comforting, calorie-laden cheddar into my mouth. "When you started playing 'Help!' so loud, I was sure you were calling for help!"

"That's the tenth time you've apologized," she said, setting down a steaming mug of cocoa on the table next to me. "I don't want to hear it again. I shouldn't have played that particular song, so we're both at fault. Of course it's the first song on the CD, so technically it wasn't my fault either, but that's neither here nor there. And Jack isn't the least bit offended that you thought he was a crazed killer. Are you, Jack?"

Jack? What happened to Darby?

"No, ma'am, I certainly am not." He shook his head, then looked at me and smiled, his cheeks flushing pink. "Fact is, I'm relieved to know you and Tressa look out for each other the way you do. It's good to have family close by when you need them. Not everyone is so lucky."

"What did you mean," I asked my aunt, "when you told Dar—I mean, Jack, 'we can work it out'?"

Darby gave out a knee-slapping roar. I shot him a glare, which unfortunately went unnoticed.

"We were discussing our favorite Beatles songs," Aunt Tressa explained, a distinct sparkle in her eye. "Jack's favorite is 'Let it Be' and—"

"—yours is 'We Can Work It Out'," I finished wearily. I'd known that since I was seven, of course. Why did it slip my mind tonight?

I wondered if Aunt Tressa had questioned Darby about Lillian. I certainly couldn't ask her while he was still here.

"By the way, where are the cats?" I asked my aunt.

Aunt Tressa and Darby both laughed. "Over there." My aunt pointed at the oversized hassock in the far corner of her living room. "When Jack set his jacket down on the hassock, they both scurried over and took possession of it. They've been there ever since."

Sure enough, Pazzo and Ringo were stretched out on Darby's flannel-lined denim jacket, looking as blissful as I'd ever seen them.

Darby's face did that familiar flush. "I should explain. You see, I always keep a smidgen or two of catnip in one of the pockets. Works wonders when I'm doing repairs in a home that has cats. Keeps them happy and occupied, and out of harm's way."

I didn't even try to make sense of that. What did he do in a home that had dogs? Rub raw liver on the linings of his pockets?

Minutes later I drained my cocoa mug and rose, my knees throbbing in protest. "I'm afraid this day tripper has had enough

132

excitement for one evening," I said, eliciting a chuckle from Darby. He made some comment about looking forward to seeing me again, but if it happened any time before the dawn of the fourth millennium, it would be entirely too soon for me.

Back in my apartment, I couldn't wait to slip between the covers and sink into dreamland. But as I'd often heard, there's no rest for the weary. One glance at the blinking red light on my answering machine told me that I had two new messages.

CHAPTER SEVENTEEN

From the journal of Frederic Dwardene, Saturday, November 25, 1950:

I visited Whalie's Jewelers in Manchester today. How mobbed it was with Christmas shoppers! Oh, they had so many wonderful things I wanted to buy for Dora! In particular was a shining topaz pendant that hung from a dainty gold chain. I have already imagined it nestled above her collarbone, its golden facets dancing in the light. On a whim, I purchased it. I plan to present it to her on Christmas, just as surely as I will portray her wearing it in the painting . . .

Please be Lillian, please be Lillian . . .

The mantra chimed through my head like a scratched vinyl record as my finger stabbed the message button.

But it wasn't her. It was someone I absolutely, positively, definitely didn't want to hear from.

"When were you going to tell me about Lillian?" the male voice barked into my machine. "Call me when you get in."

No preamble, no greeting. Not even a phone number. The fact that we'd once had a relationship was apparently supposed to mean that his number was tattooed on my hand.

Then the second message came on—a kinder, gentler version of the first. "Apple, I'm sorry. It's Daniel. I can't believe how rude I just sounded. I . . . Paul Fenton called me this afternoon and asked if I'd seen or heard from Lillian. I couldn't believe it when he told me she's been missing since yesterday. Will you give me a buzz when you get in? Please?" This time he left his phone number.

Not that I needed it, since it *was* tattooed on my hand. Or at least on the inside of my brain cavity.

I should have known Paul Fenton would call Daniel. They'd gotten to know each other when Daniel was helping Lillian through the aftermath of her cat ordeal. After news of the nineteen cats she'd been housing in her trailer became public, she'd begun receiving all sorts of harassing, even threatening calls. Local news columnists labeled Lillian a "hoarder" and a "collector," displaying no empathy for her plight. Neighbors pointed fingers at her and snickered behind her back.

I sorely wished that even one of those critics could have seen the terror in her eyes that day. The terror as she watched us collect the cats, one by one, and load them into carrying cages. The terror of believing her beloved babies were all going to be "executed." Her kitchen cabinets, we discovered, had been well stocked with food for the cats but almost nothing for herself. Lillian had been subsisting on cheap bread and boxed macaroni dinners so the cats could eat well.

Thinking about it made me angry all over again, so I forced it out of my head. My problem at the moment was Daniel. Did he seriously think I was going to call him?

My pulse was doing the Daytona 500 when I punched in his number. He answered on the first ring.

"Apple? Thank God you called! I was beginning to think something had happened to you, too."

Was he fishing? Trying to find out if I was with someone?

"It's only a little after nine, Daniel. And believe it or not, I do have somewhat of a life."

"I know, I'm sorry. I guess I'm a little out of sorts." His tone softened. "It's really good hearing your voice again, App."

About a thousand responses chased each other around my tongue, but I swallowed them all back. "So, Chief Fenton called you about Lillian."

After a moment's silence he said, "Yeah. He called my office this morning and asked if I'd heard from her. Then he told me what happened at that old mansion on Saturday. I didn't realize your aunt was a close friend of the victim."

I'm out of the loop, he was trying to say, and all my guilt feelings came flooding back.

Since I was sure Fenton had put his own twist on the story, I gave Daniel my version of that horrible afternoon. I hadn't realized how much I'd bottled it up inside. I must have chattered for a full ten minutes before taking a breath. When I was finished, a sense of relief washed through me, though I wasn't entirely sure why.

"How is your aunt taking Lou Marshall's, um, death?"

"She's doing okay." More than okay if the events of this evening were any indication.

"So you think Lillian might have seen the murderer?"

"I feel sure of it, Daniel, and that's what's scaring me. I'm terrified that someone might have hurt her, or—" I couldn't finish the thought. It was too unthinkable. "What exactly did the chief say to you?"

Daniel sighed. "Not a whole lot. I think he was hoping I knew where she was. Anyway, he told me how you and your aunt found her door open yesterday. At the time, he didn't think foul play was indicated. But I got the distinct feeling he's been seriously rethinking that opinion. He also told me you've been bugging the beans out of him about her disappearance."

"Wouldn't you be?" I snapped.

"Darned right I would be! You're preaching to the choir, Apple." Then, more quietly, "By the way, how's Elliot? Fenton said you took him home with you."

"He's fine, and he adores Cinnie. They're actually pretty crazy about each other." An uncomfortable silence followed—a silence that hugged my heart in a death grip. I broke it by asking, "When was the last time you talked to Lillian?"

"Oh, let's see, I want to say about a month ago? I try to call her every four or five weeks. If I'm in the area I usually pay her a visit, but I haven't done that in quite a while. It's a bit of a hike from Goffstown. As you know, I don't get to Hazleton as much as I used to."

As you know . . .

He was obviously trying to lay a humongous guilt trip on me. Even worse, it was working.

"Daniel, did Fenton tell you about the napkin we found on the floor in Lillian's trailer?"

"No. He basically gave me an abbreviated version of everything. I think he was hoping I might have heard from her. When I told him I hadn't, he didn't seem inclined to want to linger on the phone. But never mind that, tell me about the napkin."

I described the crumpled napkin Aunt Tressa had found on the floor near Lillian's sofa.

"Darla's Dine-o-Rama," he mused. "I think I've heard of it, but I can't remember exactly where it is. Do you think it's important?"

"I'm not sure, but I can't help thinking that whoever is responsible for Lillian's disappearance might have dropped the napkin."

For several seconds Daniel was silent. Soft clicking noises filtered through the phone. "Daniel, are you there?"

"Got it," he said. "Darla's Dine-o-Rama. It's on Route One Twenty-One in Hampstead."

"Are you on the Internet?"

"Yup. Doesn't look like it has a website, though. It's probably a small mom-and-pop type of place."

"Thanks for looking it up, Daniel," I said, though I wasn't sure that knowing where the Dine-o-Rama was located was all that critical. I was more interested in knowing who'd dropped the napkin. I also wished I'd had the foresight to hang on to Lillian's house key before Aunt Tress and I locked up her trailer.

Then I remembered something.

I knew I had to be crazy for doing this, but I couldn't stop myself. If there was even a chance we might find something that would lead us to Lillian . . .

"Um, Daniel? Don't you have a key to Lillian's trailer?"

"Actually I do. She gave it to me in case there was ever an emergency or . . . well, a problem. She was still getting some of those wingnut phone calls—which is partly why she gave up her land line—and they worried her a lot. In fact, she told me she'd started sleeping with her cell phone in her pajama pocket, just in case she had to call for help real fast."

I felt my stomach lurch. The thought of an eighty-something-year-old woman going to bed in fear every night sickened me.

"Are you thinking what I think you're thinking?" Daniel said, the animation in his tone unmistakable.

Unfortunately, I was. The idea that Lillian's worst fear might have come true trumped my own issues with Daniel.

"Maybe we'd better use your key."

CHAPTER EIGHTEEN

From the journal of Frederic Dwardene, Thursday, December 7, 1950:

Oh, but my Dora is the dearest, most beautiful creature on earth! Once again, she looked terribly sad when she came into the bank, but I immediately took her under my wing. Politely, I inquired if she'd heard from her young soldier. It was too soon, of course, for her to have received a letter, but I carefully dropped a hint as to the ease with which a soldier acquires other interests after he leaves home. (Oh, I was wickedly clever!) At first she looked stricken, but I instantly soothed her by saying I was sure her particular soldier wasn't like that. But the seeds of doubt had been planted. Here's the best part: after only a little coaxing, I persuaded her to have lunch with me on Saturday. It will simply be a friendly lunch at a respectable establishment, but it is a beginning . . .

I hated to admit it, but being inside Daniel's Crossover again felt heavenly. Waves of hot air blasted out of the little Suzuki's heater vents. The melancholy notes of a John Coltrane classic sifted softly through the speakers.

Nestled in the passenger seat, I closed my eyes for a few blissful moments. Not for the first time, I wondered if I'd been insane to break off with Daniel, a man who was the total opposite of my dad. Over the years I'd learned to love Vincent Mariani, in spite of his abandoning me in favor of an unencumbered life. When the going gets tough, men like Dad hightail it to Vegas.

But at least I've always known where he was, which is more than I can say about my mother.

As for Daniel—he'd hack off his own legs with a butter knife before he'd abandon his or anyone else's child. He was one of the most responsible, kind and caring men I've ever met.

I suddenly had to remind myself why I ended the relationship. From the moment we'd met, wedding bells had been chiming in Daniel's head.

Our relationship had been way too intense, and way too fast, and way too overwhelming.

"You warm enough?" He reached over and adjusted the heater.

I sneaked a look at him. At thirty-three, Daniel was a year younger than I. He wore his sandy hair in the spiky, gelled-up style the young guys sported these days. In Daniel's case, it made him look about twelve. He still wore the rimless eyeglasses that I'd always thought framed his gray-blue eyes perfectly. Something warm and mushy swirled inside me.

"I'm fine," I said, but only after he caught me studying him. "Your car always did heat up fast."

I immediately wished I'd phrased that differently. Why couldn't I *think* before I spoke?

The turn into Lillian's trailer park jerked me back to reality. The access road had been roughly plowed, but was still a mass of icy lumps. Daniel drove slowly, careful not to let the little car skid.

Up ahead, Lillian's pitch-dark mobile home came into view. My throat tightened as Daniel parked in front of the trailer and shut off his engine. When he turned toward me and reached out his hand, I immediately stiffened. "Excuse me, I want to grab my flashlight," he said.

He'd been aiming for the glove box, not for me. I'd completely overreacted.

My knees still sore from my floor bounce at Aunt Tressa's, I swung my legs out of the car. Almost instantly, I felt Daniel's strong grip lift me upward. My first instinct was to pull away, until I realized I was standing on a sheet of ice. "Be careful here, it's treacherous," he cautioned. With his other hand he flicked on his flashlight.

We made it to the front steps without either of us falling, which was trickier than I'd imagined. Daniel unlocked the door and we both stepped inside.

He swung the beam of his flashlight around in an arc. Then he found the wall switch and snapped it on. The overhead light in Lillian's narrow kitchen sprang to life.

"It feels like a meat locker in here," Daniel said, turning off his flashlight. He snapped on a nearby table lamp, then located the thermostat and peered at it. "Good God, it's fifty-eight degrees."

"She must turn it way down at night," I offered.

"Even at night, fifty-eight is too cold for an elderly woman." Frowning, he glanced around. "Okay, where should we start?"

"If someone dragged Lillian out of here in the middle of the night," I said, "it had to be against her will. Maybe the kidnapper left something besides a napkin."

"I'll take a thorough look around this room and the kitchen," Daniel said, snapping on his flashlight again.

I rubbed my arms. "I'll start in the bedroom."

Daniel shot me a nervous smile. "I'm glad we decided to do this. It was a good idea."

But I wasn't so sure anymore. Now that we were here, the idea of rummaging through Lillian's personal belongings seemed like a horrible invasion of her privacy. "Thanks," was all I could manage.

In Lillian's bedroom, I turned on the frilly lamp that rested on her night table. The room looked exactly as Aunt Tressa and I had left it. My heart squeezed when I saw the thin blanket atop her bed, all tangled in the lovely afghan that I was sure Lillian had knitted herself.

I started by lifting her pillow off the bed. Nothing lay beneath it. Nor was anything hidden under the mattress.

I dropped the pillow back into place, then began to inspect every square inch of the thin, wall-to-wall carpeting. Pale beige in color, it was the type of floor covering that used to be called indoor/outdoor. Except for the alarm clock, which was still on the floor, and a few stray cat hairs that were clearly Elliot's, I couldn't see anything that might lead us to Lillian's kidnapper. I picked up the clock and set it back on Lillian's night table.

Next I went over to Lillian's painted white dresser. I couldn't help smiling at the framed black-and-white photo of a big fluffy cat that rested just below the mirror. The picture was pale and faded. I wondered if the cat had been a particular favorite of Lillian's when she was a much younger woman.

Lillian's jewelry box, a rectangle of brown vinyl, rested in the center of her dresser. I opened it.

The inside had a shallow upper tray that was attached to the cover by two thin ribbons. The bottom portion was about two inches high, and held a jumble of what appeared to be costume jewelry—mostly beaded necklaces and a few of the circle pins that were popular way back when.

Piece by piece, I emptied the bottom section. I set everything down on the dresser. Nothing jumped out at me, but then again, I had no idea what I was looking for. Maybe a hidden slip of paper on which she'd scribbled the name of the murderer?

Right. As if I'd get that lucky.

Even so, I ran my fingers around all the edges, making sure nothing had been tucked into a corner. After that, I moved to the top tray, where the more delicate items were kept—a silver medal of Saint Francis of Assisi, a thin gold choker with a ceramic cat hanging in the middle, a mounted yellow gem on a gold chain—

Wait a minute. I'd seen that one before. Where? The answer swam around the edge of my memory, but I couldn't seem to reel it in. I removed the chain with the yellow stone and set it aside. Then I returned everything else to the jewelry box and closed it.

Lillian's dresser drawers were next. Feeling like an interloper, I grabbed the two knobs on either side of the top drawer and pulled it open. I found myself gazing down at Lillian's undergarments, all neatly folded and stacked. Knowing how old-fashioned Lillian was, I figured she probably called them her unmentionables. I felt around underneath them, just to be sure nothing was hidden there.

The second drawer contained an array of knitted sweaters, each one a different pastel shade. I lifted one out of the drawer. It was a gorgeous off-white cable-knit pullover that looked incredibly complicated to make. Lillian was obviously an accomplished knitter. I folded it and returned it to the drawer, then performed a careful search of the nooks and crannies. I even ran my fingers between each of the sweaters, just in case Lillian had tucked something away there. Finding nothing, I closed the drawer.

The bottom one was next. It stuck, and I had to tug hard to pull it open.

My heart did a little jump in my chest. The drawer contained two cardboard boxes, one slightly larger than the other. Since my knees were still sore, I eased myself onto the floor next to the dresser and stretched out my legs. I was lifting a box out of the drawer when Daniel came in.

"Find anything?"

I shook my head. "Not so far, but I have a feeling this drawer has a lot of Lillian's personal things. I was just starting to go through it."

He walked around Lillian's twin bed and stooped down next to me. I caught the faintest whiff of his aftershave, and the memory of the day we met curled around me.

About two weeks after the cat story broke, I'd stopped by Lillian's to deliver a bag of cat food, and also to see how she was faring. The trailer was clean, but the strong scent of deodorizer still lingered. When Daniel rang her doorbell, Lillian gripped my arm in a panic. Although he'd called first to let her know he'd be paying her a visit, the prospect of his arrival still terrified her.

I'd stood beside Lillian protectively, and together we answered the door. Daniel stood on the doorstep, little droplets of moisture from the cloudy afternoon's drizzle dotting his hair. When he smiled, kindness beamed from his eyes. Then he stepped inside the trailer and he smelled so wonderful that I never wanted to stop breathing him in.

"—see this Apple?"

"Sorry, I was thinking of something else." I stared at the box Daniel had set down on the floor between us. He'd removed the cover to reveal a slew of old photographs.

"These must go way back," I said, lifting a sepia-toned photograph out of the bunch. The photo was of a young man with hair parted in the middle and a handlebar mustache, dressed in full military garb.

"Is there a date on it?" Daniel asked.

I turned over the photo. "Nineteen twenty-seven. Lillian's father, maybe?"

Daniel shrugged and dug another handful out of the box. As we fished through more of the photos, I was beginning to feel like a voyeur. But I somehow managed to convince myself that we needed to do this if there was any chance there was something here that might lead us to Lillian.

"I wonder who this is." I held out a photo of a young man wearing a crisp army uniform.

"Handsome devil," Daniel said. "Maybe he was an old beau of Lillian's."

I turned it over. "No date on it, but my guess would be late forties, early fifties." I flipped back to the photo and stared at it for several more seconds.

"I think you're right," Daniel said, already holding up another photograph. "Look at this one. It's gotta be Lillian!"

I grinned. "It sure is. Oh, she was lovely."

Only a few hours earlier, Bernice had told me how beautiful Lillian had been in her youth. But in the crisp black-and-white photo Daniel was holding, she was positively stunning. Standing on the front porch of an old house, she was cradling a big fluffy cat in her arms. I flipped over the photograph. "Snowball and me—nineteen forty-nine, it says. This cat must have been very special to her. There's another photo of him, or her, on her dresser."

Is that why Lillian purchased the porcelain cat at the estate sale? Had it reminded her of her beloved Snowball?

"Hey, look at this one," Daniel said, holding out another one. "Lillian looks about fourteen, doesn't she?"

In the picture, a teenage Lillian stood beneath a willow tree, her arms looped through the arms of the two women on either side of her. "I'll bet that's her mother on the left," I said. "She looks a lot like Lillian. I wonder if the other one is her aunt."

"Oh, did she tell you about her aunt Alice?" Daniel smiled. "Apparently she was quite a character."

"No, but I was chatting with Lillian's friend Bernice at the nursing home earlier this evening." I related the story Bernice had told me about Lillian traveling to Pennsylvania to care for her sick aunt.

"Huh," Daniel said. "Alice would have been pretty young back then. Well, Lillian obviously took good care of her," he chuckled. "Alice lived till she was ninety-one."

I shook my head. "Must have been a different aunt, then. The one Bernice told me about died in the fifties."

It was Daniel's turn to shake his head. "She only had the one aunt, I'm pretty sure." He threw up a hand. "Anyway, it doesn't matter. None of this is helping us find Lillian."

By the time we'd rifled through the entire box, it was close to eleven. I stifled a yawn.

"Let's quickly get through this last box and then we'll go," he said. "I can always swing by tomorrow and look around a little more."

"I'm starting to feel really guilty for poking through Lillian's personal things this way." I looked at Daniel. "Do you think—is it possible Lillian *did* leave on her own? If she thought her life was in danger, could she have decided to go into hiding?"

"Without Elliot? I don't think so. You said yourself his food dish was empty when you and Tressa arrived here yesterday."

He was right. No way would Lillian leave him like that.

Daniel slid the box of photographs back into the drawer and lifted out the other box. This one contained a wealth of personal memorabilia.

On the top was a yellowed newspaper clipping, its edges disintegrating from age. I gently removed it from the box. "It's an obituary," I said. "Private First Class Anton Polerski, late of Hazleton." As I read the rest to myself, I felt Daniel reading over my shoulder.

"He died in the Korean War," I said after I'd finished.

"Usually known as the Korean Conflict," Daniel said. "The U.S. never declared war on Korea."

"I know that, Daniel. I was a history major, remember?"

He flushed. "Sorry."

I rubbed my eyes. "Oh criminy, I'm the one who should be sorry. I'm tired and testy and a terrible pill. I didn't mean to jump down your throat like that."

"Forget it," he said. "Do you think this Polerski guy is the soldier in the photograph?"

"I wouldn't be surprised." Something about this particular photo nagged at me, but I was too weary and too distracted to figure out what it was.

"Look, there's a bunch of old letters in here." Daniel dug out a handful and handed a batch to me.

The letters, addressed to Lillian, had all been written by Anton. As I began reading through them, my fatigue turned to fascination. Though he was far from eloquent, Anton's feelings for Lillian had been heartfelt.

"When he left for Korea, they were engaged," I said quietly.

I read on. As the weeks passed, Anton's letters grew more desperate, more despairing. Not because he feared he'd never return from Korea, but because Lillian had apparently stopped returning his letters. In a letter dated one day before Valentine's Day, nineteen fifty-one, he begged Lillian to write to him. *Even a postcard from you, sweetheart, would cheer my heart . . .*

Tears stung my eyes. A massive wave of fatigue suddenly crashed over me. "Daniel, why are we doing this? These are Lillian's private letters. We have no right to read them—they're certainly not going to help us find her."

He blew out a sigh. "You're right, except—. Well look, what do you think about this idea? It's hypothetical, of course, but what if Lillian was afraid to tell the police who she saw coming out of Lou Marshall's office that day, so she wrote his name down and hid it somewhere in her house, in the event something really bad were ever to happen to her?"

The same notion had flitted through my mind. Lillian's credibility had been severely compromised when people learned she'd been living in her tiny trailer with nineteen cats.

"You think she might have been afraid the police wouldn't believe her?"

"Exactly." Daniel blew out a sigh. "But you're right, we really should get going." He started to put the cover back on the box when I spotted a yellowed, official-looking document jutting out from the stack. I eased it out of the pile.

Yellowed with age, it was Lillian's birth certificate.

"She was born in nineteen twenty-nine," I said, "in Nashua, New Hampshire."

Daniel pointed at the line above that one. "And her given name was Dora Lillian Bilodeau."

My heart caught in my throat.

Dora.

The same name as Frederic Dwardene's heartthrob. Were Dora and Lillian one and the same? Had Lillian been the young woman the banker had been so desperately in love with?

She had to be. Otherwise it would simply be too startling a coincidence. And Anton must have been the handsome soldier in the rusty Chevrolet—the one Frederic was so anxious to evict from Lillian's life!

"Gosh, I'd forgotten that her given name was Dora," Daniel said.

"You knew?"

He nodded. "I learned a lot about Lillian during those dark days after the cat problem. She was very depressed, and so sad. I tried to get her to talk about what happened, but she wouldn't. She felt ashamed that the whole town knew about her and the cats. She's lived in Hazleton all her life, and the ridicule was more than she could bear. So I started asking her questions about her family, her life. That's when she really opened up and told me about her mom and her aunt, and her work at the sweater factory." Daniel touched my arm gently. "Is something wrong? You look pale all of a sudden."

"I . . . no, it's nothing. I think we should leave."

On our way out, I checked Lillian's coat closet again. The lilac coat still hung there. On a whim, I reached into the pocket where Lillian had slipped the china cat two days ago.

The cat was still there.

CHAPTER NINETEEN

From the journal of Frederic Dwardene, Saturday, December 9, 1950:

I spent an hour this morning waxing the Hudson until it positively shimmered. Freshly shaven, I, too, was looking quite spiffy when I arrived at Dora's. Her mother, a handsome woman in her forties, answered the door. Her face beamed when she saw me. A good sign, I thought—the mother already approves. (I wondered what her opinion was of Dora's soldier!) The mother introduced herself as Dora Bilodeau, and for a moment I was perplexed. She must have noticed my expression because she fluttered a hand and said, "Oh dear, I should explain—my daughter was named after me. That's why we call her by her middle name—Lillian. Otherwise it's too confusing!"

I was relieved to see that Darby's truck was gone by the time Daniel delivered me back to the duplex. Aunt Tressa's bedroom light was on, but the downstairs was dark. No doubt she was either reading in bed or watching the late news.

She probably never realized I'd left, which was just as well. I dreaded telling her that I'd spent the evening with Daniel, even if my mission had been carried out solely on Lillian's behalf. It was going to raise all sorts of questions I wasn't prepared to answer.

Better to face it in the morning, fresh from a night's sleep. Assuming I'd be able to sleep.

Daniel accompanied me to the front door. "Give Tressa my best," he said. "Tell her if it weren't so late I'd have stopped in to say hello."

I nodded, surprised to feel tears fill my eyes. I prayed Daniel couldn't see them in the dark, but since I'd left the outside light on, I knew he probably did.

"I'll call Fenton tomorrow," Daniel said. "He may know more than he's letting on. In the meantime, is it okay if you and I keep in touch daily until all of this has been resolved?"

"Of course," I said over the boulder in my throat. Regardless of my history with Daniel, Lillian's welfare had to come first. Even if the worst had already happened, we both needed to know.

After sputtering out an awkward goodnight, I fled inside. It was only after I'd kicked off my boots and shed my coat that I began to cry.

I cried all the way into the shower, without even knowing why.

A persistent ringing wrenched me out of a dream-filled sleep.

I jerked upright in bed. A baleful look at the clock told me it was twelve thirty-seven. Who was calling me this late?

I snapped on my bedside lamp, fumbled for the portable phone sitting behind it. "Hello?" I mumbled over a huge yawn.

"Bluuuu . . . blood . . ."

A river of adrenaline zinged through me. Instantly I was fully awake, and on red alert. "Lillian?"

"Bluuuuu . . ." the voice said again, and this time I was sure it was Lillian. A very drugged-sounding, very out-of-it Lillian.

But she was alive. Thank the sun and the stars, she was alive!

"Where are you, Lillian? Tell me where to find you!"

The next sound was a sharp disconnect.

"Lillian. Lillian!" I begged her to pick up the phone again, but she was gone.

Stunned, I plunked my phone back in its cradle. Where had she been calling from? Was there some way I could trace her call?

I'd never signed up with the phone company for caller ID, mostly because I couldn't think of any reason why I would ever need it. Now I was cursing myself.

Wait a minute.

I grabbed the phone again. This time I punched in star-six-nine. A robotic voice intoned the telephone number from which my last call originated. It was Lillian's cell phone number.

What had she been trying to tell me? It sounded as if she'd been trying to say *blue blood*.

Which meant absolutely nothing to me.

What turned my veins to ice was that someone had cut the call short, and I didn't think that someone was Lillian. Would her captor—and I was now sure there was one—see her as a liability and eliminate her?

For the second time in a six-hour period, I called 9-1-1. A man answered this time, and in a calm tone asked me to state the purpose of my call.

"Look, I know Chief Fenton isn't there in the middle of the night," I told him, "but I need to get in touch with him right away. I just got a call from Lillian Bilodeau, and now I'm sure she's been kidnapped. She tried to tell me something, and it sounded like blue blood but I'm not really sure that's what she was trying to say and then she got cut off and I—"

"Ma'am, please—"

"—and I'm scared to death whoever has her might hurt her now and—"

"Ma'am," the dispatcher interrupted, "please state your name."

"Sorry." I gave myself a mental slap and sucked in a deep

breath. "This is Apple Mariani. I live at One-Eighty-One-B Summer Street, but there's nothing wrong here. You've got to get a hold of Paul Fenton and tell him to call me. You see, he wasn't really convinced something bad had happened to Lillian, even though he did make a few inquiries, but now I have proof that she's—"

"Ma'am," he interrupted, "please listen to me for a moment. I will call Chief Fenton if need be, but first I need you to calmly explain what happened."

A groan escaped me. Why couldn't I get through to this guy? Hadn't he listened to a word I said?

I repeated the story, this time going back to Sunday afternoon, when Aunt Tressa and I first realized Lillian was gone. He listened patiently, then informed me that he was dispatching a patrol car to my location.

"Please don't send another police car," I said. "All I want is—"

"*Another* police car?"

I groaned. "I had an incident earlier in the evening, but it turned out to be a false alarm. But this time I really need Chief Fenton to contact me. Please. A woman's life is in jeopardy." From the foot of the bed, Cinnie sat on her haunches and gazed worriedly at me. I was sure she was wondering if I'd lost my mind.

"Ma'am," the dispatcher said, not unkindly, "a patrol car is already on its way. It will be there in approximately two minutes. If the responding officers agree that a call to Chief Fenton is in order, they'll handle that for you. In the meantime, please stay on the line."

Still gripping the phone, I leaped out of bed. I juggled it from one hand to the other while I slid my arms into my flannel robe and shoved my feet into slippers. I was on my way downstairs when my doorbell rang.

"Gotta run. They're here," I told the dispatcher.

This time I got a man and a woman. The female half of the equation was about six feet tall, and looked agonizingly thin beneath her long wool coat. Her shorter, rounder partner, who identified himself as Sergeant Dave Everhart, flashed an ID at me. "Come on in," I told them wearily.

The pair plopped onto the sofa. With a longing look at one of my throw pillows, Sergeant Everhart stifled a yawn. He dredged a notepad the size of a business card out of his jacket pocket, then stuck his hand in his pocket again and dug out a pen.

Having done it so many times by now, I related the story of Lillian's disappearance in record time. "So don't you think you should call Chief Fenton?" I prodded when I was through.

The female officer lanced me with a glare, as if I were casting aspersions on her ability to handle her job. Her partner merely shook his head. "There's no need for that. We'll make a full report. I'll make sure Chief Fenton has it on his desk first thing in the morning."

"But . . . can't you find out where Lillian was calling from? Isn't there some way the cell phone company can trace her location?" By now Cinnie and Elliot had joined us, and were waltzing around my feet. I'd have sworn Elliot shot a reproving look at the female officer, whose name I still didn't know.

"That depends on a variety of factors," Everhart said, peering at his notes. "Now if she'd called nine-one-one—"

"I don't think she did." I blew out a tired sigh. "Several months ago, Lillian had a problem with an overabundance of cats. Unfortunately it made the news, and people began labeling her as a nut. The truth is, she was just a caring woman who couldn't turn away a stray."

"I remember that," Everhart's partner piped in. "Lady had what, ninety cats in her trailer?"

"Nineteen," I corrected, "and that's exactly what I mean. The story got blown way out of proportion. It made Lillian afraid to go to the police for help. They didn't exactly shower her with empathy during her ordeal. The bottom line is that she trusts me, and I told her to call me if she ever needed anything."

Everhart's expression softened. "So you think she called you, knowing you'd know what to do."

"In a peanut shell, yes."

"I'm still confused." Everhart tapped his pen on his knee. "If she had her cell phone with her, why didn't she call you sooner? And why would the kidnapper let her keep her phone in the first place?"

"I realize none of it makes sense, Sergeant. She sounded drugged, that much I'm sure of."

"And you have no idea what she meant by 'blue blood'?"

"None whatsoever." I wasn't even totally sure that's what Lillian had said, but it wouldn't help my credibility rating to admit that.

"Does Miss Bilodeau have any substance abuse problems?" he prodded. "Does she drink? Take drugs?"

Was he kidding? "Of course not. Sergeant, Lillian is in her eighties."

The pair exchanged barely disguised smiles. "Substance abuse has no age limits, Miss. You'd be surprised at the things we see."

Yes, I would be, but maybe I was more naive than I realized. Maybe every day there were gangs of seniors prowling the streets of Hazleton, snorting cocaine as they guzzled down shots of aged whiskey.

Or maybe I was just feeling snarky.

I answered a few more questions, then gave Lillian's cell phone number to Everhart. Hoisting his plump form off the sofa, he promised to do some checking into the cell phone call, though he didn't offer any details as to what that might entail.

I followed them to the door and watched them hustle back to their patrol car. Aunt Tressa stepped out of her front door in time to see them drive off into the night. Wrapped in a red velour robe and wearing her fuzzy orange feet, she trounced behind me into my apartment. "What in the name of Jiminy Cricket is going on? I woke up and saw those crazy blue lights flashing on my window shade again. I thought I was having a psychedelic nightmare."

It was a nightmare, of sorts.

"Come on, I'll make us some tea," I said over a huge yawn. It wasn't as if I'd be getting much more sleep, anyway. "I've got a lot to tell you."

Over mint-flavored tea and a plate of Celeste's homemade buns, I told her everything. About Daniel calling me, about our visit to Lillian's trailer. And finally about the cryptic call I received from Lillian on her cell phone.

"So, you were with Daniel?" she said, a distinct look of triumph flashing in her eyes.

"That's not the point," I said wearily. "We're both concerned for Lillian's safety, that's all it was about."

She raised an eyebrow. "Uh-huh," she said doubtfully.

"Aunt Tress, haven't you heard what I said? Lillian called me, and she sounded drugged."

"Of course I heard you, and I'm just as worried as you are." She licked a glob of sugary glaze off her forefinger. "What I can't figure out is this: if she was kidnapped, why did she still have access to her cell phone? Wouldn't that be the first thing the kidnapper would take away?"

Exactly what Everhart had asked me, and I still didn't have an answer. I told her what Daniel had said about Lillian sleeping with it in her pajama pocket. "When I searched her room last night, it wasn't anywhere to be found. Somehow, wherever she is, she must have managed to take it with her. After that last call, though, I'm sure all of that's changed." A shiver ripped through me.

Aunt Tressa shook her head. "Poor woman. Wherever she is, she's probably so scared. Did you and Daniel land on anything that might have given up a clue as to where she is, or who snatched her?"

"Not really." I told her about the photos and the personal letters we found. "Some of those letters were so sad, Aunt Tress. I wish now I'd never read them."

"Yeah, I hear you. Besides, how helpful can sixty-year-old letters be?"

"Exactly what Daniel and I said."

She looked at me, then spoke softly. "Seriously, App, how was it, being with Daniel again?"

I shrugged, but my throat felt taut. "Strange. Nice. Awful." Part of me—the needy part—wanted to pour out my feelings. But my protective shield instantly slammed into place, warning me to keep my emotions to myself and deal with it privately. "For now, let's stick to figuring out how we can help Lillian, okay?"

She nodded. "At least we know she's alive."

"Yes, but after tonight, how long is that going to last?"

Aunt Tressa went to the cabinet for two more tea bags and poured us each a second cup. "We won't be getting much sleep anyway," she reasoned. "Might as well indulge ourselves."

I picked up my spoon and squished the tea bag around in my mug. The minty aroma wafted toward me, clearing my senses. I thought about Lillian's strange words.

Blue blood.

"Aunt Tress, what do you think Lillian meant by 'blue blood'?"

"Are you sure that's what she said?"

"No, but that's what it sounded like. She sort of dragged out the words, like she was having trouble pronouncing them. Which she probably was, since I'm sure she'd been drugged."

"People usually say 'blue blood' when they're talking about a fancy-pants aristocratic family."

"Which leaves out you and me and pretty much everybody I know."

"What about the Dwardenes?"

I scoffed. "First of all, there's only one Dwardene left—Blake. Second, I'd hardly consider the family aristocratic." I could still picture Blake's dad flouncing around at the graduation party in that silly bikini top.

Aunt Tressa looked at me thoughtfully. "But think about it, App—Lillian just might. In her day the Dwardenes were a staid old banking family. Wasn't it Blake's great-great uncle who founded the old Hazleton Savings Bank?"

I nodded. "And before the mansion fell into disrepair, it was probably the classiest home in town."

"I rest my case."

And I didn't like what all of this implied. If Lillian's blue blood reference was intended to mean the Dwardenes, and Blake was the sole surviving heir . . .

Squashing the thought, I turned the table on her. "Don't you have some things to share with me, Aunt Tress? First of all, I never got a full report from you about what Fenton wanted to see you about."

My aunt quirked an eyebrow at me. "A full report, officer?"

"You know what I mean. Don't play coy with me, missy."

With a sly smile, Aunt Tressa reached for another bun. "You know, even with all the healthy grains Celeste pumps into these things, they're positively scrumptious. You gotta hand it to her— the woman can bake."

"Okay, now you're avoiding. Do I have to bring out the hot lights?"

Aunt Tressa winced. "All right, here goes. I didn't want to tell you earlier because I knew you'd worry yourself into a tizzy. Three days before Lou was murdered, I . . . I broke up with him."

"What?" I was flabbergasted. She hadn't given out a single sign that anything had been amiss between them.

"I knew it wasn't going anywhere, and I could see that he thought it was. But he was never going to be another Marty, or anything even close to that, so I had to end it."

I still wasn't wrapping my brain around this. "But I thought you had a real friendship going with Lou. You both enjoyed eating out, going to movies—"

"We did. See, that's the thing. If we could have kept everything at that level, it would've been okay. But Lou wanted more, much more, and he definitely wanted . . ." With that unfinished tidbit, she averted her eyes.

"Never mind, don't tell me." I let out a sigh. This new revelation had my head twirling like a parade baton. "So what does all this have to do with Fenton?"

My aunt toyed with the handle of her red Santa mug. "On Sunday the police searched Lou's house. Including, of course, what was on his home computer and his answering machine. Seems they found the somewhat scathing e-mail I sent him last Wednesday. Not to mention the uncensored message I left on his answering machine."

"I'm almost afraid to ask."

"Let's just say Lou made a crack Tuesday night that I didn't take very kindly to, and leave it at that."

"You don't want to share the 'crack' with me?"

She shook her head. "It was nasty, repulsive, and in very poor taste. All I'll tell you is that it concerned a particular piece of my anatomy. A piece that Lou apparently found quite alluring. But it was the *way* he said it that was so offensive." She clenched her mug tightly in both hands. I was afraid that any moment it might shatter. "He dragged Marty's name into the conversation."

Good gravy on a dog biscuit. Had the man been insane? Had he been totally oblivious of the fact that Aunt Tressa worshipped her late husband?

"No wonder his 'crack,' whatever it was, set you off. I'm surprised I didn't see the explosion from my window."

"I tried to let it go, but I couldn't. When I woke up Wednesday morning, I was even madder than I was the night before. First thing I did was plunk my fanny down in front of my computer and zip off a caustic e-mail to him." She made a wry face. "Obviously I wouldn't have done that if I'd known what was going to happen."

"So now Fenton thinks you had a motive to kill him," I said, "based on one e-mail that he found in Lou's in-box, and your nasty phone message. The man is unbelievable!"

"Fenton's been trying to pin this on me from day one," Aunt Tressa said. "He has no idea who killed Lou. He doesn't even know how to investigate a murder, since Hazleton hasn't had one since nineteen seventy-one."

A million separate thoughts crashed around inside my head. "There's something I still don't understand. Why were you so anxious to talk to Lou at the mansion on Saturday?"

"After I sent Lou that e-mail, he kept calling me. Bugging me on my cell, ringing me late at night. He kept trying to explain, saying he wanted another chance. He didn't get that it was over, that he'd never been more than a friend in the first place. I knew I'd have to confront him, face to face, if I was ever going to end his bothering me, but I wanted to do it someplace where other people would be close by. The estate sale gave me the perfect opportunity."

"Were you afraid he might cause a scene? Get violent?"

"Violent, no, but yes, I was afraid he might get a bit . . . vociferous." She gave a tepid laugh. "That's why I spent all that time in the bathroom that day. I was stalling, trying to get up the nerve to go in and talk to him."

I thought about the "ick" factor in my aunt's revelation about Lou. "I'm beginning to see Lou in a whole new light," I said. "Maybe he wasn't the person we thought he was. I'm thinking now that he may have had enemies."

"I suppose. Still, I feel bad talking about him this way. Until he made that horrid remark about my—well, he hadn't seemed like a bad guy. A little clingy, maybe, a little pushy. But not a terrible person."

"Not to change the subject," I said, "but all this talk of Lou just reminded me. Do you remember seeing Vicki Pomeroy at the estate sale?"

"Yeah, she was there. When you and I first went in, I saw her gawking at something on a knickknack shelf. When she turned her head I raised my hand to say hello, but she just gave me an odd look and darted away. She's been acting strange toward me for a while now."

"I feel kind of bad for her," I said, and explained what Celeste had told me about Vicki's apparent crush on Lou.

"I guess that explains why she's been giving me the evil eye of late." Aunt Tressa's right eyebrow shot upward. "You don't think . . ."

I stared blankly at her, then realized where she was going. "That she killed Lou? Glory, no, I can't picture that at all. Even if it was unrequited love, as Celeste called it, Vicki doesn't have an aggressive bone in her body. Oh sure, she complains a lot, about *everything*, but . . ." I shook my head. "No, somehow I just can't picture Vicki doing in Lou."

"Well, I say we don't let anyone off the hook until the murderer is breaking rocks up at the granite quarry in Concord."

I chuckled. "I don't think prisoners do that sort of thing anymore."

"Pardon me. Until the murderer is sitting in his cell with his laptop, e-mailing all the members of his fan club."

"Are you so sure it was a *him?*"

She cocked a finger at me. "Interesting question."

"Isn't it?" I said. "And before you go off on another tangent, it's time you dished out the dirt on Darby."

To my surprise, my aunt did something I'd rarely ever seen her do.

She blushed.

CHAPTER TWENTY

Lillian—her middle name! I had always addressed her as Dora, and she never corrected me. Strangely, I felt buoyed by this revelation, small though it was. I chatted amiably with Mother Dora while I waited for Lillian. She tittered like a schoolgirl when I related a humorous story about one of the bank's eccentric customers. I saw, clearly, that the path to winning Dora's (Lillian's!) hand would be by earning her mother's approval . . .

"I knew it! You like Darby, don't you?"

"Like?" Aunt Tressa rolled her eyes. "You make me sound like a teeny-bopper. But yes, as a matter of fact, I like *Jack* very much. As it turns out, the man has led a colorful and fascinating life."

I crossed my arms in front of me, school principal style. "I see. So, tell me about him. How old is he? Has he always been a handyman? Does he live alone? Has he ever been married?"

"Would you like to know what he scored on his college boards, too?" she asked innocently.

I glared at her. "All right, point taken." I reached for a cinnamon bun. "Split this one with me?"

"You have to ask?"

I fetched a knife and severed the bun in two, then slid the larger segment onto her plate.

"He actually grew up in a rural town outside of Scranton.

His folks were in their thirties when they had him, or rather, adopted him. He was an only child, so they doted on him. In high school he played drums in a rock band. After high school he went to Villanova, where he graduated cum laude. Did a stint in the Air Force; always wanted to be a fly boy, but his eyesight wasn't good enough. He discovered his true calling when he took up carpentry and realized he could create just about anything with wood. He's lived all over the country: Montana, San Diego, Buffalo."

"A drifter," I said flatly.

"A consummate adventurer," she corrected, then took a long pull on her tea.

"So how did he end up here," I demanded, "in picturesque Hazleton, New Hampshire?"

My aunt hesitated. "I'm not sure, actually. We didn't quite get that far, if you catch my drift."

It was my turn to blush. "Aunt Tress, I'm so sorry about that. I honestly, truly thought you were in danger."

She laughed. "I told you, knock it off with your sorries. Besides, Jack was very impressed. He thought your courage was absolutely amazing!"

"You're joking."

"I joke you not."

"He was impressed with my charging through your front door like a rhinoceros, rolling pin raised and ready to bash him on the head?"

"Yes, he was. He thought it was one of the bravest things he'd ever seen." She popped a slab of cinnamon bun into her mouth.

"How about your dishwasher? Did he even look at it?"

"Give me a little credit, Apple. Not only did he look at it, he fixed the leak. It was just a loose screw or bolt or something somewhere in the guts of the thing. He said he was glad I called him because a repairman probably would have charged sixty bucks just to look at it, let alone repair the leak."

Of course he did.

"So what did he charge you?"

"Um, nothing, actually. He said I could consider it a courtesy repair, since it took him hardly any time at all and because I make the best hot cocoa on the planet."

I sighed in growing defeat. "All right, let me cut to the chase. Did you find out how he knows Lillian? And why he offered to build her that thing for Elliot for only ten dollars?"

"Uhh . . . no. After you, um, dropped in the way you did and the cops finally left, Jack didn't want to linger much longer. He was afraid he was keeping me up."

Of course he was.

"So essentially you found out zippo," I said.

She held up a finger. "I beg to differ. Now that I know his back story, as they say, I'm ready to move in for a closer examination of the subject."

I was way too tired for this. "Meaning?"

"Meaning I invited him to have dinner here with you and me on Wednesday evening."

"You did *what?*"

"I invited him here for homemade chicken pot pie." She slid me a sly look. "Care to invite Daniel?"

CHAPTER TWENTY-ONE

Oh, how delightful she looked when she stepped into the parlor! She wore a simple yellow dress with lace at the collar, and matching bows in her hair. I nearly gasped at the sight of her, but I kept my composure and greeted her as I would a dear friend. She looked a bit paler than usual. Nonetheless, she said it was very thoughtful of me to want to take her to lunch. I asked her if I might call her Lillian, and she smiled and said yes, of course.

Morning sneaked up behind me, then hit me on the head with a sledgehammer.

My eyes burning with fatigue, I somehow managed to drag myself into the shower, throw on a half-decent pair of slacks and a blouse, and gobble down some oatmeal in time to deliver Aunt Tressa to her office for an 8:45 appointment.

Her new clients, whom she'd yet to meet, were a couple in their sixties. They'd told her on the phone they were planning to retire to Myrtle Beach, but only if they could sell the beloved cape they'd raised their family in. At a hefty price, of course. Otherwise, their move to warmer climes would be put on hold indefinitely.

"They sounded so sweet on the phone," Aunt Tressa said, toying with the buttons on my radio. "I think I'm going to enjoy working with them."

I barely heard her. The bizarre events of the previous evening kept flouncing through my head, skipping around each other like partners in some maniacal square-dance.

Lillian. Daniel. Darby. I couldn't get any of them out of my mind.

Truth be told, I was also annoyed with Aunt Tressa. I loved her more than anyone in the Milky Way, but sometimes she had me teetering on the slippery edge of sanity.

For starters, you'd never guess she'd been up half the night gabbing with me. Her eyes were positively vibrant this morning, her makeup brighter than usual. Wearing a sparkly green scarf over her black suede jacket, her designer bag propped on her knees, she looked like a seasoned model, ready to march down the runway and take on the world.

As for me, I felt as droopy as an old spaghetti mop. If only someone would wring me out and stand me in a corner, maybe I could snag a few more minutes of sleep.

"—you heard a word I said?" My aunt's trill cut through me like a machete.

I jumped, then yawned. "Sorry, I wasn't really listening. I got about forty-seven minutes of sleep last night. Drinking all that tea didn't help."

"I slept like a cat after I went back to my apartment last night," she chirped. "I must've crashed after eating all those sugary cinnamon buns."

Not surprising. She polished off nearly five of them.

Or had it been visions of Jack Darby that sent her sailing off to dreamland with such ease?

I yawned again as I swung my car into her parking lot. "I meant to ask you—did Wilby make it home all right yesterday?"

"Yeah, he did. We called his mom, and she came by and picked him up around four-thirty. We chatted a bit, and she agreed to let Wilby have my old cell phone." She patted her massive handbag. "I've got it with me. Wilby's going to pick it up today, and his mom's going to get him added to her calling plan."

"That's good. Let me know what time your car will be ready today. Maybe we can pick it up at lunch time."

"Sure thing." She turned and studied me. "Are you going to make it through the day?"

"I'll make it," I said dully. "Tonight I'm going to bed at six o'clock, and heaven help anyone who calls and wakes me."

She laughed. "I'll be doing some cooking and baking tonight, so you won't hear a word from me."

Of course. For the Darby dinner.

"You *are* planning to attend tomorrow night," she said, "are you not?"

"Do I have a choice?"

"Not really. I was just reminding you. And don't forget what I said about inviting Daniel."

"I'll think about it." It was a lie, but I'd crossed my fingers first.

She grinned as she released her seat belt and sprinted out of the car. "Okay, then. Later!"

I waited until she was inside, then dug my cell phone out of my purse and called the Hazleton police station.

"Ms. Mariani." Chief Fenton's greeting was several notches below cordial. "Why did I guess that I'd be hearing from you this morning? Before you launch into some long-winded harangue, I've already been apprised of what happened last night. Both times," he added snidely.

I tamped down the first retort that came to mind and opted for the second. "The first 9-1-1 call was an innocent mistake. In fact, I should think the police would be glad that it was a false alarm and that they didn't walk into some horrifically bloody crime scene. As for Lillian's phone call—"

"We're already looking into it, Ms. Mariani. As soon as we

learn something, you'll be . . . one of the first to know."

I silently counted to three. It seemed like a moot issue now, but I needed to ask. "I assume you checked all the area hospitals yesterday?"

"Affirmative. They were a dead end. Now if that's all, Ms. Mariani—"

"Wait a minute. Isn't there some way Lillian's cell phone company can track where her call came from last night?"

"I repeat, Ms. Mariani, we're looking into it. We've already been in contact with her cell phone carrier. I can appreciate your concern for your friend, but you have to trust that we know what we're doing." With another half-hearted pledge to keep me informed, he disconnected.

I headed for my office.

Miniature snow mountains lined the rear of the town parking lot. The painted lines were hidden beneath packed ice, so I inserted my Honda between Sam's Buick and the aging coupe that Vicki drove.

Coffee. Right now it was all I could think about.

I picked my way carefully across the icy lot. On the sidewalk, I spotted the wire trash receptacle with its THANK YOU FOR NOT LITTERING reminder bolted onto the front. I remembered the cellophane wrapper from the mint I'd snagged at the antique shop the day before—it was still in my coat pocket. I pulled it out. I was tossing it into the bin when I spied something in the barrel that was disturbingly familiar. A chill washed over me.

On top of the myriad paper cups and candy wrappers and other assorted trash, a brightly wrapped package tied with a gold bow sat unopened. Fluttering out from beneath the bow was a hand-made tag. *Happy Holidays Vicki—Celeste and Blake.*

CHAPTER TWENTY-TWO

*Lillian's eyes widened the moment we entered the dining room
of the Hazleton Inn, which nearly sang with the scent of apples
and cloves. I saw instantly how impressed she was with the
elegant décor. She looked at me and smiled, those spectacular
blue eyes warming me to the core. My heart soared . . .*

"There she is. Apollonia Nicole Mariani, my favorite paralegal."
Blake Dwardene leaned over and dropped a quick kiss on my
cheek, then lowered his athletic form into the chair opposite my
desk.

"Well, it's nice to see you, too, Mr. Dwardene. Have a seat," I
told him. "I've got your docs all ready to sign."

"The deed, too?"

I feigned exasperation. "Of course the deed, too. Did you
doubt *moi?*"

He laughed. "Not for a moment." A yawn escaped him.
"Sorry. I've been dragging these past few days. A lot's been going on."

For the first time since I'd known him, I thought Blake looked
stressed. His handsome face was drawn and pale, his expression
weary. I hazarded a guess. "Not sleeping?"

"No, it's not that. In fact, I've been sleeping pretty well. It's
just that . . . well, ever since Lou's murder, I've been having
these crazy, jumbled dreams. By morning I can't even remember

them, but I wake up feeling more draggy than when I went to bed."

"I can sympathize. I've been having some nutty dreams myself. I think Lou Marshall's murder's had a creepy effect on all of us. Hopefully you'll be able to put it all behind you once you land in New York."

He nodded, but looked unconvinced. "Yeah, I hope you're right."

"Celeste and I chatted for a while yesterday," I told him. "Oh Blake, she is so excited about the move. I'm really thrilled for both of you. And thank you both for the delectable culinary gift. My aunt and I made a hefty dent in those babies last night!"

"Oh, gosh, you're welcome. Celeste was just itching to deliver those packages to all of you yesterday. She loves showering her friends with her baked goods."

"I know she does." I didn't tell him that one of those packages was sitting, unopened, in a trash barrel.

"It's going to seem strange, though, living in New York." He looked away thoughtfully. "I've never even lived outside of Hazleton, let alone in a big city. I just hope Celeste won't be disappointed if everything doesn't pan out as quickly as she thinks it will."

"What do you mean?"

He blew out a breath. "Well, she's banking all her hopes on starting her new business there, lassoing in all kinds of rich and famous customers. I keep trying to remind her, gently, that it might not be all that easy. The competition will be fierce, especially against all those established gourmet bakeries and catering services. It's not like it is here, Apple. I mean, it's the big bad city."

I smiled. "You make it sound so decadent. I think you need to have more faith in Celeste. She's a smart woman. She knows what she wants, and she's going for it. I really admire her."

"Yeah, I know. Look, I'm nuts about her. She's the best thing that ever came into my life. I want her to succeed beyond her wildest desires. She—" He shook his head and looked away.

I waited. I could see that he was struggling.

"She had it so tough growing up," he finally said. "Well, heck, you remember her in school, right? Wasn't she in your trig class?"

"My trig class and senior English," I confirmed, a sudden, awful memory leaping into my head.

I'd been in tenth grade, juggling a pile of books, hurrying to get to trig class on time. Celeste had rushed in behind me, her unruly blond hair framing her thin face like a fuzzy wig. Instead of one of the faded blouses she typically wore, she had on a beautiful cashmere sweater—dark red with tiny pearls on the cuffs. The bell rang, and everyone scrambled into their seats. Then, from the back of the classroom, a squeal erupted. "Oh good glory, I recognize that sweater!" The voice belonged to Kirsten Davis, one of the junior varsity cheerleaders. She was pointing a manicured finger at Celeste. "It used to belong to my sister. Before she donated it to Goodwill, that is!"

Several of Kirsten's friends—her fellow squad members—burst into unmerciful giggles. Pleased with herself for providing such hearty entertainment, Kirsten gave a little bow.

I remember wanting to cry for Celeste, wanting to lash out at her tormentors. Mr. Decker, our trig teacher, had ordered immediate silence, but the snickering and whispering went on for several minutes. Celeste stared at her desk during the whole period, never raising her head. When class was over she raced out. I didn't see her the rest of that day.

"I remember," I told Blake quietly, "that her mother cleaned houses for a living. She didn't earn enough to buy Celeste new clothes very often. Some of the snooty girls, mostly Kirsten Davis's crowd, were always poking fun at the way Celeste dressed. They were horrible to her."

"I know, and I'm embarrassed to say I was one of the guys who never looked twice at her then. She had brains and beauty, but I was too dumb to see beyond the frizzy hair and the dowdy duds." He shook his head. "What a jerk I was."

"Don't be too hard on yourself," I said. "Besides, Celeste showed everyone, didn't she? Bested them all, especially Kirsten Davis. Last I heard Kirsten was working at the mall in Manchester, selling candles at one of those kiosks. She's been married and divorced twice, and now she's living with her dad."

Blake chuckled. "Really? Now that's what I call karma."

"What about Celeste's mother?" I asked him. "Are they close?"

"Nah. Those two were never close. Marie is all about Marie. Always has been, always will be. She hops from one slimy boyfriend to the next, if I may be so blunt. The only relative Celeste was ever close to was her grandmother."

"Celeste told me a little about her," I said. "She still misses her, doesn't she?"

"Yeah, a lot. Poor old lady smoked herself to death, but she loved Celeste like crazy and Celeste adored her. I think Celeste pushed herself to succeed mostly to make her gram proud."

"Well I, for one, am enormously happy for both of you." I slid a packet of documents in front of Blake and dug my notary seal and some ballpoint pens out of my desk. "Have you, um, heard anything more about Lou's murder? Do you think the police might be close to an arrest?" I was fishing without so much as a pole, but I hoped Blake might have a tidbit or two to share about the investigation.

"The crime scene people spent all day Sunday at the mansion. According to Fenton, they inspected every nook and cranny of that room. Problem is, there were so many people at the estate sale that day, the crime scene was compromised from the get-go."

"Compromised?" I smiled. "You sound like an investigator yourself."

"Yeah, well, it's in my best interest to see the murderer nailed so we can put this all behind us as quickly as possible. Fact is . . ." He brushed an imaginary speck from his sleeve. Again, I waited. "I'd had a little go-around with Lou earlier that afternoon. The day of the murder," he added ominously.

"Go-around?"

"An argument." He shifted uncomfortably. "Shoot, but the man could be a pain in the butt. A lot of the stuff that was still in the house that day was supposed to have been delivered to the antique shop in town early last week. That was Lou's job, but he didn't do it. He said there'd be plenty of time after the estate sale, that he had the mover all lined up."

"You know what they say about the best-laid plans."

"Yeah, exactly. And those daggers," Blake said darkly, "shouldn't have been in the house at all. The collector who was buying them offered to pick them up two weeks ago, but Lou wanted the daggers to stay there until after the estate sale. He claimed they'd draw a bigger crowd, since lots of people knew Edgar collected them."

"Even if they weren't for sale?"

"That's just it, see?" Blake twirled his finger next to his ear. "Lou's thinking was a little warped. I mean, the guy knew his collectibles, and as an auctioneer he was unrivaled. But he was the worst procrastinator I'd ever seen. Everything had to get down to the wire with him."

I nodded, thinking. I was beginning to see Lou Marshall from an entirely different angle—an angle that cast a slight shadow over his pristine reputation.

"So is that what you two argued about?"

"Pretty much, yeah. There was also some personal stuff, but I won't even get into that."

"Do . . . did the police consider you a, um, person of interest, as they say?"

Blake laughed. "Oh yeah, along with Celeste, and your aunt, and that jerk Josh Baker. Oh, would I love it if Josh turned out to be the killer. You do know, right, that he was the one who found Edgar's body that day?"

"I'd heard that, yes," I said evasively. What I didn't know was why Blake disliked Josh so intensely. "Blake, what is it about Josh that bugs you so much?"

"Come on, Apple, get real. Young guy moves in with an old codger like Edgar, pays practically nothing in rent. The guy's a user, a gold digger. He was worming his way into Edgar's good graces, hoping he'd inherit something when Edgar finally bought it."

"I don't know, Blake. I had the impression Josh was genuinely fond of your uncle. Josh didn't have much of a relationship with his own father, you know. The man traveled all the time on business and was never around. I know this sounds kind of trite, but I think Josh bonded with Edgar. I think they became friends."

"Anything's possible," Blake conceded. "But personally, I'm not buying it. And I don't believe Edgar gave him the car. I think Edgar *sold* him the car, and after he died Josh decided he didn't want to pay for it. The guy's an actor, Apple, pure and simple."

Another old memory grabbed me. Little Josh, barely eight years old, playing the role of coroner in *The Wizard of Oz* at the now defunct Children's Playhouse in Hazleton. I was fourteen or fifteen at the time. I'd attended the performance with one of my high school buds and her mother, an elementary school teacher. We'd all been impressed by Josh's performance. For such a young boy, he'd been quite a skilled actor.

"Well, since we're never going to agree about Josh," I said

lightly, "why don't we get these docs signed so you can be on your way to New York."

"Sounds like a plan, although I had to postpone my trip to New York until tomorrow." He gave me a weak smile. "Hey, look, I'm sorry to be so contentious. Lou's murder threw a major wrench into the works, for all of us. Celeste has been a trouper, but it's been tough on her, too. She can't wait to say good-bye to Hazleton and hello to the big city."

The grass is always greener, I thought.

After a cursory read-through of the deed and the seller's closing affidavits, Blake signed everything. I took his acknowledgment and notarized the documents.

"I'm kind of sorry I won't be here to meet the buyers," Blake said. "But I've got a meeting in New York on Thursday with a new client—a vitamin company based in Toronto—that I can't afford to miss."

"Well, rest assured that Aunt Tressa will take good care of them. She's meeting them in her office Thursday evening to go over some last-minute details. They'll do the final walk-through early Friday morning. Assuming they find everything in order, they'll close here at eleven."

"Think you'll be able to record the deed the same day?"

"Sure, barring a Nor'easter sweeping in and preventing me from driving to the Registry." The Rockingham County Registry of Deeds was in Brentwood, about a forty-minute drive from Hazleton. Blake was clearly anxious for the estate to receive the sale proceeds. Once the mansion was sold, Sam could file the final account with the probate court and disburse Blake's rightful inheritance. "I assume the house is completely empty now?"

"Yeah, it should be." He set the ballpoint pen I'd lent him back on my blotter. "Oh, except for the desk."

I looked at him. "Your uncle's antique desk? The one Lou was using when he—?"

Blake nodded. "The very same. The buyers fell in love with it when they first viewed the mansion. Insisted we make it part of the deal. Have you seen it?"

"No, I . . . didn't go into that room."

"It's a stunning piece of furniture, custom made in the early nineteen forties. Has lots of cubbies on top and two large drawers on the bottom. Originally it belonged to my great-uncle Frederic, but it's gotten pretty battered over the years. It'll be gorgeous once it's refinished."

"Frederic was your dad's uncle, right? I recall from the title search that when Frederic died, his entire estate went to his brother Mason."

He pointed a finger at me. "Good memory, App. My grandfather, Mason Dwardene, was Frederic's only brother. Frederic left everything to him, in spite of the fact that the two despised each other."

"Why did they dislike each other?"

Blake shrugged. "It was before my time, but from what I understand, they had totally clashing personalities. Frederic was a fussy type, an old-school banker who was particular about everything. His wife died from influenza in her late thirties, right after they'd lost their little boy to polio. Supposedly Frederic got a little strange after that. In spite of it all, he was well respected in the community. He was also a talented artist. You might have seen some of his paintings at the mansion."

I nodded distractedly. Frederic's artistic bent had also been evident in the flowery, overblown prose he'd penned in his journal.

Blake's mouth twisted. "My charming grandfather, on the other hand, was a hard-drinking, rough-talking oaf. He browbeat everyone around him, including my poor grandmother. She always kowtowed to him in order to keep the peace."

Yikes. To say the least, Blake's grandfather didn't sound like a nice person. Which brought to mind something I'd been curious about.

In performing the title search, I'd had to review Mason Dwardene's probate file. In his will, Mason had bequeathed his entire estate, including the mansion, to his son Edgar. Albert had received a pittance—a token bequest of Mason's extensive gun collection. It seemed as if Albert has been intentionally snubbed.

"Blake, forgive me if this sounds like prying, but why do you think your grandfather left everything, except for his guns, to Edgar?"

Blake's expression darkened. "Because he was a nasty piece of work, that's why. Mason always favored Edgar over my dad. Even as an adult, Edgar was the quintessential obedient child. Don't get me wrong, he was a decent guy, but he was nothing like my dad. My dad was a fun-loving free spirit who always did what he thought was right, in spite of his father's bullying. Unlike his own father, my dad treated people—all people—with kindness and respect." Blake's eyes grew misty. "I couldn't have asked for a better role model."

Inwardly, I gave myself a solid kick. "I'm sorry, Blake. I shouldn't have brought it up."

"No, it's okay. I'm glad you did." He looked drained. Quietly, he said, "Do you know why my grandfather left Dad his gun collection? It was to taunt him. My dad refused to take up the glorious sport of trophy hunting, and that irked the spit out of my grandfather. But Dad got the last laugh on him. Except for this one gun that reminded him of an old cowboy six-shooter, he turned every last one over to the state police. I could almost hear my grandfather bellowing from his grave." Blake's laugh had a sharp edge.

"Your dad was a special guy. You'll always have good memories of him."

All the talk of the estate had reminded me of something. "Blake, before I forget, when I was at the mansion Saturday I grabbed a set of John Jakes's books from the library. After, well . . . everything else happened, I never got the chance to pay for them. I owe you—"

He was already waving a hand at me. "Are you kidding? Consider them a gift from Celeste and me. It's the least we owe you for all your hard work."

"You're sure?"

"Positive." He glanced at his watch and rose. "Hey look, I gotta run. I need to be home for a conference call at 10:30."

He didn't move, though. He stood there staring at me, his expression unreadable. I had to force myself not to squirm under his gaze.

"Hey, App?" he said at last. "Did you ever think there was a time when"—he fluttered his hand back and forth between us—"you know, that you and I might have gotten together? As a couple?"

A couple? Blake and me?

Actually, there had been a time when I'd thought about it. Or maybe fantasized would be more accurate. But that was back in high school, half a lifetime ago. It was worst of clichés—the straight A's overachiever harboring a crush on the school's star quarterback. I'd tutored him in history and we became good friends, but that was the extent of it.

Besides, Blake had other interests then.

Curvier, sexier interests.

Then college intervened, and . . . well, frankly, I grew up.

"No, because you've always been too good a friend," I said lightly, knowing how utterly lame it sounded. "And you should be grateful because you ended up finding the love of your life."

His smiled looked wistful. "Yeah, you're right. I am a lucky man. Thanks for everything, App." He leaned over and hugged me, a bit longer than I felt comfortable with.

Then he left, and for the first time I realized something. I'd probably never see him again.

Chapter Twenty-Three

The rest of the meal went smoothly, though Lillian (oh, how strange it sounds to suddenly be calling her by a different name!) was still very quiet. I daresay her appetite compares to that of a sparrow, though I did coax her into sampling the Inn's famous pumpkin pie. I almost inquired about her soldier, but didn't want his name to spoil our lovely meal. I've thought about him a lot, wished that any number of terrible fates might befall him . . .

With the aid of three cups of French vanilla coffee and a doughnut hole from the pastry box Sam had left beside the coffee maker, I managed to keep my eyes propped open through the morning.

Not surprisingly, Heidi had called in sick. I only hoped the poor girl was getting some much-needed rest.

Vicki and I had been taking turns listening for the phone, but calls had been sparse all morning. Sam had gone to the probate court in Brentwood to file some documents for a new estate he was handling. For the second day running, he'd been acting strange. Abnormally quiet. In fact, with only Vicki and me there, the office felt like an echo chamber.

At one point, Vicki popped out of her chair, minced into my office and sputtered, "I heard you cough. Three times."

I didn't recall coughing, not even once, but I also didn't keep track of things like that. Vicki apparently did. "Take two of these immediately," she'd ordered, unscrewing her treasured bottle of zinc tablets. She tapped out two of them onto my blotter and twisted the cover back on, ensuring that my germ-infested hands didn't sully her bottle.

"Thanks, Vicki," I said. "I'll get some water from the kitchen."

Which I did, and which I swallowed down in one long gulp. When I was sure Vicki was ensconced back in her office, I scooped the zinc tabs off my blotter, shoved them in an envelope and dropped them into the bottom drawer of my desk.

With the office having a painfully slow week, I decided to play catch-up on some of my post-closing backlog. I was zipping off follow-up letters to lenders about delinquent mortgage discharges when Aunt Tressa called.

"Hey, I've got a surprise for you. Any way you can get some time off this afternoon?"

Actually, I'd been contemplating asking Sam if I could take my annual "Christmas shopping afternoon" today—a tradition old Mr. Quinto started ages ago. He'd always believed that since women got stuck with most of the planning and shopping and cooking around the holidays, the least he could do was give each of his employees a paid half-day in December to spend any way she pleased.

"I think so," I said. "I may even take off the whole afternoon, but I've got to run it by Sam first. Why, what's the surprise?" I was almost afraid to ask.

"Well, the Caddy'll be ready to shake, rattle and roll by two, so we can swing by the dealership to pick it up. But first . . ." She paused, dragging out the suspense. "I'm going to treat you to a hot plate special at Darla's Dine-o-Rama!"

"Darla's Dine-o-Rama? You know where it is?"

"Of course! I Googled it. I called first to be sure the place was open, and some woman with a voice like the Wicked Witch of the West rattled off today's special. Ever hear of Yankee

Doodle Noodle Strudel? Anyway, listen to this. The restaurant's only about three miles past the dealership, on Route One Twenty-One. We can eat at Darla's, do some nosing around. Who knows, maybe somebody there knows something about Lillian."

I suddenly wished I had a recent photo of Lillian. Was there someplace I could get my hands on one?

"Sam should be back any time," I told her. "I'll see what I can do and call you back."

I quickly got on to the Internet and Googled the Hazleton Knitting Club.

Nothing.

Not that I'd thought Lillian and her band of knitters had a website, but it was worth a shot.

Next I logged onto the *Hazleton Bugle,* a weekly paper jammed with local interest stories. The *Bugle,* fortunately, maintained a sizeable online archive of back issues. In the search box, I entered the words *Hazleton* and *knitting.* As I'd hoped, an article popped up. Dated September nineteenth of last year, it was a cheery account of the Club's annual Knitting Extravaganza, which Lillian had won for the third straight year.

And there was her photo.

It wasn't the best likeness of Lillian I'd ever seen, and it wasn't in color, but her features were reasonably clear. The photo depicted her standing between the first and second runners-up, each one proudly holding up a knitted afghan. Lillian's looked familiar. With a sinking sensation, I realized it was the one I'd seen on her bed, all tangled in the top sheet.

I clicked on the print icon and retrieved the article from my laser printer, just as I heard the front door open. UPS, I figured, since they delivered something nearly every day. Instead, it was Sam. He looked thoroughly wrung out.

"Hi, Sam. Everything go okay at the probate court?" I was

careful to keep my tone neutral.

He unbuttoned his lined overcoat and roughly tugged off his scarf. "Thing's choking me," he grumbled, sweeping past me. Ignoring Vicki's mumbled greeting as he passed her door, he tramped down the hallway and into his office. I followed.

"Yeah, everything went fine," he said. "Judge Harper allowed the will. No surprise there."

"So Mrs. Anders is the executrix?"

Sam tossed his briefcase onto the leather chair opposite his desk and shot me a look. "Of course she's the executrix. Who'd you think the judge was going to appoint, one of Santa's elves?"

Embarrassed, I shrugged. "I'm sorry, Sam. I was making small talk. When you came in you looked . . . well, stressed. I thought maybe something was wrong."

He stared at the floor for a moment, then blew out a sigh. "Close the door and have a seat, will you?"

Hesitantly, I pushed the door shut. My mental antennae were zipping up and down like automatic car windows gone mad.

"First I have a question," he said, lowering himself into his chair. "I don't suppose you've heard anything new about Lou's murder?"

"No, nothing useful. Rumors, mostly."

Which wasn't entirely true.

Aunt Tressa's revelation about her breakup with Lou was a fact. As was Blake's admission that he'd quarreled with Lou not long before Lou was stabbed. But I had no intention of sharing either of those disclosures with Sam. Not yet, anyway.

I did consider whether or not I should tell him about Lillian's disappearance. I decided to hear what he had to tell me first.

Sam walked around his desk and dropped into his chair. His face was as pale as the frozen ridge of snow on the window pane outside. "Apple, Lou called me Saturday, on my cell phone. It was right before—" He pressed his fist to his mouth and shook his head.

"Right before he was murdered?" I finished.

Sam nodded. "Mary and I were in the supermarket at the time. I can never hear my phone when I'm in there. When we got in the car, I realized I had a message. It was from Lou. His voice sounded so strange, kind of . . . like he was trying not to be overheard. In a very urgent voice he said, *'I gotta talk to you right away. Something's not right. Sam, I think there's been a terrible mistake.'* He started to say something else, but the call got cut off."

Something tumbled inside my stomach. "What did you do?"

"First I tried calling him back, but he didn't answer. So I drove Mary home and ran the groceries inside for her. Then I headed over to the Dwardene place, but by then the snowstorm was getting bad. When I got there . . ." He looked away and released a heavy sigh. "When I got there, it was too late. I saw the police cars in the driveway, and I knew something bad had happened."

So that's why we saw Sam leaving the mansion that afternoon. "Did you tell Chief Fenton about the call?"

"I told him right away, that afternoon. I played the message for him. Problem was, I had no idea what Lou was trying to tell me," Sam said miserably. "What kind of mistake was he talking about, Apple?"

I shrugged helplessly. "I don't know, Sam. It could be just about anything. He didn't say that *you* made a mistake—just that there'd been a terrible mistake."

"I know, but I've been worried sick over it." Sam rubbed his hands over his eyes.

"Of course you have. You're a worrier by nature." I didn't want to say that I'd be worried, too, if I'd gotten that call. Sam was already agonizing over it. No need to make him feel worse.

"Fenton's already called me twice to ask if I've made any sense of Lou's message yet. Nothing like a little pressure," he said sourly. "I came back here last evening and went over the probate file again with a fine-tooth comb. I couldn't find anything amiss."

"See? It probably has nothing to do with you. You're just the one Lou called to confide in. Leave it to the police, Sam. They'll solve Lou's murder and everything will be explained." I wasn't entirely sure I believed that, but at this point a little good faith was in order.

Sam expelled a long sigh. "Maybe you're right. Mary says I blow everything out of proportion."

We talked for about another five minutes, during which Sam managed to quiet his frayed nerves. I decided to tell him about Lillian, starting with her disappearance and ending with her middle-of-the-night phone call to me.

"I hate to say it, but none of that sounds good, Apple. I'll have a chat with Fenton, see if I can light a fire under him. Seems to me, Lillian Bilodeau might be the missing link to the murderer."

"My feeling exactly," I said. "And thanks, Sam. I really appreciate it. But now I have another favor to ask." I told him about Aunt Tressa's idea to check out Darla's Dine-o-Rama before we picked up her car.

"Sure, go ahead. Today's as good a day as any." He cast a dreary glance at the stack of mail teetering on the corner of his desk. "I'll corral Vicki into helping me get through some of the correspondence I've been neglecting."

"And I'm sure Vicki'll be glad to be rid of me for the afternoon. She told me I coughed this morning, three times, to be precise."

He raised his arm and pointed at the door. "Then take thy vile germs and hie thee hence, contaminant!"

I was grateful to see he'd recovered his sense of humor. My hand was on the doorknob when I thought of something else. "Hey, Sam, did you ever think it was odd that Edgar Dwardene didn't leave a will?"

He frowned. "That came out of the blue. Why do you ask?"

"I don't know. Wouldn't it have been the sensible thing to do?"

Sam shrugged. "I suppose, but look at it this way. Edgar only had the one heir—his nephew Blake. Even if he'd made out a will, who else would he have left his estate to? To my knowledge, he wasn't particularly interested in any charities. Maybe he figured a will was a waste of time. And money."

"Yeah, I guess," I said. "He was awfully frugal."

Oh, God.

Unless that was the mistake Lou tried to tell Sam about. Had Lou found a will when he was cleaning out that desk? A will that changed everything?

A will that someone would kill over?

I felt my chest tighten with anxiety. I was getting as bad as Sam, thinking the absolute worst.

Forcing myself to calm down, I thanked Sam for letting me bail early. After letting Vicki know I'd be gone for the afternoon, I phoned Aunt Tressa from my office.

"I'm working on the contract for my new listing," she said. There was a lilt in her voice I hadn't heard in a long time. "Can you pick me up around one?"

"Won't you be starving by then?"

"Normally, yes, but I zapped a frozen pizza to hold me over."

A microwave pizza would have held me until dinner, but for Aunt Tressa it was a mere canapé. With a promise to swing by around one, I hung up. I realized I was feeling a bit hungry myself.

I could only hope that Darla's Dine-o-Rama would live up to its napkin: *New Hampshire's best eats!*

CHAPTER TWENTY-FOUR

From the journal of Frederic Dwardene, Thursday, December 14, 1950:

The weather has grown cold and dreary. Since the day of our delightful luncheon, I have not seen any sign of my Lillian. She did not come to the bank today to make her usual weekly deposit. My worst fear is that she might be avoiding me. Oh, I pray it isn't so! Perhaps she is only sick with a cold, or with some other minor illness . . .

Aunt Tressa emerged slowly from the Honda and slammed the door shut. "Well, curl my hair and call me a poodle. Darla's Dine-o-Rama is a dump."

I was already out of the car, but I hadn't yet locked the door. I stared at the squat white building that housed New Hampshire's best eats. The place was in dire need of a paint job, if for no other reason than to cover the rust stains caused by the leaking gutters. The front steps consisted of two sagging concrete slabs that looked as if something had chewed their edges. Around the perimeter of the grimy front window, a string of red and green lights blinked anemically.

Only two other vehicles occupied the lot—a salt-encrusted pickup and a red SUV.

"Still want to eat here?" I figured it wasn't too late to save ourselves.

Head down, Aunt Tressa made a determined beeline for the

entrance. "I promised you a hot plate lunch, and a hot plate lunch you're going to get."

Lord help me.

A tinny bell jingled as we pushed open a door that screamed for a shot of WD-40. With the exception of a lone diner sitting at a window table forking up globs of some gravy-covered conglomeration, the Dine-o-Rama was empty.

I know it sounds cliché, but the place smelled vaguely of boiled cabbage—sharp, sour and nauseating all at the same time. To our left, six round stools stretched along a chipped Formica counter. One of the stools listed sideways, its red seat charmingly adorned with crisscrossed strands of duct tape. At the far end of the counter, a scratched display case boasted an assortment of gooey, gunky-looking pastries.

"I guess the lunch rush is over," my aunt remarked.

"Think anyone works here?" I whispered.

"Yeah, where's Darla?" Aunt Tressa strode over to the large chalkboard propped on an easel near the counter. I stood slightly behind her and read the daily offering.

Yankee Doodle Noodle Stroodle
All you can eat ~ $7.95
Includes a king size slab 'o Darla's famous cornbread!

Aunt Tressa looked all around, growing clearly annoyed. "Stay here, I'm going to go find someone. After driving all this way, the least we can do is find out if anyone has seen Lillian. Hello!" she called out. "Anyone here?"

"Maybe there's someone in the kitchen," I said, dipping my head in the direction of the metal door behind the counter.

Aunt Tressa followed my gaze. Handbag propped over her shoulder, she marched toward the swinging door and pushed her way through.

I meandered over to the lone customer, who was staring

blankly through the dirty front window, a toothpick bobbing between his lips. The table in front of him was littered with crumbs—cornbread crumbs, it appeared. Darla's *stroodle*—if that's what he'd ordered—must have been scrumptious. The man's plate had been licked dry, save for a few swirls of brown sauce.

"Sorry to bother you, sir." I unzipped my purse and pulled out the photo of Lillian I'd printed. "Have you ever seen this woman, the one in the middle? I think she may have eaten here once or twice."

Ignoring the photo, he stared up at me as if it were the first time he'd ever seen a human of the female persuasion. I was inching the photo farther under his nose when a cry of distress, followed by a loud thump, made us both swivel around.

Aunt Tressa burst out from behind the swinging door and threw herself onto the nearest stool. "Oh God, Apple. *Oh. Dear. God.*"

Dropping the photo, I rushed over to her. Her face was chalky. One red-gloved hand was clamped firmly over her mouth. I grabbed her shoulders. "Aunt Tress, what is it? Are you all right?"

"Horrible . . ." she gurgled out. I half expected her to heave all over me. "Dead . . . everywhere . . . hanging . . ."

I felt my stomach drop with the force of an anchor. What kind of carnage had my poor aunt stumbled into back there? Were the two of us even safe, sitting here like this? Abruptly, I jerked around, half expecting the lone diner to be standing behind me with a gun. Instead, the table he'd occupied was empty. As was the restaurant.

I squeezed my aunt's shoulder. "It'll be okay," I soothed, digging out my cell with my free hand. "I'm calling the police—"

"No." She closed her hand over my phone and shook her head. "Don't. They won't come. Go . . . see for yourself."

Mouth open, I stared at her.

She nodded bleakly. "Go ahead. Go look. It's . . . beyond description."

I turned slowly and shuffled toward the swinging door. I had the odd sensation I was headed for the gallows. My fingers felt like rubber pins as I gingerly pushed my way through. The door swung shut behind me with a squeak, but I barely heard the sound. I was in the kitchen, gazing at a sight so surreal that my knees almost gave way.

Dangling from the ceiling—in quantities that boggled the imagination—were rolls and rolls of fly paper. Coated with the mortal remains of unwary flies, the hideous things hung everywhere. Two were suspended directly above the grease-coated grill, three more above the scarred wooden cutting board. The rest were distributed in willy-nilly fashion throughout the kitchen. Unless the room was shifting, they all seemed to be swaying to the rhythm of an unseen air vent.

They all looked as if they'd been there since the Reagan administration.

For several moments, I couldn't breathe. Or maybe I was afraid to breathe. I pictured tiny, decomposing fly wings drifting through the air, landing on everything. No wonder Aunt Tressa had nearly swallowed her teeth. To her this must have looked like a house of horrors.

Beyond the kitchen's work area, a protruding row of tall metal shelves was stacked with supplies. Could Darla be hiding back there? Finding my voice, I squeaked out, "Hello? Is anyone back there?" I moved forward a few steps, which unfortunately brought me closer to the grill. On top of the grill, a battered metal pan held remnants of the stroodle—globs of twisted noodles soaking in the same brown sauce I'd seen on the lone diner's plate. I stifled a shudder.

A door that led into the back of the building suddenly banged open. Someone carrying a large cardboard box trudged through it and into the kitchen, then kicked the door closed with a booted foot. The box dropped to the floor with a thud. A tall woman in a bulging pink uniform, her orange hair swirled into a messy beehive, stood glaring at me. "Who are you?" she demanded.

"I . . . I'm Apple Mariani. Are you Darla?"

She moved toward me, her eyes narrowed into slits. "I am," she said. "Who wants to know?"

I swallowed. "Actually, I'm looking for someone who might have patronized your . . . establishment," I said.

Was it my imagination, or did she look relieved?

"You're probably wondering," she said, swirling her finger at the ceiling, "about all the fly paper. 'Bout seven years ago I had a bad fly problem. Couldn't get rid of the things for nothing. Finally got sick of swatting 'em and invested in some fly paper. Lucky thing the hardware store still had some in their stockroom. The stuff's hard to find these days. Can you imagine?"

Oh, yes, quite easily. "Is that so?" I said weakly.

"Yeah, and it did such a good job killing the little buggers that I decided just to leave it there. No flies on me, right?" she cackled.

Somehow I sputtered out a polite laugh. "Oh, yes, right. Um, is there someplace we could talk? I'm here with my aunt, and we'd like to ask you a few questions."

"Sure! Hey, you hungry?"

I might be hungry, in a week or so. "Thanks anyway, but I've already eaten." It wasn't really a lie. I'd eaten breakfast.

"Well, that's a shame. You're missing out on my homemade stroodle, you know. I'd be willing to bet you've never tasted anything like it!"

I'd be willing to bet she was right. "Can we chat for a minute, Darla? Out there?"

"Oh, sure, no prob." She bounded through the swinging door. I trailed in her wake.

Aunt Tressa was still sitting on the stool, clutching her handbag to her chest so it wouldn't touch anything. I was glad to see her looking a bit more relaxed. Her color was definitely better.

"I found Darla," I said. "Darla, this is my Aunt Tressa."

Darla grinned, displaying two rows of stained teeth. "Pleased to meet you, Tressa. Man, I like that name. Real pretty. And you"—she pinned her gaze on me—"how'd you get a name like Apple? Your mom have a passion for apples or something?"

"It's actually Apollonia," I explained for the nine hundred forty-seventh time since my birth.

"Oh, yeah, like that babe in the movie! I gotcha. Now Tressa"—she turned to my aunt and looked her up and down—"you look like a lady who could use a good meal. How about a nice plate of my homemade noodle stroodle? Give it to you half price, since the lunch rush is over."

To her credit, my aunt managed not to gag visibly. Instead, she coughed into her gloved hand. "Thanks, but I think I'm coming down with something. I'm not really hungry."

Darla shook her head, dislodging a few strands of the beehive. "Well, that's too bad. You don't know what you're missing."

"Darla," I said, "we've been trying to locate someone who might have eaten here recently. We haven't been able to reach her for a few days, and we're worried about her because she's elderly." I omitted the fact that we thought she'd been kidnapped. "She might have come in here with a group of friends. Can I show you a picture of her?"

Darla scratched one side of the beehive with a jagged fingernail. "Yeah, sure, I guess."

I reached into my bag, then remembered that I'd dropped the photo when Aunt Tressa had fled in terror from the kitchen.

"Excuse me a minute," I apologized. I scooted over to where the lone diner had sat. The photo was upside down on the floor, marred by a big brown footprint. I picked it up by one edge and shook it.

"This is her," I said, handing it to Darla. "The one in the middle."

Darla took the sheet of paper from me. I watched her face for any sign of recognition, but her expression remained blank. "Nah, I haven't seen her," she said, thrusting the photo at me. "I'd remember an old dame like that. I'd definitely remember a bunch of old ladies coming in together. Actually, just about all my customers work at the parts plant down the road." She nodded in the direction of the front window. "Or at the insurance company across the street."

Frustrated, I folded the photo and stuck it back inside my bag. That's when something oddly familiar attracted my attention.

Inside the Plexiglas pastry case was a strange-looking cruller. It was about half a foot long, with a bloated mound at one end. The mound had been swirled in dark frosting and then plunged into a vat of chocolate sprinkles.

My stomach did a mini-flip.

Only once before had I seen a cruller like that.

"Ah, you can't fool me," Darla crowed at me. "You've got your eye on my last lion's tail, haven'tcha?" She walked around to the other side of the counter, and with an exaggerated wink opened the pastry case. Using her bare fingers she plucked the lion's tail off the tray and slapped it onto a paper plate. "Here you go. No charge, either. I close this place up at three, and if I take it home with me my fat old bulldog'll just eat it. And he needs that like he needs another flea, if you catch my meaning." She grinned and pushed it over in front of me.

Oh, Lord, now what? No way was I going to eat the thing,

not with visions of decaying fly corpses dancing in my head.

"Apple," Aunt Tressa said sharply. She pointed a finger at me. "Don't even think of eating that after what your doctor told you last week."

For one surreal moment I wondered if the sight of all the fly paper had driven her totally insane. Then, feeling like a dolt, I realized she was coming to my rescue. Duh.

Darla stuck her hands on her hips and gawked at me. "What, are you sick or something?"

"I—"

"Her cholesterol was up to three forty," Aunt Tressa told Darla helpfully. "Something like that pastry there could kill her in one fell swoop. She's supposed to be sticking to a low-fat, high-fiber fruits and vegetables diet, the way I do."

I'm glad I hadn't been drinking something—I'd have choked to death.

Darla looked at Aunt Tressa, then smiled ruefully and shook her head. "Man, I'll never understand you grainy granola types. Shame, really. All's I can say is, I'm glad my customers don't eat the way you do. I'm grateful they appreciate the kind of good old-fashioned, hearty cooking I'm known for—the kind of food that sticks to your ribs."

And your gums. And your arteries.

"Yeah, once in a while I get these peddlers comin' in here," she droned on, "wanting me to sell their healthy muffins or crappy whole wheat doughnuts or some other such nonsense to my customers . . ."

Darla prattled on, but her harangue had faded to the lower chatter of a squirrel because my thoughts were now fixed on something I'd spotted through the restaurant's front window.

The sign on the building across the street.

"—I mean, some of their baked goods looked like they swept the floor and dumped it all into the batter, for corn's sake,"

Darla was still whining. "I mean, get real, right? I can't sell crapola like that to my customers!" She scooped the lion's tail off the plate and stuffed the business end into her mouth. Chocolate sprinkles dripped everywhere. Chewing vigorously, she brushed them off her pink uniform, scattering them onto the floor.

"Well, we'd better get going," I said brightly to my aunt, using eye movements to signal that I needed to talk to her. "We've taken up enough of Darla's time."

Aunt Tressa nearly leaped off her stool.

"Hey, sorry I couldn't help you out with that old lady," Darla said. She swiped her lips with the back of one hand. "You think she's okay?"

"We're not sure," I said truthfully. "It's not like her to go away without telling anyone."

"Why'd you think she might've come in here?" Darla asked.

"We found one of your napkins crumpled up on the floor of her living room," Aunt Tressa explained. "If she didn't leave it there, then we want to know who did."

Darla looked away thoughtfully. "Yeah, I can see where you're headed with that. This lady rich or something?"

"No," I said. "But she may have witnessed a . . . crime, and we're concerned for her safety."

"Whoa." Darla's eyes widened. "Look, why don't you both give me your numbers, and I'll keep my eyes peeled for her. If she comes in here, I'll get right on the horn and give you a fast ringy-dingy. Mind if I keep the photo?"

I didn't hold out much hope that Lillian would be dropping into Darla's any time soon, but I wrote down Aunt Tressa's and my numbers on the back of Lillian's photo and gave them to her anyway. "Here, and you're welcome to the picture. I can always print more."

Darla stared at the photo again and her face softened. "Poor old gal. Reminds me of my Aunt Nellie, God rest her soul. Hope she's okay."

"We hope so, too," I said.

In the parking lot, I grabbed my aunt's arm as she paraded toward my car. "Aunt Tressa—"

"Did you notice how insects were a recurring theme in there?" my aunt was ranting. "First the dead flies and then her dog's fleas. And that hairdo—"

"Aunt Tressa, stop for a second and listen to me. Look at that building across the street."

She stopped short. "Yeah, so? It's an insurance company."

"Yes. *Diamond Crown* Insurance."

She tapped the side of her head. "Call me dense but I'm still not getting it. Why do we care?"

"Because Josh Baker works there, remember? And yesterday I saw him eating one of those fat bombs Darla calls a lion's tail."

Chapter Twenty-Five

From the journal of Frederic Dwardene, Friday, December 15, 1950:

I've known, of course, that Lillian works in the sweater factory in Manchester, but lately I've been quietly observing her routine. (How fortunate that as a banker my work day ends at 3!) The bus drops her off on Elm Street each morning at 7:50 AM, and she walks the block or so to the factory. Her shift runs from 8 to 5:15, then she catches the 5:35 bus back to Hazleton. I will be grateful when she does not have to work anymore, when I can take care of her every need . . .

"So Josh eats at Darla's," my aunt repeated for the sixty-fourth time. "That doesn't make him a kidnapper. Or a murderer."

We were sitting at a table in a local burger joint next to a harried mom with three curly-haired hellions who didn't look far apart in age. The poor woman was mopping one tear-stained face with a napkin, while the other two toddlers were gleefully squirting packets of ketchup at each other. Aunt Tressa, oblivious of the family drama, feasted on a double-cheeseburger and fries while I picked without much interest at a chef's salad.

Outside, tiny white flakes were floating from a graying sky. The bright sun of earlier in the day had taken a sudden powder.

"You do realize," I pointed out, "that you are defending the Great Tulip Thief. The one you wanted to have shipped off to reform school for . . . oh, let's see if I remember, was it thirty years to life?"

She swallowed a mouthful of burger. "Okay, so I was overboard about the tulips. Give me a break. They were the only thing I'd ever been able to grow. Besides, that was almost twenty years ago."

I laughed, but then I got serious. "Look, I'm not accusing Josh of anything. But you have to admit, it's quite a coincidence that he works across the street from the Dine-o-Rama."

"It is, but that's all it is."

"And here's another weird thing." I briefly filled her in on Celeste's account of finding the dead baby birds.

Aunt Tressa put down the fry she was holding. "That is pretty horrible. Did she really think Josh killed the birds?"

I sighed. "He was the only one living there, remember? Edgar had already died."

My aunt chewed silently for a while, but I could see her mind churning. When she'd finally devoured her meal down to the last pickle, she said, "I guess we've reached an impasse, haven't we? The cops still have no idea who killed Lou, and we're no closer to finding Lillian than we were on Sunday."

"I agree." I pushed aside my unfinished salad and tossed my napkin on the table. "I don't even know where to turn next."

"You barely ate half of that," Aunt Tressa pointed out. "Why didn't you get a bacon burger? I thought that was your favorite fast food."

I shot her a wry look. "My cholesterol is three forty, remember, Miss Grainy Granola?"

My aunt sniffed and waved a hand at me. "At least I rescued you from having to eat that . . . that thing. Sad part is, something gooey and sugary like that would normally appeal to me, but after seeing that kitchen . . ." She shuddered.

"What I don't understand is how that place ever passed a Board of Health inspection," I said. "I liked Darla, but I really think someone ought to drop a dime on her. Maybe it would force her to clean up her act."

"Not our problem." Aunt Tressa pushed back her chair. "We've got bigger things to worry about right now."

True enough.

"Let's go pick up your car," I said wearily, buttoning my coat. "Maybe we'll come up with an idea on the way."

"Sounds like a plan, but actually I tend to think better when I'm alone in the Caddy. And there's something I want to talk to Marty about today."

I tripped over my own boot, and had to grab the table to stay upright. "What did you say?"

Aunt Tressa's cheeks sprouted two pink circles. "Sometimes, when I'm alone in my car, I talk to Marty. Call me crazy, but in my heart I know he's always there, listening, watching out for me."

A lump the size of a golf ball formed in my throat. "I know he is, Aunt Tressa. And who knows, maybe he'll think of something that we haven't."

She smiled at me, her eyelashes damp. "Yeah, maybe he will at that."

Ten minutes later we arrived at the dealership. The Caddy was parked in front of the service department, its maroon paint gleaming as if it were showroom new.

"Looks great," I said. "They washed it."

Aunt Tressa smiled lovingly at the car. "Yeah, it sure is a clean machine. Meet you back at the house? After that we can do some Christmas shopping. Hey, maybe we should get our eyebrows threaded again at the mall."

"Sure!" I said with mock perkiness. "How about in a year that begins with the number four?"

"Oh come on, it didn't even hurt. And it was over within a minute or two."

A minute or two too long, in my book of *Hair Removal Methods I Wish I'd Never Heard Of.*

In a sudden burst of memory, I recalled something Blake had said earlier. "Not to change the subject, Aunt Tress, but do you still have a key to the Dwardene place?"

"Of course I do. I'm the listing broker." Light dawned. "You want to go inside?"

"Actually, I do. Blake told me Edgar's old desk is still there. The people buying the house are purchasing it from the estate."

"That's right. I should have remembered that. What do you expect to find in the desk, though? Don't you think the cops have already torn it apart?"

In truth, I didn't know what I'd hoped to find. But even if it turned out to be a fool's errand, what did we have to lose?

"Maybe, maybe not," I said, remembering the valentine Lou had given Aunt Tressa right before he was murdered. Why had he instructed her to "give it to Apple"? Did he really want me to have it for my postcard collection? Or did the valentine contain a clue to Lou's killer that I hadn't picked up on?

It didn't seem likely. Surely a poem written in the nineteen fifties by a lovesick man had no connection to Lou's murder. Still, a twinge of guilt ripped through me when I thought about the valentine. I'd shoved it in the junk drawer of my kitchen and forgotten about it.

I resolved to turn the valentine over to Chief Fenton. After I made a copy for myself.

There was always the risk, of course, that Fenton might accuse me of withholding valuable evidence. In that case, I could truthfully say that I had no idea the valentine would be of any use whatsoever to the investigation. Let the handcuffs fall where they may.

"I want to check out the desk for myself," I told my aunt. "I mean, maybe the police didn't search the desk at all. It's not as if they had a reason to believe a critical clue was hidden in there."

Aunt Tressa shrugged. "I suppose. But I'll have to pop over to my office first to grab the key. Why don't you meet me there, then we'll head over to the Dwardene place."

I hopped inside my Honda and started it. Before I shifted into Park, I pulled my phone out of my purse and tried Lillian's cell number again.

Nothing.

A sick feeling burrowed its way into my stomach. Lillian was in trouble, and I had no idea how to help her.

Maybe it was already too late.

CHAPTER TWENTY-SIX

From the journal of Frederic Dwardene, Monday, December 18, 1950:

Late this afternoon I parked near the bus stop in Manchester, waiting for Lillian to arrive. It was a frigid day, the kind that turns ears bright red and clouds one's breath. Pretending I'd just come from the smoke shop on Elm Street, I greeted her with feigned surprise as she walked toward the bus stop. The poor darling looked frozen, and far too pale. Insisting that she allow me to drive her home, I took her by the elbow and escorted her into my Hudson . . .

"This place is downright creepy," Aunt Tressa said in a loud whisper.

We were stalking up the staircase in the Dwardene mansion, toward the second story. I had to admit, the house felt cold and eerie. The silence was almost palpable. I didn't believe in ghosts, not for a minute. Still, the air seemed thick and strange. If otherworldly spirits did exist, I had the feeling they were hovering close by.

"Why are you whispering? There's nobody here," I said. Was I trying to convince her or myself?

I stopped in front of the doorway to the room where Lou had met his gruesome demise. The mahogany desk sitting against the far right wall was a dead giveaway.

Aunt Tressa came up behind me, then moved past me and

stepped into the room. She skimmed her gaze all around. "Looks like the room has been cleaned."

I nodded in agreement, then pulled off my gloves and shoved them into one of my coat pockets. "Once the police released the crime scene, Blake must've gotten a cleaning crew in here right away. I'm sure he wants the house to look perfect for the walk-through."

"Well, they did a good job. I don't even see any—"

"Blood?" I finished.

Nodding, she swallowed and moved gingerly toward the desk.

I strode over and stood next to her. Blake was right—the desk was an absolutely gorgeous piece of furniture. Almost as tall as I was, it had a central door flanked by three cubbyholes on either side, all of which rested atop a table that I thought looked like pencil inlay. Two wide, brass-handled drawers formed the bottom portion of the desk. The entire thing was dull and scratched, but I was sure that a good refinishing job would restore the wood's original sheen.

I opened the central door of the desk. It had a single shelf that divided the space into two compartments, the top one slightly shallower than the lower one. Both were empty. Even so, I reached my hand in and probed all around with my fingers, in case something had been stuck in the back or taped to the top.

Nothing.

Next I searched each of the cubbyholes the same way, hoping to find something stuck in a crevice, or even a secret compartment. Once again, nothing.

Aunt Tressa, meanwhile, was staring at a point on the wall next to the desk. "That's where it was," she said. "The portrait we saw in the antique shop. It was propped up against a bunch of other paintings."

The painting. I'd almost forgotten. The topaz necklace Daniel and I found in Lillian's jewel box was exactly like the one the woman in the painting had been wearing.

Which meant the woman in the painting had to be Lillian—Frederic Dwardene's beloved "Dora."

All of which reminded me of something else. I'd promised to update Daniel if I heard anything new about Lillian, and I still hadn't called him. He didn't know that Lillian had tried to reach me last night.

I dreaded calling him. He was going to bombard me with all sorts of questions I wouldn't be able to answer. Worse, he was going to try to worm his way back—

No, don't go there. Daniel wasn't important right then. Finding Lillian was the only thing that mattered. I'd call Daniel when I was good and ready.

Turning my attention back to the desk, I chucked my purse onto the floor. "I'm going to pull out the bottom two drawers."

"All the way out?"

"Yep. I want to be sure there's nothing hidden back there."

I eased open the bottom drawer first. It was empty, save for a few faded ink stains that marred the old wood. With my aunt's help, I removed the drawer completely and set it gently on the floor.

"Let's flip it up," I said.

Very carefully, we rotated the drawer and rested it on one side. Half hoping to find a handwritten will taped to the bottom, I blew out a sigh of disappointment. I rested the drawer against the wall, and Aunt Tressa and I removed the second one.

The second drawer was empty as well, and there was nothing taped to the underside. Although—

"What's this?" I said. At the very back of the drawer, a tiny sliver of paper, yellowed with age, was stuck in one corner. Using my thumb and forefinger, I gently pulled it out. It was barely a shred, but something about it looked awfully familiar.

"Wait a second. I think I know where that came from!" Aunt Tressa cried. "Remember the valentine Lou gave me right before—" She cleared her throat. "One corner of the envelope was torn. I'll bet you anything that's what this is from."

"I think you're right. Aunt Tress, that envelope must have been stuck back there for a long time. Lou was probably checking the drawers, making sure the desk was empty, when he found the envelope stuck back there."

"But why would that silly valentine be important? It's over sixty years old!"

"I know," I said, my mind swirling. "That's why I think something else was in that envelope."

"Like what, a will?"

"That would be my guess. But we'll never know now, will we?"

"We won't?"

I shook my head. "If the killer has an ounce of intelligence, he's already destroyed it."

An unwanted thought tiptoed into my mind, sowing seeds that threatened to sprout into firmly rooted suspicions. I tried snatching them out and discarding them, but for every one I purged, another sprang up in its place.

"Okay, wait a minute." Aunt Tressa held up both hands. "Are you suggesting that Edgar Dwardene wrote out a homemade will, and then folded it up and hid it away with some old valentine that his uncle wrote?"

"I know it sounds nutty, but yes, I do."

My aunt looked at me skeptically. "But why?"

"Oh, Lord, I don't know." I groaned and dropped my head into my lap. I hated what I was thinking. Hated the thought that someone I'd known for more than half my life might be a murderer.

"All right, Apple, 'fess up," Aunt Tressa prodded. "You suspect someone, don't you?"

My head still on my knees, I nodded.

"Who?"

Slowly, I sat up and looked at her. "Oh Aunt Tress, what if it's Blake? He was never close to his uncle. That's common knowledge. And Josh had grown really fond of old Edgar. I think they'd truly become good friends. What if Edgar secretly wrote out a will and left all—or even half—of his estate to Josh? And what if Blake—"

"May I remind you," Aunt Tressa interrupted, "that barely an hour ago Josh Baker was at the top of your suspect hit parade?"

"He wasn't at the top," I said dully. "I was only brainstorming to see how he might factor into all of this. He's like a puzzle piece that doesn't quite fit anywhere, you know?"

Aunt Tressa gave me a sympathetic look. "I know."

I stared dejectedly at the scrap of paper in my hand, then slipped it into my pocket. "Let's not talk about it now. I really need to mull over everything in my head. Come on, help me put these drawers back, will you? Then we can do something fun, like some holiday shopping. I don't suppose you know what you want for Christmas yet."

She averted her gaze. "I do, but for now I'm keeping it close to the vest."

Normally I'd start hounding her after a cryptic comment like that. But right now I was too discouraged, too disheartened, to even come up with a snappy retort.

We returned the desk drawers to their rightful slots, and then I grabbed my purse and we headed out of the room.

Aunt Tressa had started to descend the staircase when I noticed something. To the right of the staircase, perpendicular to the bathroom, was a narrow door. I tugged on her coat sleeve and pointed at it. "Is this a linen closet?"

"No, there's another staircase behind there. It leads to the tiny entryway at the back of the kitchen pantry. In the olden days it was used by the servants, I think."

My heartbeat revved up a notch. "So someone could have killed Lou and then scooted down those stairs?"

"I suppose," she said. "Assuming the killer knew the stairs were there, and where they led."

I paused for a moment, thinking. Then I reached for the knob and turned it. The door opened silently. I peered down into a narrow stairwell, but it was too dark to see much of anything. "Do you know if there's a light?"

Aunt Tressa reached a gloved hand around the corner and felt for the switch. A bright white glow illuminated the stairs.

"I'm going down," I told her. "I want to see where this comes out."

"All right, but be careful. This place is feeling weirder by the minute."

While Aunt Tressa watched from the top of the stairs, I made my way slowly down. The treads of the wooden steps were worn, almost dangerously so. Even as I tried to move carefully, my boots hit each one with a reverberating thud. After five steps, I reached a landing, then the stairway turned and went the opposite way. I was almost at the bottom when I heard a deep voice, followed by my aunt's explosive yelp.

Jet propulsion had nothing on me. I spun around and flew up the stairs so fast that I nearly fell headlong into the second story hallway. What stopped me cold was the glaring face standing directly behind Aunt Tressa.

"Josh! What are you doing here?"

"Scaring the butter beans out of me, that's what he's doing." Aunt Tressa whirled on him. "Between you and that horrible spider of yours, you're determined to do me in, aren't you!"

I trounced through the open doorway and slammed the door

shut behind me, blood pounding in my ears.

"What do you mean what am *I* doing here?" Josh demanded, a lock of his dark hair falling over his left eye. "The real question is what are you two doing here? It seems like every time I turn around, there you both are. Are you following me?"

Aunt Tressa opened her mouth. Hard as it was to believe, nothing came out.

"How could we be following you? We were here first, remember? And since my aunt is the listing broker, she has every right to be here. So I'll ask you again—what are you doing here?"

There. I'd put him on the defensive. I hoped.

He took a halting step backward. "I . . . came to get a few boxes that I left in my closet."

"Really?" I was feeling bold now. "Why aren't you at work? Don't you work in the building across from Darla's Dine-o-Rama?"

"Yeah, as a matter of fact I do, but I took a few days off to move into my new place." He narrowed his eyes at me. "You know where Darla's is?"

"We saw it when I drove my aunt to pick up her car today."

Josh was silent for a few long moments. We'd had to drive nearly three miles past the dealership to find Darla's, something he would obviously be aware of since he traveled that road every day. I wondered if he was connecting a few dots in his mind.

"You still haven't told me what you two are doing here," he reminded us, crossing his arms over his chest.

"The buyers are doing a final walk-through Friday morning," Aunt Tressa told him. "Since I had no idea what condition this room would be in after . . . you know . . . I wanted to be sure I didn't have to get a cleaning crew in here."

Josh smirked. "Yeah, right."

I edged closer to Josh and looked deep into his eyes. Aren't the eyes the mirrors of the soul? He met my gaze with nary a blink. I couldn't help wondering if it was the act of an honest man, or of a man simply playing a part—a modern, twisted version of his childhood role as coroner in *The Wizard of Oz*.

He looked away first.

"Josh," I said, taking a desperate plunge, "do you know Lillian Bilodeau?"

He snapped his head back toward me. "You mean the crazy cat lady?"

"She's not crazy. She's an elderly woman who got in over her head trying to care for too many strays. Is that the only reason you know her?"

"Yeah, plus my mom knows her from being in the club with all those old ladies who knit stuff for charity."

"Your mother was in the Hazleton Knitting Club?"

"A long time ago she was. She wasn't much of a knitter, though, so she quit. What does Lillian Bilodeau have to do with anything?"

It was a calculated risk, but I spilled out the story again, ending with Lillian's strange, late-night phone call to me. He listened quietly, then brushed past Aunt Tressa and me and went into the room where Lou had been murdered. I followed him. He stood there, silently, staring at the desk we'd just searched.

"It was so bizarre," Josh said, a tremor lacing his tone. "I came in here that day to tell Lou that whether he and Blake liked it or not, I was going to have the Hudson towed away on Monday. It was my car, and they had no right lumping it in the appraisal with the other estate assets. Anyway, it was weird because the door was closed. That didn't make sense. I knocked once and didn't hear anything, so I opened it. Lou was . . . sprawled face down on the floor. That big dagger was sticking out the back of his neck. His shirt . . . God, it was soaked in blood." Josh covered his face with his hands. "It was surreal, you know? I can't stop having nightmares about it."

He'd deftly avoided the subject of Lillian. Had that been intentional?

Josh went on. "And his laptop—I'd never seen anything like it. It was practically chopped in half. The hard drive was totally destroyed. Whoever killed Lou must've stabbed the laptop, too."

That was news. Something the police had obviously withheld from the public.

"Josh, did you see Lillian before you came in here and found Lou?"

He thought about it for a minute, or at least appeared to. Then he shrugged. "I don't remember seeing her, no. The snow was coming down hard by then, and people were starting to leave."

That much was true. The crowd had thinned out fairly quickly once the roads started to get bad.

"By the way, Apple, what were you doing on those back stairs?" Josh asked abruptly.

My aunt and I exchanged glances. Though she knew precisely where the staircase came out, she kept silent. "I wanted to see where they led," I told him honestly. "Because it occurred to me that those hidden stairs made the perfect escape route for the killer."

"Then come on, I'll show you."

I looked at Aunt Tressa, and we both fell in line behind Josh.

"Be careful," he warned as we picked our way down the narrow staircase. Josh's leather boots echoed noisily, and we sounded like a herd of hippos clumping down the stairs. At the bottom was another door. Josh opened it and the three of us stepped inside an old-fashioned pantry. The room was about eight feet square, with yellow painted shelves that lined the walls from top to bottom.

"Wouldn't you love to have this kind of storage space?" Aunt Tressa quipped. "My kitchen cabinets are overflowing."

"No one builds anything the way they used to," Josh said sourly.

Following him through a doorless entryway directly opposite the staircase, we found ourselves standing in a huge kitchen. Tall, glass-front cabinets lined two of the walls. The counters and flooring were hopelessly outdated, but with this much space to work with, the possibilities for renovation were endless. I felt a twinge of envy for the two lucky doctors who were buying the house.

"Edgar could've modernized the kitchen," Josh said, "but he didn't see the point in wasting money like that." He shook his head and chuckled. "The fridge wasn't even self-defrosting. Sometimes the freezer looked like the polar icecap."

Josh's tone had sounded wistful. Once again, I saw how much he seemed to miss Edgar. Or was living in this intriguing old manse the only thing he missed?

"You two better go," he said suddenly.

"I second that motion," Aunt Tressa said. She looked at Josh, a slight glint in her eye. "Need any help getting those boxes into your car?"

After a momentary hesitation, he shook his head. "No. They'd be too heavy for you two anyway."

We left him standing in the kitchen and hurried out to my car. The sky was a yellowy gray, and the temperature had dropped considerably. I shivered as I slid into my car and started the engine.

Aunt Tressa looked unusually pensive as she snapped her seat belt into place. "Apple, do you think it was a good idea to tell Josh about Lillian? What if it *was* him Lillian saw that day?"

Actually, the same thing had occurred to me. If Josh had

something to do with Lou's murder, I was taking a risk revealing that we knew Lillian was missing. And that we'd been trying to find her.

"I know, Aunt Tress, but it was time to go proactive. I can't help thinking Lillian's time is running out."

If it hasn't already.

And something else was sticking in my brain—something that someone had said. Unfortunately, I couldn't seem to pluck it out long enough to expose it to the light. I couldn't even remember who'd said it.

With a silent prayer that it would come to me, I rummaged through the compartment that held my CDs. I was about to pop in the Spice Girls when I remembered one of my favorite Christmas CDs. I found it and pushed it into the player. The lush, powerful sounds of the Trans-Siberian Orchestra began roaring out of my speakers. One of my favorite songs—"A Star to Follow"—came on.

If only there was a star I could follow that would lead me to Lillian.

Chapter Twenty-Seven

From the journal of Frederic Dwardene, Tuesday, December 19, 1950:

Until now my progress has felt plodding, but I now feel a sense of renewed hope. The biting cold and snow have worked in my favor, for nearly every day Lillian allows me to drive her home. Since the bank closes at three, there is always ample time for me to make the fifteen-minute drive to Manchester to greet her at the bus stop. Some days she looks unwell, and I fear for her health. Even worse, I am afraid she is pining for her soldier . . .

I was delivering Aunt Tressa to her realty office to retrieve her Caddy when we spotted Wilby camped out on her steps. The moment he saw us, he leaped down the stairs and sprinted toward the passenger side of my car, his grin the width of the Merrimack River.

"Miss Tressa! Look what I did!" His ears and nose a matching shade of rose, he wiggled his new cell phone in front of her window. "I already took seven pictures!"

Aunt Tressa smiled at me. "He doesn't have cell service yet, but I showed him how to use the camera feature on the phone. I swear, he was more excited than a kid with a Christmas puppy. Let me see, Wilby!" she trilled, swinging her legs out of the car.

I hopped out, too, and went over to where Wilby and Aunt Tress were viewing the pictures. The air felt raw and biting. I turned away and coughed several times, then peered over my aunt's shoulder at Wilby's new toy.

He giggled as he pointed at the first image. "My mom got kinda mad when I took this one at breakfast this morning. She told me to *never* take her picture again before she has her face on!"

Peeking at the tiny snapshot on the phone, I could totally understand where she was coming from. Wilby had captured his mom with her hair uncombed and her eyes half closed, glaring at him over the rim of her coffee mug. I laughed. "You're quite the photographer, Wilby."

He beamed. "Keep going. There's more."

"Oh, App, look at this one." Aunt Tressa held up the phone so that I could get a better view. Wilby had taken a picture inside Hazleton's Food Mart. The three deli clerks—sporting jolly Santa hats and boasting silly smiles—had posed for him. The remaining images were nondescript scenes Wilby had taken in downtown Hazleton.

It was the last one that caught my eye.

The image was crooked, but the building was instantly recognizable—my office building. In front of the building, a woman stood on the sidewalk. She appeared to be staring through one of the office windows. With her back to Wilby's camera, I could discern only one thing about her—she wore a long fur coat.

"Could I see that one?"

Aunt Tressa handed me the phone. I rotated the tiny image every which way, then located the *zoom* feature. On the first floor of Quinto and Ingle, in the second window from the right, a faint shadow was visible. It could have been a trick of the light, or even my imagination. But I didn't think so.

Unless I was completely imagining it, the woman in the fur coat was watching someone.

And the only two people in the office this afternoon would

have been Sam and Vicki.

Two hours later I was back in my apartment, warming my hands around a mug of steaming cocoa. Aunt Tressa and I hadn't managed to squeeze much holiday shopping into our dwindling afternoon, but we'd stocked up on wrapping paper and ribbon, so the trip to the mall wasn't a total loss. My stomach felt queasy and my head ached, so I was glad to be home alone on my comfy, sagging sofa.

I'd retrieved the old valentine from my kitchen drawer, and was analyzing it for about the twentieth time when Cinnie and Elliot joined me on the sofa. Elliot tickled my neck from behind with his whiskers while Cinnie sprawled in my lap.

Aunt Tressa, meanwhile, was busy in her own apartment, cooking up a culinary storm for her Wednesday evening dinner with Darby. The man had clearly cast a spell on her, a fact I would simply have to tolerate.

For now.

But since I was going to have to endure at least one meal with him, I'd already decided I would use the time as an opportunity to pry into his psyche. His ten-dollar deal with Lillian was sticking in me like a three-pronged thorn. No one offered to do that much work for so paltry a fee unless he wanted something. But whatever it was Darby wanted from Lillian, I couldn't fathom. For the most part, Lillian subsisted on Social Security. Her lifestyle was what I would euphemistically refer to as modest. Surely Darby didn't think she had money hidden away somewhere?

No, something else was going on. I only wished I had a clue as to what it was.

With an exasperated sigh, I snatched the old journal off my end table. I wasn't surprised to realize that the handwriting on the valentine matched the flowery entries in the journal.

Frederic Dwardene had been obsessed with a woman he barely knew, a woman whose delicate beauty and quiet tenderness had sent him over the moon.

Lillian.

I wondered how Lillian had felt about him back then. Had he managed to persuade her to fall in love with him? Was that why she hadn't returned any of Anton's letters?

I opened the journal and turned to an entry written five days before Christmas.

Wednesday, December 20, 1950

The painting continues to progress nicely, though I am struggling with blending the hues for Lillian's golden hair. Without a photograph of her, I must paint from memory, but that is easy, since her face is always foremost in my mind. I am sure, now, that I will have the painting completed by February 14th, at which time I will present it to Lillian and ask her to marry me.

I flipped ahead a few days.

Friday, December 22, 1950

I was wise to befriend Lillian's mother, for I've been invited to have Christmas Eve dinner at their home. Lillian's only aunt, a woman who lives in Pennsylvania, arrived three days ago to spend the holidays in Hazleton. I can hardly contain my joy at being invited! Already I am feeling like a family member, which I will be, very soon . . .

Lillian's only aunt.

If that was true, then Daniel was right. Lillian had had only the one aunt—her Aunt Alice. Not that it mattered, but I couldn't help wondering why Bernice thought Lillian's aunt had died in the fifties.

Oddly, there was no entry for Christmas Eve. On Christmas

Day, however, Frederic's words were bittersweet.

Monday, December 25, 1950
It is Christmas, and I am alone. Lillian was very quiet on Christmas Eve, though she seemed delighted to be with her Aunt Alice. I must say Alice was a charming woman, bubbly and full of fun. No one mentioned the soldier all evening, which I took as a positive sign. Lillian's mother—clearly my ally— showered me with food and eggnog. We ate and drank in the tiny parlor as the snow fell outside. Tinsel sparkled among the red and blue lights on the small Christmas tree. I waited till just the right moment to present the prettily wrapped topaz necklace to Lillian. Lillian's mother and aunt gasped with delight as Lillian removed it from its velvet box. Aunt Alice immediately fastened it around Lillian's neck, as Lillian smiled at me and murmured a quiet thank you. I confess I'd hoped for a stronger response, but I know that Lillian is shy and reticent, so I forgave her that . . .

I forgave her that.

The words sent a shiver through me. Frederic was beginning to sound creepy. I read ahead, through several more entries.

Saturday, December 30, 1950
I have not seen or heard from Lillian since Christmas Eve. I know she took days off from the factory to spend time with her aunt, but surely the woman must have returned to Pennsylvania by now. I will spend all of New Year's Eve working on the painting. The second half of the century will soon dawn. I must be ready . . .

Thursday, January 4, 1951
Lillian came into the bank today with her savings deposit, looking more somber than ever. Oh, if only I knew what troubled

her so! Is it because of the soldier, who has clearly lost interest in her? Risking the wagging tongues of the tellers, I asked her to come into my office. She sat down, and I expressed my concern for her health. She insisted she was perfectly fine, if a bit weary from the dreadful weather we've been having.

Saturday, January 6, 1951
Today I returned to Whalie's Jewelers, for I cannot bear to see Lillian looking so blue! Thinking that a small gift might cheer her, I purchased a lovely china cat, white with green eyes (like her own cat!). It is imported from England and truly quite special. I will drive her home from work on Monday and present it to her then . . .

A china cat.

From Frederic's description, it sounded like the one Lillian purchased at the estate sale. Could it be the same one?

I read on, wanting desperately to know if Frederic ever gave the cat to his beloved Lillian.

Monday, January 8, 1951
Today I gave Lillian the gift box with the china cat nestled inside. We were sitting in my Hudson, in front of her home, when I presented it to her. The sky was dark and scattered with a million stars. In the meager glow from the porch lamp, I saw Lillian's look of surprise as she untied the bow and removed the cat from the box. I wished desperately for her to lean over and kiss my cheek! Instead, her eyes filled with tears as she thanked me in a hoarse voice . . .

Poor Lillian. Frederic had really been putting the pressure on.

What didn't make sense were his statements about the soldier losing interest in Lillian. If the soldier in question was Anton—

the one who died in Korea—it didn't jibe with the genuine pleas of love Anton had expressed in his letters. Hadn't he begged Lillian to write to him?

I could think of only one possibility.

Lillian had never received the letters.

Only a dozen or so pages remained in the journal. Turning to the next page, my thoughts kept tripping to the valentine, which was resting on my end table. Something in the poem had stuck in my memory. What was it?

I'd no sooner reached my hand over to grab it off the table when a thunderous crash from Aunt Tressa's apartment made me leap out of my socks. In a matter of seconds I was out of my apartment and pounding frantically on her door. I heard her mutter a long string of expletives as she stomped across her living room and yanked open the door.

"My Lord, I thought a meteor fell through your roof! What happened?"

"Come see for yourself."

At the entrance to her kitchen, I came to an abrupt halt.

What on Planet Earth . . . ?

Spread all over the floor, like an overflowing pond, was a cream-colored, chicken-flecked disaster area. In a prior incarnation, the mess had obviously been the filling of a chicken pot pie.

"I can't believe I did this," Aunt Tressa sputtered. "I was carrying the pot from the stove to the counter when Pazzo jumped right in front of me. I stopped short and my foot slipped, and—"

"Oh, my gosh! You didn't get hurt, did you?"

"No, of course not." She swiped at a glob of gravy that had splashed onto her arm. "I didn't even fall. I just dropped the pot. I was afraid Pazzo might have gotten splattered with hot gravy, but he's fine. He bolted like a rocket when the pot hit the floor. Poor thing didn't know what was happening."

Sure enough, Pazzo was peeking into the kitchen from around the corner, his big green eyes flicking nervously over the scene.

"It wasn't his fault," Aunt Tressa said with a sigh. "He was only coming in for a snack. It was his timing that was lousy."

"I'll help you clean it," I said, coughing into my arm.

"Your eyelids are sagging and you look pale. Go home and go to bed. This will take me five minutes to clean up."

"Give me a break, Aunt Tress. A haz-mat team couldn't clean this up in five minutes."

She relented, and fifteen minutes later we had the kitchen looking as freshly scrubbed as an operating room. In other words, the way Aunt Tressa's kitchen normally looked.

"What are you going to do about your dinner tomorrow?" I asked.

She poured each of us a glass of wine and set out a plate of cheese and crackers. "Start over," she said brightly. "I have more boneless chicken in the fridge, so it's no biggie. Hey, can you believe it? Jack doesn't like veggies in his pot pie either, so it'll just be chicken and tiny white potatoes in a luscious gravy, with a flaky biscuit topping. And for dessert I'm making a decadent chocolate mousse cake."

"Sounds like you've met your culinary soul mate," I said in a resigned tone. For someone who claimed she didn't like to cook, everything she made always tasted delicious.

"Have you decided if you're going to invite Daniel?" She took a sip from her wine goblet.

Daniel.

Hearing his name sent an avalanche of guilt through me. I still hadn't called to fill him in about the strange phone call from Lillian.

"I haven't had time to think about it," I hedged. "Right now I'm more worried about you. I sense that you're a bit . . . well, infatuated with Darby, and it scares me. A little voice in my head tells me he's hiding something. I only wish I knew what it was."

Slowly and precisely, Aunt Tressa set down her glass. "Apple, this has got to stop."

Her tone had gone flat, setting off an alarm in my head. "What's got to stop?"

"This excessive worrying about me. You've been doing it for a long time and it's gotten out of control. I want it to end. Now."

I felt a hard lump swirl inside my stomach. My aunt had never spoken to me this way.

"It started when I had the cancer scare three years ago," she went on. "Thank God that turned out to be nothing, but ever since then you've been treating me like one of those delicate animals made from hand-blown glass."

Had I wandered into some crazy time warp? Another dimension in space?

"What are you saying?" My voice rattled. "That I shouldn't care about you? That I shouldn't worry about what happens to you?"

"Of course not." Aunt Tressa's tone softened. "Listen, I know I can be off-the-wall at times. But I'm a grown woman who's perfectly capable of taking care of herself, and of making her own decisions. Especially when it comes to gentleman callers."

I swallowed, but the painful lump in my throat refused to budge. All this time, I'd had no idea Aunt Tressa felt this way. Why hadn't she told me this before?

The answer was obvious. She was afraid of hurting my feelings, of wounding my ego. I shook my head, willing away the tears that were trying to burst through the gates.

"It must've been awful, the day you found out Dad was never coming back. That you were *stuck* with me," I added bitterly. I was in full pity mode, now, dredging up ancient history as if it had all happened yesterday.

Her expression morphed into something I'd never seen before—a cross between amusement and fury. "You mean the day I realized it was going to be just you and me against the world, to put it bluntly? The day good ole Vince Mariani hauled his sorry patootie off to Vegas and never looked back?" She sat back and grinned at me, a distinct gleam in her eye. "Oh, yeah, that was quite the banner day."

"I remember it too," I said softly. "Not as distinctly as you, maybe, but there's one thing I'll never forget."

She leaned forward, serious now. "What was that?"

"The day before he left for good, Dad drove me over to my friend Ashley's to play. I think he was sick of seeing me mope around and sniffle, always asking him when Mom was coming back. You'd been staying with us for a while—"

"Eight days," Aunt Tressa confirmed.

"But I hadn't warmed up to you. All I wanted was my mother. Anyway, when he picked me up from Ashley's that day, the first thing I asked him when I hopped into the car was, *Did Mommy call yet?* That did it—he exploded. He started shrieking at me that she was never coming back and that I'd better get used to it, because there was nothing he could do about it."

"I never knew that," Aunt Tressa said.

I sucked in a long, calming breath. "I started to bawl, and I couldn't stop. I kept sobbing and sobbing. We happened to be driving past Mrs. Howell's place when he told me about Mom— you know that old clapboard house with the circular window at the top? I've hated that house ever since. Any time I drive by it I look the other way."

I paused to take a sip of wine, until I realized it didn't appeal to me at all. "When we got home, Dad got out of the car and stormed into the house. He left me sitting there alone, crying. Eventually I cried myself out and went inside." I looked away.

"Apparently I didn't close the porch door all the way."

Aunt Tressa blanched. "Oh, no."

I nodded. I couldn't say the rest because my throat was clogged, but she already knew what happened. My adorable tortoiseshell cat, Pebbles, who'd always stayed inside, managed to sneak out. Dad found her the next morning. She'd been run over by a car.

"You blamed yourself for that, didn't you?" Aunt Tressa said.

"Yes! It was my fault—I left the door open!"

"It was *not* your fault. Your father shouldn't have left you in the car. You were seven, for pity's sake. If I'd known he did that I'd have ripped him open a new one with a rusty can opener."

"Dad left that day and never looked back," I said. "I don't recall ever asking for him, though, or wondering if he was coming home again."

"You didn't." Aunt Tressa leaned closer and crossed her arms on the table. "You turned sullen, painfully quiet. I wasn't sure what to do."

I swiped at my damp eyes. "Poor Aunt Tress. Young and single, stuck with a sad little girl who only wanted her mother. I can't imagine what was going through your head."

"I wasn't sure myself, frankly." Aunt Tressa drained her wine glass. "At first I wondered what in the name of Sergeant Pepper I'd gotten myself into. I knew my brother well, and I had little doubt that he was gone for the long haul. I decided I had two choices."

I laughed. "Was one of them the orphanage?"

She waved a hand at me. "Get out. Option one was to deliver you to my mom and dad's house. They'd have fussed over you and cooked for you—Lord, they'd have had a field day taking care of you."

"So why didn't you?"

"Look, my folks were wonderful people, but they were very

set in their old-fashioned ways. Plus, they both had health issues." She swallowed and shook her head. "But that wasn't the real reason. The real reason was that I was selfish, so I chose option two—to keep the little girl I'd already grown to love as if she were my own. It took me all of about ten seconds to reach that decision."

My eyes filled with tears. "I remember now. That was the first time you made the kooky macaroni."

"I didn't know what to give you for supper that night, so I had to make do with what was on hand. You were a fussbudget, but you liked macaroni and you liked cheese and for some oddball reason you liked black olives. I threw the ingredients together with a can of spicy tomato sauce and some crumbled burger, baked it in a casserole dish, and voila! You loved it. When you asked me what it was, I made up the name kooky macaroni."

"After that I asked for it all the time."

"That you did. Now listen to me." She pointed a finger at me. "You're pale and exhausted, and I want you to go home and go to bed."

"Yes, ma'am," I said with a tepid salute.

I was beginning to feel better, at least emotionally. Talking about that agonizing day had been cathartic. I'd always blamed myself for Pebbles getting killed in the road. It never occurred to me that Dad as the adult should never have left me alone in the car.

As for Aunt Tressa, I'd never realized that my fretting over her health and her safety had reached the point of overkill. Not that I'd ever stop worrying about her, but from now on I'd do it more surreptitiously.

I pushed away my wine glass and glanced at her. Her expression was aglow with, what . . . dreams of a new love? "Hey Aunt

Tress," I said softly, "did you ever have your conversation with Marty?"

Eyes sparkling, she grinned. "I did, and as usual he came through. He reminded me that I'd had the answer all along, that it's always been inside me." She splayed her hand over heart.

After a long moment of silence, I glared at her. "Are you going to tell me what it was?"

With a laugh she said, "Of course! When the song came on the radio, I knew it was Marty sending me a sign. *All you need is love.*"

Oh, boy. Aunt Tressa had it bad.

I rose and delivered my nearly full wine glass to the sink. My head felt as if someone had pumped it full of air and was using it for basketball practice.

Bidding my aunt good night, I stumbled back to my apartment. Something about that valentine was still poking at my brain.

It was going to drive me batty until I figured out what it was.

CHAPTER TWENTY-EIGHT

From the journal of Frederic Dwardene, Friday, January 12, 1951

I haven't seen Lillian since Monday! Why hasn't she come into the bank? I thought by now I might have received a tiny note, thanking me for the china cat. But no, nothing . . .

It was almost seven thirty when I remembered that the last solid food I'd eaten was the chef's salad I'd barely touched early in the afternoon. Oddly, I still didn't feel very hungry.

After coughing through *Wheel of Fortune*—during which I alternated between shouting guesses at the television and re-reading the valentine—I made myself a plate of graham crackers slathered with peanut butter. My kind of comfort food. But the first bite made me grimace. Something tasted off. Had my peanut butter dallied past its expiration date?

Eeech. I didn't want to know. I set aside the crackers and picked up the valentine again. *Concentrate,* I told myself.

With weary eyes, I gave it another read-through. The saccharine sentiment hadn't changed. It was the same sugary drivel.

I read it again. And then once more.

> *You've dwelt within my heart, dear love*
> *From that first and shining day*
> *Your eyes of blue and locks of gold*
> *Within my dreams did reign*

And so, dear sweet, to you I pledge
My essence and my soul
Now we shall dwell within this home
Which shall be yours to hold

This time something sparked inside my head. Like a tiny match struck over and over until the flame ignites. Something about the last line of the poem. No, the last *two* lines.

Now we shall dwell within this HOME
Which shall be yours to HOLD

I read the two lines, over and over. What was it about those words that bothered me?

But the spark was gone. Fizzled.

Maybe after a solid night's rest it would come to me. I reached for the envelope and slipped the valentine back inside.

And then I saw the numbers.

The numbers that someone, probably Lou, had written with a felt-tipped pen on the back of the envelope. Until now, I'd been ignoring them.

1199-0540. Written exactly that way.

I was back to my original question. Why had Lou wanted me to have the valentine?

All at once, I saw those numbers the way I see them every day.

Book and page numbers in the Registry of Deeds.

My laptop was on the kitchen counter. Heart hammering, I skidded into the kitchen on stocking feet and dragged it over in front of me. "Come on, come on," I muttered, booting it up.

A decade must have elapsed before I was finally on the Internet. The site for the New Hampshire Registries of Deeds— nhdeeds.com—was at the top of my browser. Within seconds, I was in the grantor indices of the Rockingham County Registry.

In the prompt for "Book" I entered 1199, and in the one for "Page" I entered 0540. I clicked View Document.

After twenty or so seconds, a copy of a deed appeared. Handwritten, it was penned in the same elaborate script as the valentine.

Know all men by these presents that I, Frederic Dwardene, an unremarried widower, for consideration paid, hereby grant to Dora Lillian Bilodeau, with quitclaim covenants, the following described property:

My stomach clenched as the deed went on to describe the parcel of land that the mansion sat on. At the bottom, Frederic Dwardene had signed it, dating it February 2, 1951. His signature had been properly witnessed and notarized. The Registry's date stamp at the bottom showed he'd recorded the deed the same day.

Now we shall dwell within this home which shall be yours to hold . . .

The words now made perfect sense. A mortgage banker by profession, Frederic would have been familiar with the term "holding title."

Lovestruck Frederic had conveyed his home to Lillian. If my guess was right, he'd enclosed the deed inside the envelope with the valentine.

It was his Valentine's Day gift to her. A gift that was never delivered.

Nausea gripped me. Bile rose in my throat.

For starters, I'd done the title search on the property and failed to find this deed. In my line of work that was a deadly omission—every title searcher's living nightmare. How had I missed it?

My hands shook as I brought up the indices for nineteen fifty-one. I entered the name DWARDENE. Since it wasn't a common name, it was an easy one to search. Names like "Smith" and "Jones" were the bane of title searchers.

But the only "Dwardene" document listed under the year nineteen fifty-one was a mortgage from Mason Dwardene to the Hazleton Savings Bank—a mortgage that encumbered the home Blake's dad had grown up in.

There were no entries under Frederic Dwardene, or even under *F. Dwardene* or *Fred Dwardene*.

I checked some alternate spellings, though I knew I'd already done so when I searched the title. Names that sounded like Dwardene but could be spelled differently. *Duardene. Doardene.*

Nothing.

I went back to the beginning of the "D" names and scanned every name slowly.

And there it was. A deed recorded in Book 1199, Page 0540. Indexed under the name Dawrdene, Frederic.

Dawrdene.

All this time, the deed had been indexed under the wrong spelling—two of the letters had been transposed. In Registry lingo it was a scrivener's error. That's why I hadn't found it during my search.

A chill crept over me.

My fingers numb, I entered Lillian's name in the indices, beginning with the year nineteen fifty-one and coming forward all the way to the present. Maybe she'd somehow learned about the deed and conveyed the property back to Frederic.

But there was nothing.

Lillian owned the property that Blake and Celeste were planning to sell in three days.

That's why Lou had left the cryptic message in Sam's voice mail. *I think there's been a terrible mistake . . .*

My heart sank to my stomach like a dead weight. All this time, the mistake had been mine—not Sam's. I'd failed to find the misindexed deed when I searched the title.

While cleaning out the desk, Lou Marshall had found the deed.

And so, apparently, had the killer.

CHAPTER TWENTY-NINE

From the journal of Frederic Dwardene, Saturday, January 13, 1951

I've tried three times this past week to drive Lillian home from work, but she wasn't at the bus stop at her usual time. I'm terrified that she is avoiding me. Either that or she is gravely ill and on her deathbed. I have resolved to contact her mother . . .

Fatigue instantly abandoned me. Adrenaline zinged through me like a live power line.

Blake had obviously found out about the deed and killed Lou to keep him quiet. The afternoon of the estate sale, Celeste had said Blake was cleaning out the basement. But at some point he must have gone upstairs to talk to Lou. Had Lou told Blake about the deed? Or had Blake simply wandered into Lou's makeshift office when Lou was on the phone trying to reach Sam? Either way, Blake must have panicked, realizing Lou was about to blow everything. In which case, Blake and Celeste's plans for their big move would be derailed, maybe permanently.

Right now the more important question was: where was Lillian? Assuming she was still alive, where had Blake hidden her?

And then—like the lightning bolt that struck Michael in *The Godfather* when he first saw Apollonia—it came to me.

Blake's cabin in Weare. The one he inherited from his dad. It was the perfect place to stash a hostage. But he couldn't keep

Lillian prisoner forever, could he? That scared me more than anything.

Weare was in Hillsborough County. My fingers moved at warp speed as I went back to nhdeeds.com, this time logging onto the Hillsborough County Registry. Unlike Rockingham, whose online indices went back to the sixteen hundreds, Hillsborough's ran from nineteen sixty-six to the present. If Albert Dwardene bought the cabin any time after nineteen sixty-five, I should be able to find his deed.

Luck and the angels were with me. A deed to Albert Dwardene for land in Weare was recorded in nineteen seventy-nine. I clicked the link to view it and scanned the legal description. The property was on Deer Trail Road in Weare. Unfortunately, deeds don't offer driving directions.

But the town's website might reveal a street address. Fingers flying, I did a quick search and pulled up Weare's assessment records. It felt like an eon before the assessor's card for Albert's parcel came up, but it was probably only five or six seconds.

And there was the street address: 29 Deer Trail Road.

In the upper left corner of the card was a mini-photo of the cabin. I enlarged it. A log cabin with a pitched roof came into view. Two windows flanked the front door. They looked fairly low to the ground, maybe four feet at the most.

I did a fast MapQuest search and printed out directions. On a good day, the drive was about forty minutes from Hazleton. But in the winter . . .

I thought of calling Aunt Tress. Then I pictured her bustling about in her kitchen, preparing for the Darby dinner, more animated than I'd seen her in a long time. Instead, I punched in the main number of the police station and asked for Chief Fenton. I didn't want to talk to anyone else. It would take too long to explain. I felt sure that Lillian's time was running out.

Fenton was off duty, so I left a long message on his voice

mail. I told him what I'd discovered and where I was headed. That way if anything happened . . .

But it wouldn't. If Lillian was still alive, I was going to find her and bring her home. The police would have to deal with the rest.

I bundled up. Hat, gloves, ski jacket, boots. I put fresh D batteries in my flashlight and loaded my car with blankets for Lillian. I had no idea what condition I'd find her in, so I wanted to be prepared.

Cursing myself for not owning a GPS, I memorized the directions to the cabin—no easy task with a head that felt like a punching bag.

Then I was off.

CHAPTER THIRTY

From the journal of Frederic Dwardene, Monday, January 15, 1951

Lillian's mother was thrilled to hear from me. I confided that I was worried about Lillian, and she agreed that her daughter has not been herself at all. I confessed that by now I'd hoped my friendship with Lillian might have blossomed into something deeper. Her response was most encouraging. Between us, we've resolved to formulate a plan . . .

First order of business: check out the parking lot at Blake's condominium.

My digital clock read 8:43 when I swung my car into the complex. Cruising slowly along rows of parked cars, I scanned every one, my tires crunching over the frozen snow. In front of Blake and Celeste's building, I spotted Blake's black SUV. Two spaces over from that was Celeste's white sedan.

I breathed a quiet prayer of thanks. With any luck, they were both hunkered down for the night. If nothing else, the fact that both cars were here would buy me enough time.

The traffic was light on Route 114. I pressed the gas pedal harder and felt my little Honda skid slightly to the left. Much as I wanted to find the cabin, I had to pace myself. I couldn't afford an accident. Not now, not when I was so close. Gritting my teeth, I tamped down my impatience as I mulled over what I'd learned.

Blake was a murderer.

I'd tutored him in high school, helped him earn a much-needed B in history so that he could remain on the football team. I'd always considered him to be a decent guy, if a bit self-focused. Still, he'd been a friend. I never saw his dark side, never realized he had one.

After finding the deed inside the valentine, Lou Marshall must have done exactly what I did: check the Registry's indices to see if Lillian had conveyed the property back to Frederic. What did he do when he realized that she hadn't? Did he tell Blake they'd have to cancel the closing? Did he burst his bubble with the bombshell that Lillian held title to the mansion?

And Lillian, had she seen the deed when she went into that room to pay for her china cat? Had Lou told her what he'd found? Something had clearly upset her that day. What else could it have been?

Oh Lillian, if only you'd confided in me, I could have helped you . . .

Right now I felt nothing but disgust for Blake.

Disgust and red hot rage.

I expelled a sigh of relief when I crossed over the Weare town line. A mile and a half later I turned onto Windsor Road, which would dump me onto Deer Trail Road. From there it was only a short distance to the cabin, if the directions were accurate.

Traffic was almost nonexistent. As I made the turn onto Deer Trail Road, a pair of headlights momentarily blinded me. For a few seconds I lost my bearings. I slowed down and checked my odometer. Seven-tenths of a mile to go.

Flanked on both sides by tall pines, the road grew impossibly dark and narrow. What if I passed by the cabin without realizing it? So far, I hadn't even spotted a driveway, let alone a dwelling.

Without warning, Celeste popped into my mind. I thought of how devastated she was going to be by all of this. It was bad enough that her hopes and dreams were going to be blown to bits, her life torn in half. She would also have to suffer through the nightmare of learning that the man she loved was a murderer.

Don't think about it now. Find Lillian first and bring her home.

I continued driving slowly, concentrating on the road, my headlights burning twin tunnels into the inky night. I glanced at my odometer again. I'd gone sixth-tenths of a mile and hadn't seen a single house. Pressing the brake lightly, I let the car inch forward. And there, curving off to the right, were the faint remnants of tire tracks.

Fearful of missing the turn, I snapped my wheel to the right. I followed the path made by the snowy tracks, maneuvering my way along the rutted mess that apparently served as the driveway. It was a dirt drive at best, not designed for winter use. It would have been a breeze for Blake's SUV to navigate, but although my little car handled like a dream, it didn't have the weight of an SUV. Fir trees rose high on either side of me, smothering the sky.

Worse, the tire tracks began to snake steadily uphill. The cabin must sit at the top of a rise. Any second now, I expected to get—

Oh, God.

—stuck.

My left tire had slipped into a frozen rut.

No, please. Not now . . .

I jammed my foot against the accelerator and held it fast. The Honda rocked forward violently, then fell back again. The rut was only getting deeper.

I tried three more times. Bubbling with frustration, I slammed the car into Park and hopped out. Leaving the door wide open, I trudged around it and peered at the tire. Yes, it was a tire all right—stuck in one of the rings of Hades.

The same tire Fenton claimed wouldn't pass inspection.

I fumed for a minute, squashing the urge to kick it. Then a thought smacked me on the back of the head. I clomped around to the back of my car and threw open the hatch. I hoisted out the bag of kitty litter I'd bought the night Elliot came home with me. With all the bizarre events of the past few days, I'd forgotten to haul it inside my apartment.

Thank heavens.

I dragged the bag around to the front of the car and tore it open—not easy to do wearing gloves. With any luck, the coarse litter would give the front tires some purchase.

I spread some litter all around, emptying the bag as I scooted farther up the drive. When I'd used it all, I tossed aside the bag and jumped back into the car. I slid the gearshift into Drive.

With a silent prayer, I pressed the accelerator and steadily increased the pressure. This time the Honda jerked forward, then shot out of the rut like a bullet. "Yeesss!" I cried as the car roared up the drive.

And then, like a shimmering lake materializing in the desert, a snow-covered log cabin came into view.

The same one I'd seen in the photo.

I killed my engine, grabbed my flashlight, and got out of the car. Looking down, I saw oval indentations in the snow—the telltale remains of footprints.

Someone had definitely been here.

I glanced at both of the cabin's windows. No light shone from within.

I followed the prints to the door of the cabin, then tried the doorknob. It was locked. I'd expected as much, but my heart still dropped. I pounded my fist on the door. "Lillian? Are you in there?"

I turned the knob again, this time throwing all my weight against the door. But it was rock solid and wouldn't budge.

Frustrated, I stepped backward and examined the two windows. In the photo they'd looked barely four feet off the ground. In reality they were more like five. That extra foot made all the difference. Even if I could break one of the windows, there was no way I could pull myself up to climb through.

The cold air was starting to chill me now. Beneath my gloves, my fingers felt like icicles. With a shiver, I flicked on my flashlight and shone the beam all around. I needed to find something I could stand on.

But there was nothing. I was rapidly growing disheartened. And desperate.

Drained of energy, and of ideas, I clumped around to the left side of the cabin, my boots sinking into the hardened snow. Maybe I'd find something I could use—a trash barrel, an old milk crate, anything . . .

Luck was with me. Stacked against the back of the cabin and covered by a tarp was a mound of cut wood. With a cry of triumph, I ripped off the tarp.

I shoved my flashlight into my pocket. Working as fast as my weary legs would carry me, I lugged chunks of wood to the front of the cabin. One by one, I stacked them in front of the closest window, forming them into a makeshift stepstool. By the time I'd made a pile about two feet high, my arms felt as if they were going to snap off at the elbows.

Flashlight in hand, I mounted the wood pile. My boots wobbled and my head spun slightly, but I kept my balance. Planting my feet securely, I directed the beam inside the cabin.

Rustic would be a polite word for the interior. It was a room about thirty feet square, adorned with the barest of furnishings. A sagging sofa bed rested against one wall, a wood stove against another. In front of the sofa was a low table made from a rough slab of pine. The back wall boasted a rack of fishing poles. Cut into the rear wall was a narrow door that I assumed led to a bathroom. If there was a separate room for sleeping, it wasn't obvious.

There was no sign of Lillian.

My gaze jolted back to the pine table. A blue plastic bag rested on top, its organic contents splayed out in front.

Blue *bread*. Blake had left one of Celeste's loaves of bread there for her to eat—a loaf encased in screaming blue cellophane. That's what Lillian had been trying to tell me. She wanted me to make the connection!

But where was she?

Fear coursed through me. Had Blake come out here one last time and disposed of her?

"Lillian!" I screamed as loudly as I could, tapping on the window with my flashlight. "Are you in there?"

I waited but heard nothing. Hot tears streamed down my frozen cheeks.

Maybe Lillian had never been here. Maybe I'd gotten it all wrong.

Maybe I was totally insane.

I shone the beam around one last time, illuminating every crack and corner. My heart hammering, I doused the light and stepped off the wood pile.

In my car, I cranked up the heat as high as it would go. My entire body shivered as I slid the gearshift into Reverse. I had to pull myself together. Backing down the icy drive was going to be dicey, at best.

I was releasing the brake when something caught my eye—a flash of pink in the window. It disappeared as quickly as it came. Had I imagined it?

I waited another minute, but saw nothing. Dejected, I started back down the drive.

Then it flashed again, a circle of bright pink. This time it stayed in the window for several seconds. The color was dazzling, almost like neon—

Lillian's necklace! The one she received for winning the Knitting Extravaganza.

I shut off the engine and flew out of my car. One leap and I was atop the woodpile, cracking the window with my flashlight. With my gloved hands I pulled out shards of glass and tossed them into the snow. Using both arms, I hoisted myself over the lip of the window and tumbled inside head first.

I landed on the floor with a thud. Beside me, someone cried out faintly.

I pulled myself into a sitting position and aimed my flashlight at the sound. Propped against the wall beneath the window was a rolled-up braided rug. Lillian's pale head and one thin arm jutted out from the top. The necklace hung in a limp tangle from her fingers.

My heart rate did a wild spike. I set the flashlight down and gently clasped her shoulders. "Lillian, are you all right? Are you hurt?"

Her head lolled slightly, and her eyes looked glassy. She moved her cracked lips but couldn't seem to form any words.

"Let me get this off," I said. Very gently, I peeled away the rough carpet. The sour stench of human captivity wafted toward me, making me cough. Beneath the carpet, Lillian had been wearing her quilted bathrobe over a pair of yellow pajamas. Tears stung my eyes. Blake must have snatched her from her bed in the dead of night and tossed her into his SUV. Thank heaven she'd gone to bed still wearing the robe. It probably saved her from freezing to death.

Her lips moved again.

"Don't try to talk, Lil. I'm going to get you out of here."

I reached inside the pocket of my jacket and dug out my cell phone. I wasn't sure how 9-1-1 worked from a cell, and didn't have time to learn now. I pulled off a glove and punched in

Aunt Tressa's number. I gave her the address and told her I needed an ambulance, fast.

A hand clawed weakly at my sleeve. "C-c-co . . ." Lillian tried to push out the word in a raspy voice.

Cold.

No wonder. The cabin was a freezing dungeon. How could Blake do this to a helpless woman? When did he become such a monster?

"Help is on the way, Lillian. Hang in there." I peeled off my hat and snugged it over her head, covering her ears. Then I pulled off my jacket and tucked it around her frail form.

Seized by a sudden bout of coughing, I slid open the bolt on the cabin door and hurried out to my car. I returned with two blankets and a bottle of water. Lillian was still propped against the wall beneath the window, her tiny body lilting to one side. I tucked both blankets over her and uncapped the bottle. "Here's some water, Lil." I tilted the bottle to her lips.

She surprised me by taking several gulps. I should have realized she'd be dehydrated. I had a sinking feeling she was also suffering from hypothermia.

I rubbed my hands over her arms, hoping to massage some warmth into her. "Lillian, do you know what he drugged you with?" I wanted to give as much information as I could to the paramedics.

Lillian frowned in confusion. She shook her head, but couldn't seem to form the words to utter a response.

"Never mind. You'll be at the hospital soon," I promised.

Somewhere in the distance, the squeal of a siren pierced the night. Tears slid down my cheeks as the sound grew closer. Less than a minute later, I saw red lights flashing in the window.

By the time the police and paramedics burst through the door, I was sobbing uncontrollably. They worked quickly to get Lillian onto a stretcher and immediately started tending to her.

Curled up on the floor now, I vaguely saw plastic bags and other things I didn't want to think about. My stomach was roiling. Every bone throbbed.

One of the paramedics bent close to me. "It's okay," he said kindly, touching my cheek. "It's all over now."

I protested when I saw them bringing in another stretcher. "I don't need that. I'm fine," I told them. "I just need to get home and go to bed."

"Uh . . . I don't think so, miss. Pardon me for saying this, but your face is the same color as the hairball my cat upchucked this morning."

With that, I threw up all over the cabin floor.

A silly thought popped into my head.

I should have swallowed Vicki's zinc tabs when I had the chance.

CHAPTER THIRTY-ONE

From the journal of Frederic Dwardene, Thursday, January 25, 1951:

I needn't have worried about Lillian's soldier. Her mother today confessed to me that she's been hiding his letters to Lillian. It explained my darling Lillian's distress these past weeks, but oh, how sweet to have such a powerful ally in this war of love! How uplifting to know the elder Dora has been conspiring on my behalf all along!

"That son of a bad girl," Aunt Tressa spat, her eyes dark with fury. "Killing Lou wasn't bad enough—he had to put poor Lillian through all that torment."

I wanted to respond, but another bout of coughing seized me.

"As for you," she railed on, "I still can't believe you went out to that place alone." She tucked my comforter high around my neck, a little too tightly, I thought.

I was back in my own deliciously comfortable bed, pumped with flu meds and floating high on the knowledge that Lillian was safe. When I saw her at the emergency room, the doctors were confident she was going to be all right. Wrapping herself in that grimy old carpet had probably saved her from freezing to death. She was a clever lady, and a survivor.

My eyes teared up again. "I'm so thankful she had that pendant from winning the Knitting Extravaganza. She'd rolled so close to the window that I couldn't see her. If she hadn't been able to signal to me with that neon necklace . . ."

"Never mind the necklace," Aunt Tressa said, swiping a finger over her eyes. "If you hadn't figured out what those numbers on the envelope meant, Lillian would probably be dead."

I didn't want to think about it anymore. Not right now, at least. All I wanted was to sleep for a week. The entire evening had been one surreal nightmare. I still had trouble believing it had all happened.

Blake, I was happy to learn, was in police custody. My deepest wish was that they'd serve him gutter water and wet crackers and green liver for breakfast and for every other meal for the rest of his life. Part of me still ached like crazy, knowing what he'd done. He'd been my friend for more than half my lifetime. Now he was nothing but a monster in man's clothing.

Through all this, I couldn't stop thinking about Celeste. I felt so bad for her. She was strong and capable, but she was also in love with Blake. They'd planned a glorious future together. I was afraid this was going to destroy her.

Aunt Tressa was leaning over me, examining my face.

"Don't get so close to me," I said with a sniffle. "I've got the worse flu ever. Believe me, you don't want to catch this one."

"I never get the flu," she reminded me. "But I still, still, *still* can't believe you went there alone."

"I didn't want to bug you while you were getting ready for the Darby dinner," I whined at her.

She twitched her lips into the tiniest of smiles. "All right, all right, point taken. God, it's after two," she said over a vociferous yawn. "Try to get a good night's rest and I'll be back in the morning. You can sleep all day tomorrow."

Exactly what I was planning to do.

" 'Night," I mumbled, burying my head in my pillow. The comforting weight of two furry forms curled around my feet.

Then a multiringed hand squeezed my shoulder for the briefest of moments.

All's well that ends well, I thought.

With that soothing notion, I drifted off to nowhere-land.

My brain pounded like a thousand hammers. I tossed, turned, twisted, but the sound wouldn't go away. It was like—

Someone knocking on my front door.

It couldn't be Aunt Tressa. By now she should be sound asleep. And why would she come back, anyway?

Was it the police, coming back to question me? Did they need another statement from me?

My head felt like a water-filled balloon as I shrugged on a robe, shuffled into my slippers and lugged my aching body downstairs. "I'm coming," I muttered to the insistent knocker.

I trudged over to the front door and flicked on the outside light. Expecting the police, I jerked open the door without asking who was there.

A ghostly pale woman wearing a full-length fur stood shivering on my front porch. Her eyes looked glazed. Her hair was the wild, frizzy mop I hadn't seen since high school.

Celeste.

Oh, my God. Celeste.

I pulled her inside and closed the door. Only a sudden fit of coughing and the fear of contaminating her with my flu germs stopped me from enveloping her in a hug.

"Come in, Celeste. Sit down. Can I make you some tea?" I didn't have the strength to fetch her so much as a glass of water, but her fixed expression had made me offer it without thinking.

For several moments she stood near the door, stiff as a plank, both hands stuffed deep in the pockets of her luxurious fur coat.

Fur coat . . .

I'd seen that coat before. Where?

"Blake's at the police station." Her voice was strange and low. "It's over now. Everything's ruined. My plans, my dreams, my future . . ."

"Come in and sit down, Celeste. You need to get warm." My heart was breaking for her, even more so because she was trying to remain stoic. In her place I'd be sobbing my brains out. I couldn't begin to imagine what she was going through.

Cinnie and Elliot had crept down the stairs, no doubt curious about my late-night visitor. Both cats stood about ten feet away, watching Celeste warily.

"Can I get you something?" I asked her again.

She looked at me, and for a moment it seemed she was staring straight through me. Feeling a sudden wave of dizziness, I hauled myself over to the sofa and plunked down on it. "Sorry, but I've picked up a nasty bug. I have to lie down for a minute." I rubbed a hand over my throbbing eyes. When I slid my hand away from my face, my insides went from solid to liquid.

"Celeste, what . . . are you doing?"

She was standing over me, her beautifully manicured fingers curled around the handle of a silver gun. I knew instantly what it was.

Albert Dwardene's old six-shooter.

CHAPTER THIRTY-TWO

*From the journal of Frederic Dwardene, Friday, February 2,
1951*

*The deed is done, and I mean that literally. Today I transferred
title to the mansion to my darling Lillian. The deed is recorded,
but for now I will keep it a secret. Even Lillian's mother mustn't
know. In her excitement she might reveal the surprise, and it
must be saved for Valentine's Day! Surely, when I present Lillian with this undeniable evidence of my devotion, she will see
the wisdom in becoming my wife. And I will make her love me.
I will!*

For a nanosecond, I thought I'd fallen down a deep, dark rabbit
hole.

I tried to ease backward, away from Celeste, but my sofa
cushions would only give so far. Terror gave me an adrenaline
rush, but even so I was trapped. Only twelve or so feet separated
me from the barrel of her gun.

"You've spoiled everything." Her voice was a low hiss. "In a
few more days, I was going to be out of this butthole of a town.
Hazleton, New Hampshire, was going to be nothing but an ugly
memory."

"Celeste, I know you're distraught over Blake, but it doesn't
mean your life is over. You've got so much going for you. You're
successful, you're super smart—"

"Shut up. Suffice it to say, Miss Apple Polisher, that you've wrecked things for me for the last time."

Miss Apple Polisher?

"That's how I used to think of you in school. Always sucking up to the teachers. Disgustingly helpful and dependable."

"And boring."

"True, but everyone admired you." She gave out a cold laugh. "Unlike me, Celeste the Mess. And don't deny it—I know all the girls called me that."

"A few of them did," I admitted. "But you turned out better than any of them. And you did it on your own, without help from anyone."

"You're wrong, I did have help." Her eyes softened, but only for a second—a momentary blip of normal in an otherwise unbalanced mind. "My gram helped because she loved me. She was the only one who ever did. She told me I could do anything I wanted, be anything I wanted to be. Every problem has a solution, she used to say. I simply had to find it."

"Don't do this, Celeste. You had no control over the monstrous things Blake did. You can still go on, move forward with your life and your career. Put the gun down and we'll talk about it."

She shook her frizzy blond head. "I gave you too much credit, Apple. You still don't get it, do you? Blake didn't kill Lou Marshall. I did."

No . . .

"He left me no choice. He was cleaning the remnants out of the old desk when he found the deed. Lou was no dummy. He knew what it meant. He was online, looking at the Registry indices, when I went in to ask him about a vase someone wanted to buy. The look on his face said it all. Something was very wrong."

"Did he tell you what it was?"

"Not until I prodded him. When he told me what he'd discovered, I offered him money to keep his mouth shut. His eyes lit up for a second or two, but then he shook his head and told me no, that he had to tell Sam about the deed."

I coughed again, my lungs on fire. "So you killed him?"

"First I left the room to think. About a minute later I went in again. Lou's back was to the door so he didn't see me. He was on his cell, trying to reach your boss."

Sam, I think there's been a terrible mistake . . .

"I had to stop him. All my plans depended on the sale proceeds from the mansion. I grabbed one of those daggers from the wall display near the door. Before Lou could even turn around, I jammed it into the back of his neck. He didn't make a sound—he just sank to the floor. I looked at his laptop to be sure he hadn't e-mailed anyone, but he was still on the Registry website. There was another knife on the rack, a smaller one, so I used it to smash up the laptop. I wasn't sure if the cops had a way to figure out what he was viewing before he died."

At the edge of my vision, I saw Elliot creep up quietly behind Celeste. I uttered a silent prayer that he wouldn't do anything to provoke her.

"Lou's scarf was draped over the back of the desk chair," she went on. "I grabbed it and swiped it over the knife handles, then I returned the smaller knife to the rack. Within seconds I was tiptoeing down the back staircase, the one that leads to the pantry. No one even saw me."

In a sudden, swift motion, Elliot leaped onto the arm of the sofa near my feet, barely a yard from where Celeste was standing. She jumped slightly and shot him a nasty look. Elliot sat there, unmoving, his golden gaze fastened on her face.

"You took a huge risk," I said. "Anyone could've walked in—"

"I'm *aware* of that. I did what I had to do. For every problem there's a solution, remember? Why Frederic deeded the house

251

to Lillian I'll never know, but that's water over the dam now. What I want to know is how you missed the deed when you did the title search." She grinned coldly at me.

I knew why, but right now I had bigger worries. Was her gun loaded? Didn't a six-shooter hold six bullets?

"That day, at the estate sale," she said, "Lillian Bilodeau was coming downstairs as I was heading up to talk to Lou. I didn't think anything of it at the time, but she looked distracted, as if she'd seen a ghost. Afterward, I realized what had happened. Lou had obviously told her about the deed when she went up there to pay for that china cat."

Poor Lillian. No wonder she looked so dazed when she came downstairs that afternoon. She must've been stunned to discover she owned the Dwardene property.

"I knew once she grasped what it meant, she'd have her hand out. Blake wouldn't be able to sell without getting a release deed from her. She'd have wanted big bucks for that. Problem was, we needed every penny for the loft in Tribeca. And I wasn't giving that up. Not for *anyone*."

"What you did to Lillian was terrible," I rasped.

She swallowed, and her eyes turned glassy with unshed tears. "I didn't want to hurt her. She reminded me so much of my gram. Gram was a real beauty once. Before she got sick, she looked a lot like Lillian. She had those same stunning blue eyes. Age and smoking ruined her looks, but she was always beautiful to me."

"How did you get inside Lillian's trailer?"

Her six-shooter still trained on me, Celeste moved closer, sidling around my coffee table until she was standing at the foot of the sofa. "Late Saturday night I drove over there in Blake's SUV. I'd dressed totally in black and covered my hair. I figured out which room she slept in and tapped on the window. I'd brought a rolled-up towel with me, and I held it against me like it was an animal. Once I'd woken her and gotten her attention, I cried pitifully, 'Help me, my boyfriend's going to kill my cat. You have to hide her for me!' Believe me, you never saw an old lady move so fast. When she opened the door I was ready. I pulled out my duct tape. I slapped a piece over her mouth, grabbed her, and hoisted her over my shoulder. She weighed nothing. It was like carrying a doll."

Something tickled my brain. The same something I was trying to recall earlier.

Once in a while I get these peddlers comin' in here, wanting me to sell their healthy muffins . . .

"You weren't as clever as you think. You left a napkin from Darla's Dine-o-Rama on the floor in Lillian's trailer."

After a moment of surprise, her turquoise eyes hardened. "Josh was always yammering about how good Darla's food was. He took Edgar there every Sunday for breakfast. It sounded like a kitschy place, so I decided to check it out. I thought it might be a good venue to sell my whole-grain cinnamon rolls." She rolled her eyes. "The second I walked in I knew I'd made a mistake. The place was filthy. Darla looked like something out of a trashy sitcom. I told her I'd planned to offer her my healthy breakfast buns to sell, but that they were far too superior for that dive. Do you know she actually stuck her tongue out at me?"

Go, Darla!

"Before I left, I made a show of snatching a napkin off the counter so I wouldn't have to touch the door handle." She frowned. "I must've stuck that napkin in my coat pocket afterward. It was the same black coat I wore the night I took Lillian. The napkin probably fell when I pulled out the duct tape."

"That night, didn't Blake wonder where you'd gone?"

She gave me a feral smile. "Not after all the medication I put in his wine. I had a ton of prescription painkillers left from when my gram was dying. Anyone who says drugs lose their potency after a year has no idea what they're talking about. Of course I upped the dosage a bit."

"Did you drug Lillian, too?"

"Of course. I couldn't take the chance she'd find her way out of that cabin. There was water in the bathroom, and I made sure she had food—my delicious whole-grain bread."

Except that Lillian was too drugged to get to the bathroom. And the cabin had no heat.

"She nearly froze to death," I snapped.

Celeste looked thoughtful, as if she were actually sane. "I thought about lighting the wood stove, but I couldn't risk someone seeing the smoke." She laughed. "The old girl was sharper than I thought, though. She must have had her cell phone in her bathrobe pocket. I caught her trying to call you when I showed up Monday night to check on her. Luckily she was too drugged to make any sense. I quickly disposed of her phone so it couldn't be traced."

"What were you going to do with her? Leave her there to die on her own?"

For the first time, she looked nonplussed. "At first I thought I'd drive her somewhere in the middle of the night. Leave her someplace where someone would find her." She shook her head. "It wouldn't have worked. Once the drugs wore off, she'd have still remembered the deed. After Blake left for New York, I was going to . . . get rid of her. Somehow."

"I know why you didn't kill her right away," I taunted. "Lillian reminded you so much of your gram—killing her would've been like killing your grandmother, the only woman on earth who ever loved you, who ever cared about—"

"Shut up!"

Out of the corner of my eye, I saw Elliot move—that undulating motion cats make when preparing to pounce. "Do you think your gram would be proud of you now, Celeste? Do you think she'd condone murder?"

She leaned toward me, her face infused with rage, just as Elliot leaped onto the arm of her fur coat and hissed in her ear. Surprised, she flung her arm aside, sending Elliot sailing across the room. He landed among the jumble of holiday candles clustered atop my bookcase, knocking a large jar candle to the floor.

"God, I hate cats," she spat out.

Poor Elliot cowered against the wall. He looked unharmed, but terrified. I wanted so badly to gather him in my arms and make sure he was all right, but I didn't dare move. Celeste's gun hand had remained remarkably steady. Any hope I had for escaping this nightmare was rapidly fading.

"You're contemptible," I said. "But you're not dumb, so you can't seriously think you're going to kill me, too, and get away with it."

She gave me a look that chilled me to the core. "Of course I don't. The moment the police took Blake away, I knew it was over. Tonight I'm going to join my gram, but I'm not going alone. First you have to pay for ruining my life."

Everything inside me curdled. "*Au contraire*, Celeste. You won't be joining your gram. Not where you're going."

Her blue eyes flared. "You miserable—"

The ringing of the phone jolted us both. My portable phone was on the coffee table, directly behind Celeste. "It's Aunt Tressa," I said, dread squeezing my gut. "The commotion must have woken her up."

She pointed the gun at my face. "Don't even think of answering it."

The last thing I wanted was to endanger my aunt. But I knew if I didn't answer, she'd panic, use her key, and come barging in. Celeste would kill us both.

"Please," I said. "I'll get rid of her fast. If I don't answer, she'll only come storming in here. She has a key."

The phone rang again.

Celeste smirked. "Not a problem. I have enough bullets for both of you."

"Celeste, listen," I pleaded, "since you're . . . planning to kill me anyway, it'll be the last time I ever talk to her. Just let me get rid of her and she'll go back to sleep."

I was appealing to a sociopath, but it was the only chance I had. For the first time, she looked uncertain. Wondering, no doubt, if she could pull off shooting both of us at the same time.

She pushed the phone in front of me, then snapped her head toward Elliot. "Say one wrong word and I'll use that furball for target practice. Got it? The other one, too. I've got six bullets—plenty for everyone."

That answered the bullet question.

"I'm only going to let her know I'm okay. I promise." I was as far from okay as I've ever been, but I had to stop Aunt Tressa from walking into a death trap.

She gave a sharp nod and I picked up the phone. "Hello?" I yawned loudly. "No, no, it was nothing. I couldn't sleep so I came downstairs for some tea. The cats followed me, and Elliot got rambunctious and starting knocking things off my book-case."

Celeste was staring hard at me, her gun aimed between my eyes.

"I will, don't worry. Go back to sleep. And . . . Aunt Tress? Thanks again for coming to the hospital last night." My voice shook. Tears smudged my vision. "You're always there for me, and"—I swallowed—"I acted like such a jerk last night, making a scene over that song you were playing. You know, the one you blasted through my wall when your friend was visiting? I know it was loud, but I shouldn't have been so nasty about it. It's not like *I* never played loud music, right?" I managed a pathetic laugh. "Yeah, okay, I just wanted to apologize. Talk to you tomorrow. Later."

Slowly, I returned the phone to its cradle. The idea of never seeing Aunt Tressa again tore at me. Even worse was the thought of her finding my body.

"Well, that was heartwarming." Celeste laughed mirthlessly. "You really are a dreary soul, Apple. I suppose having your mother desert you at an early age didn't help your confidence any, though you had me fooled for a long time. My own mother was a swine, but at least she didn't fly the sty on me."

I glared at her, determined to keep her talking. Every second I stayed alive was precious.

My bleary gaze landed on her fur coat.

Fur coat. Of course—that's what she'd picked up from storage at the dry cleaners. Something grazed my memory. "You were staring through my office window yesterday afternoon, weren't you? Who were you looking at?"

She gave me a wicked grin. "I was just having a little fun with Vicki. She caught me destroying the baby birds' nest the day she came over to drop off some probate docs for Blake to sign. Stupid things had nested over the drain pipe—I had to get rid of them. Bad timing on my part, though—I'd forgotten Sam was sending Vicki over with those forms. She squealed like a rusty hinge when she saw what I was doing. I didn't want her blabbing about it, so I explained to her, in some excruciating detail, what would happen to her precious parakeets if she told anyone."

No wonder Vicki had tossed Celeste's buns into the trash. She was petrified of her!

Mentally and physically depleted, I dropped my head on the

sofa. I couldn't fight Celeste. I had the strength of a wet noodle, and there was nothing I could use for a weapon. I thought of the people I'd never see again.

Aunt Tressa.

Daniel.

My mother, if she was still out there.

My last hope dwindling, a chilling revelation washed over me. "You killed Edgar, too, didn't you?" I said quietly.

Her gaze went flat. "I had to. He had too many good years left in him. Even with the sorry shape the mansion was in, it was still worth a cool half mil." She shook her head with disgust. "Do you know I actually had to talk Blake into selling the place? He originally wanted to renovate it, turn it into a happy little home for the two of us and a couple of rug rats."

"Now that's a scary thought," I said.

"What is?"

"You raising kids."

She gaped at me. "You're a nasty little witch when you want to be, aren't you?"

"And you're a sociopathic fiend."

A faint shadow drifted across my vision. A sneak peek into the beyond? A glimpse into the next life?

Celeste's gaze turned stony. She aimed the gun at my face. "Wave bye-bye, Apple. It's time to—"

"Put the gun down, Ms. Frame. *Now.*"

CHAPTER THIRTY-THREE

From the journal of Frederic Dwardene, Wednesday, February 7, 1951

Lillian's mother called me today at the bank. I nearly spilled the beans about the deed, but then wisely held my tongue. For now, it is my secret alone. I did, however, tell her about the painting, and she squealed with delight. We have agreed that on February 14, I will treat her and Lillian to a sumptuous dinner at the Inn, after which they shall both visit my home, where I will propose to Lillian . . .

With a gasp, Celeste swung her head around. I used the opportunity to pull back my knees and kick at her with both feet. As kicks go it was pitifully weak, but it was enough to knock her off balance. She tumbled over the coffee table, shrieking as she landed with a thud.

Within seconds, Paul Fenton had her hands cuffed behind her with her face pressed into the carpet. Two uniformed officers quickly flanked him, their firearms leveled at Celeste.

During the ten seconds or so that it took for all of this to go down, Aunt Tressa had soared into the room like an F-15 with a tailwind. I vaguely heard Fenton reading Celeste her rights as my aunt grabbed me and hugged me so hard I thought my ribs were going to crack.

"You're squishing me," I groused, clinging to her for all she was worth.

She laughed as tears sprouted from her eyes. "I knew I raised you right," she said. "Thank God I called you when I did."

Aunt Tressa had obviously zeroed in on my plea for help. But I still didn't understand how the police had gotten here so fast. Barely two or three minutes had elapsed since her phone call. How did Fenton and crew get here so quickly?

As if he'd read my mind, Fenton turned and faced me. He looked exhausted and elated at the same time. "We've been questioning Blake Dwardene for hours. He vehemently denied any involvement in Marshall's death, or in Miss Bilodeau's kidnapping. But it wasn't until we told him about finding Miss Bilodeau in his cabin that I knew something was off. Blake looked genuinely shocked, and I don't mean shocked that we found her. I mean he was totally stunned that Lillian was even *in* the cabin." Fenton shook his head. "By then I was starting to get a bad feeling. I know you think of me as a small-town gendarme, Ms. Mariani, but I've seen my share of bad eggs. Thing is, I was sure Blake Dwardene wasn't one of them."

I suddenly felt terrible for all the bad things I'd wished on Blake. How could I have had so little faith?

"His fiancée, meanwhile"—Fenton glared at Celeste—"had already been questioned and released. The woman puts on a good performance, I'll give her that. She's quite the little actress."

He had that right.

"Anyway, Blake suddenly clammed up tighter than a new jar of pickles. He demanded a lawyer, which effectively put the interrogation on hold."

I coughed. "Did he call Sam?"

"Yes, but only for a referral. Sam contacted a criminal lawyer he knew in Concord. Since nothing was going to happen until the woman got there, I snagged a couple of my guys and we drove over to Blake's condo. Imagine our surprise when we saw that Ms. Frame's car was gone. *Not.*"

"She could've gone to her mother's," I pointed out.

"That was our next stop, Ms. Mariani. Mama Frame answered the door in a nightgown I could've read the sports section through. Bottom line, she hadn't seen Celeste in months." Fenton's shark-like grin was growing ever more triumphant.

I stole a glance at Celeste, now propped between the two officers, her hands behind her. Her expression was unreadable. I couldn't begin to imagine what was going through her messed-up mind.

"By this time I knew she was up to her pretty little earlobes in this whole mess," Fenton said. "We were headed back to the station—I wanted to get an APB out on her—when I got your aunt's call. Luckily we were on High Street, not even two minutes from here. Your aunt ordered me to get my, uh, posterior over here *toot sweet.* Said she'd be waiting with the key."

"Thank you, Paul," Aunt Tressa said earnestly. "You saved Apple's life. Well, you and the Fab Four."

Fenton looked baffled. "The *who?*"

"Not The Who, the Beatles," she said, rolling her eyes skyward.

I thanked my lucky stars that my aunt had homed in on the message I was trying to get across on the phone. She'd obviously picked up on the real reason for my phony apology—to convey my desperate plea for "Help." If Aunt Tressa and the police hadn't acted so quickly, I'd probably be . . . well, some place I didn't want to think about.

Like the morgue.

Fenton's weary eyes lasered in on my aunt. "We'll chat again tomorrow, Tressa Krichner. Meanwhile, we're going to let you ladies get some sleep." He leaned toward me and lowered his voice. "Truth is, Ms. Mariani, when I first came in here I was afraid you'd already been shot. Forgive my bluntness, but you look like death on buttered toast."

"Thank you," I said, meaning it. "As long as I'm still alive, I don't care what I look like."

Elliot had quietly padded over to us. Now nestled in Aunt Tressa's lap, he purred softly. I cupped his head and looked again at Celeste. She caught my gaze and her face seemed to collapse inward. For a moment I felt a twinge of pity.

Then I thought of Lillian and Lou and Blake, and the moment died.

Celeste wouldn't be joining her gram any time soon.

And the wait was going to be misery.

Chapter Thirty-Four

From the Hazleton Bugle, February 14, 1951

Prominent banker Frederic Dwardene was killed yesterday morning in Manchester when he was struck by a milk truck on Elm Street in front of Whalie's Jewelers. According to police, Dwardene was crossing the bustling main thoroughfare when he slipped on a patch of ice. The driver of the truck, Lonnie Paxton, told police he attempted to stop when he saw Dwardene fall, but his brakes locked, causing his vehicle to skid. Dwardene was pronounced dead at the accident scene. No further investigation is anticipated. The police have confirmed that no charges will be filed against Paxton.

"More hot mulled cider, Lillian?" Aunt Tressa's dangly earrings twinkled like blood red chandeliers as she offered another helping from her Beatles collector teapot.

"Oh, no thank you, dear. Although I must say it's quite delicious. What is that spice that makes it so special? Nutmeg?"

"The cloves, probably," I said. "They give it that extra little zing."

Lillian smiled wistfully, and for a moment I saw the beautiful young woman in the painting. "It reminds me of the wassail my aunt used to make every Christmas Eve," she said. "She would simmer it on the stove all day and serve it in a fancy punch bowl. I looked forward to it every year."

Two days after her dramatic rescue from the cabin, Lillian

was released from the hospital. All she could think of was her poor Elliot, and how badly he must have missed her. The morning Aunt Tressa and I learned she was being sprung, we delivered Elliot to her mobile home and filled an entire cabinet with cat food and kitty treats. I put out a fresh litter box, while Aunt Tressa stocked the fridge with fresh staples from the Food Mart—things like milk, juice and eggs. As for bread, Aunt Tressa refused to buy anything with the words "whole" or "organic" in the ingredients. Instead, she bought Lillian a round of hearty white Italian and a luscious-looking loaf of cinnamon raisin.

Her ordeal notwithstanding, Lillian was faring well. Her color was good and her blue eyes were clear and bright, though she was still a bit too thin. Over the past week, Aunt Tressa and I had delivered home-cooked meals to her nearly every day, trying to put a few needed pounds on her.

With Christmas less than a week away, Aunt Tressa had put up a small tree next to her sofa. Chock-a-block with blue mini-lights and shiny, silvery bulbs, it cast a soothing glow over the entire room. Pine-scented candles flickered on the fake mantel, infusing the air with a cozy holiday aroma. Beneath the tree were a few odd-shaped packages, one of which had been clawed open, its contents pillaged.

Aunt Tressa plopped down on the sofa next to Lillian, who sat in the center. Resting on the coffee table was a poinsettia-shaped platter that bore a variety of delectable cheeses. My aunt snagged a wedge of smoked gouda from the tray. "Where's Daniel?" she asked me. "Didn't you tell him four o'clock?"

"I'm sure he'll be here any minute."

I'd been wondering myself why he was late. It was ten past four, and Daniel was normally punctual. Over the past week we'd seen each other twice, both times over dinner. After some heavy-duty talks, we were now on firmer ground. If it was meant to be, and I had the feeling it was, our relationship would move forward at a pace we could both live with.

Pazzo, his pink nose twitching, jumped onto the sofa and wedged himself between my aunt and Lillian. Lillian smiled with delight as his gorgeous green eyes surveyed the cheese tray with undisguised envy. My aunt rubbed the cat's head lovingly, then gave him his own morsel—a tiny block of Jarlsburg—to munch on.

"Where's Ringo?" I asked.

"The moment my back was turned, he tore open one of his Christmas presents and fled the scene. Last I saw, he was rolling around on my bedspread with a catnip aardvark clenched in his jaws."

Which explained why Pazzo was now under the tree, lounging on top of the torn wrapping paper while he savored his square of cheese.

The doorbell chimed. Aunt Tressa popped out of her seat like a bagel from a new toaster and scurried toward the door.

"Look who I found hanging around on the front porch," Daniel said as he and Jack Darby stepped inside. The two had only met last week, and already they'd bonded like hot glue to paper. Daniel was clutching a large shopping bag in one hand and a platter of goodies in the other, while Darby held out two bottles of wine.

Daniel grinned when he saw me. "Hey," I said. We kissed lightly, and then I nodded to Jack Darby, who was still on my "wait and see" list. "Good to see you again, Jack."

"Thank you, my dear. I'm so pleased to have been invited."

Aunt Tressa took their coats, and Jack gave her the wine bottles. "Oh, Jack, it's the Beaucanon chardonnay! My favorite," she gushed.

"Already chilled," he added, that familiar flush tingeing his cheeks.

"Excellent! In that case, we can all have a glass right now."

Daniel tucked his shopping bag next to the tree, then set his platter down next to the cheese tray and popped off the plastic cover. The tray was jammed with an assortment of mini-desserts, each one looking more scrumptious than the other.

Suddenly, Lillian rose. Her face beaming, she went over to Jack and took his hand. With the kindest smile I'd ever seen, he leaned down and kissed her cheek. "You look quite lovely, Miss Lillian. Like a Christmas angel."

Her pale cheeks blushed pink. "Will you sit next to me?"

"Of course."

Stymied, I stared for a moment, then offered to help Aunt Tressa with the wine. We headed into the kitchen.

"What gives with Lillian and Jack?" I asked her, setting five wine glasses on a tray.

She shrugged, avoiding my gaze as she uncorked one of the bottles and filled each of the glasses. "What do you mean?"

"I don't know. She just seemed overly delighted to see him."

Aunt Tressa graced me with a smug smile. "I keep telling you what a good man he is."

Scooping the tray of wine off the counter, she toddled back into the living room. Still perplexed, I followed in her wake.

She bent toward Lillian first. "You'll have a glass, won't you, Lil?"

Lillian chuckled. "Oh my, I haven't had wine in years. This is such a treat." She carefully lifted a glass from the tray.

When we all had our glasses in hand, Jack raised his. "To family," he said, "and to good friends. May we all enjoy peace this Christmas."

Lillian sipped her wine, then looked at each of us. "I feel so lucky to be with all of you," she said, a catch in her voice. "Apple, you saved my life. I can't imagine how I'll ever repay you."

I swallowed, emotion swelling inside me. "You already have,"

I told her, "by being safe and healthy again."

"I feel terrible about what happened to poor Mr. Marshall," she said. "I can't help feeling it was my fault."

"Don't you blame yourself, Lillian," Daniel gently chimed in. "You're not responsible for the actions of a greedy, grasping woman who cared only about her own warped needs."

Lillian sighed. "I know that. The sad part is, I would have been happy to sign a deed. All she had to do was ask me. It wouldn't have occurred to me to ask for money."

"Frederic loved you very much, didn't he?" I asked her.

"Yes, I'm afraid he did. But he was so much older than I was. Besides, my heart had already been pledged to Anton, the man I loved. He died in Korea in November of nineteen fifty-one."

She looked at Jack Darby, a question in her eyes. Nodding, he took her hand. "It's all right, Miss Lillian. Tell them everything."

I shifted in my chair, my curiosity piqued.

Lillian fortified herself with another sip of wine. "Anton and I were nineteen when we met. Oh, he was such a darling man, and so handsome. We were deeply in love. Neither of us had much money, but we knew we wanted to get married. We saved our pennies like crazy. Then Anton learned he was being sent to Korea." Her eyes grew moist. "I was devastated. I was sure I'd never see him again."

Guilt washed through me. Lillian didn't know that Daniel and I had read Anton's letters.

Before I could interject, Daniel jumped in. He explained that when we'd gone into her mobile home to look for clues as to where she might be, we found Anton's letters and read many of them.

"It was terrible of us, I know," I confessed. "But we were genuinely afraid for you. We thought you might have written the murderer's name on a slip of paper and hidden it somewhere."

Lillian smiled. "Oh, Apple, that's quite all right. You did it for all the right reasons. But as I told the police, I never saw the murderer."

"But you found out about the deed, right? Did Lou show it to you?"

She gave me a baffled look. "Is that what everyone thought? That I found out about Frederic's deed to me?"

"Yes," I said. Including Celeste.

Lillian sagged. "Is that why—? Oh my."

"You mean you didn't know about the deed?" my aunt said.

"No, I didn't find out about it until I was out of the hospital."

Aunt Tressa looked bewildered. "But you looked so dazed when you came downstairs that day at the estate sale. Did something else happen?"

"Yes, it was the painting. I saw it when I went upstairs to pay Mr. Marshall for the china cat. It was resting against the wall in front of some other paintings. My poor old legs nearly went out from under me when I saw it. I never knew Frederic had done a portrait of me. Imagine my shock when I saw myself, sixty years ago, staring back at me from a painting. For the first time, I realized how extreme his obsession had been. It was most unsettling."

"These days he'd be called a stalker," Aunt Tressa said darkly.

Lillian nodded. "You're right. He would wait for me to leave the factory at the end of my work day and offer to drive me home. I knew I shouldn't have accepted the rides, but it was a bitterly cold winter and I'd been feeling so poorly. He gave me gifts, as well. The china cat I bought at the estate sale? Frederic had actually given me that cat. While it was lovely, I knew I had to stop accepting his gifts. When he wasn't looking I removed the cat from the gift box and slipped it under his car seat. I'm sure he was disappointed when he found it, but I had to do it."

"I found his diary in the antique shop, Lillian," I said. "He was planning to give you the painting on Valentine's Day, the same day he was going to present you with the recorded deed."

"Yes. Shortly before my mother died she admitted everything, although I'm sure she didn't know anything about the deed. She'd been conspiring with Frederic in his pursuit of me. For her only daughter to marry a respected, well-to-do banker would have been a dream come true."

"Her dream, not yours," Aunt Tressa noted.

"That's right. Unfortunately, my mother saw to it that after I got Anton's first few letters, I never received any more. I was crushed when his letters stopped coming, so I stopped writing to him." Her eyes filled with tears. Aunt Tressa thrust a green cocktail napkin into her hand.

Lillian dabbed at her eyes. "Then the strangest thing happened. That February—it was nineteen fifty-one—Frederic was crossing the street in downtown Manchester and he slipped on the ice and fell. A milk truck struck him and killed him instantly."

"So that's how Frederic died," I said.

And the recorded deed languished inside the valentine. No one ever found it—not until Lou Marshall cleaned out the old desk.

"I was sad to learn how Frederic died," Lillian went on, "but I had bigger worries. You see, right around then I realized I was . . ." Lillian blushed a deep crimson. ". . . I was going to have a baby."

I set down my wine glass. Frederic's diary entries about Lillian looking unwell now made perfect sense.

"Anton's child," I said.

"Yes, he was the only man I ever loved. I tried to deny it, but by the end of February I was sure. My mother, of course, was furious. For a whole week she barely spoke to me. She sent me to Pennsylvania to live with my aunt until the baby was born.

The child went to an orphanage and was adopted by a middle-aged couple. The records were sealed, so I never knew who they were."

A weird feeling clawed at me. A host of odd-shaped puzzle pieces began tumbling into place.

"Giving away that baby was the hardest thing I've ever done," Lillian murmured. Then her face lit up and she broke into a smile. "How lucky for me that my child has found me. Apple, Daniel . . . Jack is my son."

I felt Daniel gasp. I was grateful he didn't spill his wine on me.

Jack's arm slid protectively over Lillian's shoulder. "I'd been looking for this beautiful lady for a long time. When at last I had success, I immediately moved to Hazleton so I could be near her. I didn't know how she would take the news, so I decided I'd try to get to know her first. I'm afraid I became a bit of a stalker myself, but only so I could watch out for her."

"You should have told me right away," Lillian scolded, but her eyes held a world of joy. "Jack didn't give me the news until after I was out of the hospital."

I shot a look at my aunt, who was grinning like the conspirator she was. "You've known for days, haven't you? Why didn't you tell me?"

"It wasn't my story to tell, or my place." She popped a miniature peppermint cheesecake into her mouth.

She was right. Only Lillian had the right to disclose her secret.

"By the way," my aunt said, "I got a call from Darla this morning. She was so psyched when she heard about Lillian's rescue that she invited us all there for a special New Year's Eve celebration. Lil, she asked me what your favorite dish was, so I told her I'd ask you."

"Oh, how thoughtful of her! But she really needn't go to all that trouble."

"She wants to," Aunt Tressa assured her. "So how about it, what tickles your palate?"

"Well, let's see. Perhaps a roast chicken dinner? Would everyone enjoy that?"

We all heartily agreed, so roast chicken it would be.

"It's curious, isn't it," I said pointedly to my aunt, "that right after you and I visited Darla's, someone reported her to the state board of health?"

Aunt Tressa examined her shimmering ruby manicure. "Yeah, I thought that too," she said, frowning at a nail. "Anyway, the industrial-strength cleaning company she hired will be done with the overhaul right before Christmas. After that all the new appliances have to be installed. By New Year's Eve, she'll be ready to rock in a sparkling clean environment. And we're going to be her first customers!"

"Seems happy endings are the order of the day," Daniel said.

"Let's not forget Blake Dwardene," Jack quietly reminded us. "Poor fellow's got to be feeling pretty low right now."

Stunned was more like it. I'd spoken to Blake twice this past week. I had the feeling he hadn't totally absorbed all the things Celeste had done. It would be a while before he got past the hurt and the anger. Lou had apparently warned Blake that his fiancée was not all she seemed, but Blake had been too in love to take him seriously.

In the meantime, the sale of the mansion had gone through without any glitches. Over Lillian's protests, Blake insisted that once the estate was closed, half the proceeds would go into a savings account in Lillian's name. After that, Aunt Tressa and Jack were going to take her house shopping.

"I do feel strange about him offering me all that money," Lillian fretted. "In spite of Frederic's obsession with me, I never loved him."

"But he loved you, Lillian," I said. "And Blake truly wants

271

you to buy a comfortable little home for yourself. It's the least you deserve after everything Celeste put you through."

"We'll find a house with plenty of room for Elliot to have a friend," Tressa piped in gleefully.

"That will be nice." Lillian's blue eyes twinkled at me. "Looks like you and I will both be making a trip to the shelter, Apple. Your Cinnie needs a friend, too."

That was undeniably true. Cinnie missed Elliot something awful. I'd already decided that after the holidays I would adopt another cat.

A muffled, trilling sound filtered through the wall from my apartment.

Once.

Twice.

"Someone's calling you," my aunt chirped.

I shrugged. "Well, since my nearest and dearest are all in this room, it can't be anyone who matters."

I wondered briefly if my dad was trying to reach me. Three days ago he sent me a flower bouquet the size of a small tree, then called to see how I was doing. Truth be told, I was thrilled to hear his voice. He promised to visit next summer, when the heat in Vegas would be unbearable.

My phone had no sooner stopped ringing when Aunt Tressa's started up. Excusing herself, she traipsed into the kitchen to answer it. A moment later, she signaled to me.

"I'll be right back," I said to the group.

Aunt Tressa held out the phone. "A woman, for you. Didn't say who she was. Voice sounds kind of hoarse, though." With a shrug, she breezed away to give me privacy.

"Hello?" I said to the caller.

No one responded.

"Hello? Is anyone there?"

Again, no one spoke, but in the background a catchy little

tune began to play. A Christmas song, one I hadn't heard in years: "I Saw Mommy Kissing Santa Claus."

My first reaction was to smile—I'd loved that song as a kid—until I remembered that the caller hadn't spoken. "If you're there, say something," I said crisply, losing patience now.

A few more seconds elapsed. Irritated, I started to hang up the phone when the faintest of whispers reached my ears. "I love you, Apple."

I sucked in a startled breath. "Mom?"

In the next instant she was gone, leaving in her place a silence that felt oddly warm and comforting.

Slowly, I set the phone back in its cradle. Had that really been her? Or had it been only my imagination, playing a crazy trick on me?

No, deep in that place where old memories cling to the heart, I felt sure the caller had been my mother.

I scooped up a tiny cream puff before reclaiming my seat next to Daniel. "The caller hung up," I said, willing my voice to sound natural instead of giddy. "Probably kids, playing with the phone."

Aunt Tressa, meanwhile, had a strange look on her face. My stomach fell. Was something wrong?

She looked at each of us, then grinned wickedly at me. "Don't look so scared, Apple. Everything is fine. But I do have an announcement to make. Once Lillian is settled in her new home, I'm going to retire from the real estate business. Permanently."

"What?" I shrieked.

She nodded. "The housing market's been in a slump for so long, I'm not sure I want to wait for it to recover."

I looked at Jack, who was nodding slowly, absorbing her every word.

"Anyway, it seems silly to continue pouring money into that office space. My last commission—the Dwardene sale—gave my nest egg a sweet little boost, so I'm going to use it to start an entirely new business. Something I really love."

For several interminable seconds everyone was speechless. "And that is . . . ?" I said finally.

"I'm going to open a designer handbag shop." Her eyes sparkled, and I could see she was already imagining it. "But it won't be only designer bags. I'll sell vintage bags from the sixties, too—funky stuff like that." She looked at Lillian. "And maybe the ladies in your knitting club would like to sell some of their felted purses. I love those!"

"Oh, I'm sure they would," Lillian said, looking happier than I'd ever seen her.

"I'll be glad to build display cases for you, Tressa," Jack offered. "Any kind you want."

She touched his hand. "Thank you, Jack. And now, I think it's time to open that other bottle."

Jack reached over and squeezed her hand. "I'll get it. You stay put."

Aunt Tressa beamed like a harvest moon as he strode off into her kitchen. He returned a minute later with the open wine bottle and refilled each of our glasses.

Daniel was first to lift his. "A toast," he said, "to the three most perfect ladies on Earth, all of whom happen to be in this room."

We chuckled and sipped our wine. The chardonnay sent a pleasing flash of warmth through me. In spite of all the bad things the past few weeks had dumped in our laps, at this moment I was feeling pretty darned lucky.

"By the way, what are you going to name your store?" I asked Aunt Tressa.

"Oh, I'm sure if we all put our heads together we can come up with a good name. In fact," she said slyly, "that's exactly what I'm counting on."

ABOUT THE AUTHOR

Linda S. Reilly lives with her husband in southern New Hampshire. When she's not writing, she can usually be found prowling the stacks of a bookstore or library, hunting down a good mystery.